SOUTH, AMERICA

South, America

///

A Novel

ROD DAVIS

NewSouth Books

Montgomery

NewSouth Books
105 S. Court Street
Montgomery, AL 36104

Library of Congress Cataloging-in-Publication Data

Davis, Rod, 1946–
South, America : a novel / Rod Davis.

pages cm

ISBN 978-1-60306-315-9 (pbk.)
ISBN 978-1-60306-316-6 (ebook)

1. Murder—Investigation—Fiction. 2. New Orleans (La.)—Fiction. I. Title.
PS3604.A975S68 2013
813'.6—dc23
2013020424

Design by Randall Williams
Printed in the United States of America

For Jennifer, Moriah, Hailey, and Noelle

"Seems, Madam? Nay, it is. I know not 'seems.'"

— *Hamlet*, ACT I, SCENE 2

1

The body was splayed out face down across a busted-up curb in the Faubourg Marigny, downriver of the Quarter but not quite in the Bywater. Weeds and a high fence lined one side of the street, decaying duplexes and a boarded-up grocery store the other. Two bone-thin brown dogs trotted over from a ripped-up garbage bag, but, seeing me, turned back.

It was early, especially for a Sunday, not even seven. The autumn night had been cool and a thin fog put everything in soft focus, as if the city really were easy. My goal, or so I had thought, in the same way you think the sun will rise and set every day, was a big mug of Guatemalan at RJ's, somehow surviving among the abandoned warehouses and urban detritus near the docks. I hadn't slept well—maybe too much fun at the Blue Frog or too many worries about the practicality of my move here, or both.

At first I figured the corpse for a drunk or a junkie, sleeping off another lost night. Then I got closer. I couldn't see the face, buried as it was into the concrete and half-obscured by one arm, but the clothes were smart: black slacks, tan cotton shirt, simple Italian lace-up shoes. A small, slender figure, all but unobtrusive in other circumstances. He was black, but you could barely tell given the dull gray color of what skin I could see. I gently nudged his left side with the toe of my sandals. Nothing. I bent down and touched the small of his back with my fingers.

I stared for a few moments. I knew the look on my own face: I'd seen it at crime scenes a dozen times back in Dallas when I worked the news. More than that when I was a first lieutenant working intelligence. Nobody ever likes to see the bodies. Whatever the reason. Nobody who's not fucked up. I didn't like to think about it. One thing I had learned hard—people are completely without sophistication around death. Completely.

I heard something and stood up, but it was just the rattle of an old car with bad suspension somewhere in the distance. Given the hour, I was almost certainly the first person to have come by. Except for whoever left him that way, with the back of his head smashed flat, close-cropped hair a carpet of blood and whitish ooze.

I hadn't brought my cell with me but there was a pay phone up near a grocery on Franklin and I went to call. The receiver was spray-painted purple and crawling with turf codes, but at least the cord was intact and the line was good. I dialed 911 and told a dispatcher what I'd found, and where, and went back to wait.

I was surprised how quickly a squad car showed, lights flashing but no siren. A young cop, strawberry blond, got out. He popped the nightstick from his belt and held it low in his right hand. He told me to step back, which I did, and asked for some ID, which fortunately I had in my jeans. He asked me what I did for a living and to keep things simple and mainstream I told him I wrote advertising copy. He looked me over fairly closely and then sort of relaxed. He gave me a cop name, initials only—J. F. Mallory.

I told him how I'd come across the body. I could see him writing down a few things: "male," "African-American," "head wound" and so on. When I said all I knew he told me I could leave, but that he might need to get in touch and I gave him my home phone number. I walked away slowly, half-wondering if there were a story I could work up and sell. What I didn't tell the officer was that while I was trying to figure out a line on my future I was doing some freelance writing and the occasional unlicensed PI investigation for a divorce lawyer/ex-Army buddy on the West Bank. But I didn't want to hang around and take a chance that someday Officer Mallory might remember he'd seen me when I was down at the police station doing business, so I just headed back to my apartment. Another squad car pulled up. The place would soon be thick with onlookers.

At home, I sidestepped a pile of unread magazines and went into the kitchen to fix the coffee I never did get from RJ's. I was out of everything except a French Market chicory mix, but that was my favorite anyway—had been since I'd gone to college in Baton Rouge. Things seemed more straightforward then.

I cleaned a few dishes and looked out the window into the courtyard. It was one of those Creole row-house duplexes common to the neighborhood, where the front half faces the street, and the rear unit is set back behind a garden. In this case a well-tended one, thanks to my landlords, Eula and Art Becker, a retired couple who relocated ten years ago from Memphis. He had been in the hotel business and she had been a public school teacher. They liked the city and had bought this place back when the Marigny was cheap and undiscovered. I guess Art had a good eye for a deal.

We didn't have a lot to do with each other since I was gone a lot or liked to work alone, but they had given me a fair rate for the back half and they always kept everything up, unlike some of the other places on the block. Case in point: the four-plex next door. Only one of the units was rented. The others were in such disrepair that it was a constant effort on all our parts to keep wandering junkies from squatting, especially in the two narrow one-bedrooms in back. Periodically, we'd chase them off, but they always left behind their needles, condoms, pizza boxes, and beer bottles.

The owners of the mostly vacant place lived up North and Art told me the city couldn't seem to do anything to make them shape up. If the absentee owners were to show up and any locals spotted them, I'm not sure what would have happened. Here, you watched for a while and then you found the best thing to do. It didn't have to involve rules of law.

I kept my own apartment as tidy as my mood permitted. An Uptown belle once dismissed my décor as Asian Southwestern—a haphazard combination of Mexican blankets, wood and leather couches, highly eccentric taste in tables, chairs, and dinnerware, and a bedroom with a futon and a Zen mat that I used about as much as a lapsed Catholic goes to Mass. Actually I did tend to look to Asia in my head, when it got all mixed up. On the other hand, Asia was where a big chunk of the mixing-up started.

The living room next to the kitchen was also my office, with a wooden desk in one corner and a side bookshelf filled with things I thought I might need when I came here a year ago from Dallas. I'd worked for a TV station. I was a pretty good reporter and weekend anchor with a decent audience. But it's a volatile profession. One day I got into an argument with my boss and slammed him against a newsroom wall. They don't let you stay after that. Since he'd been throwing a punch at me at the time, the dust-up was kept out of the police blotter but not the grapevine. I walked away with a decent settlement "to pursue other interests."

I wasn't sure what other interests were. I was paying the bills with the freelance and PI gigs and looking into maybe using some of my CBS-7 cash-out to open a specialized high-end tourist agency. Mostly I was laying low, trying to get a bead on what I would do if I could do anything I wanted. In New Orleans. Anno Domini 2000.

All that's a long way of saying that as uncertain as things were for me in the Big Easy, I felt a lot better and a lot healthier than I had in the Big D. And if you are getting healthier in New Orleans, you definitely know you were not doing well previously.

THE DAY PASSED IN the usual routine. I put on WWOZ and listened to jazz while knocking out a few pages on a no-brainer story about Biloxi for a travel magazine. The real creativity was in making up an invoice to send to Ray Oubre, my lawyer friend, for photos I took of a Mr. Clive Tauberly with the wrong woman at a chic hotel on Gravier Street. Actually that's where I had gotten the idea for a tourism business. "Weekends on the Wild Side"—something like that. By early evening I was sitting on a wobbly wrought-iron barstool with a cracked red vinyl cushion at Berto's, a little tavern near Frenchmen. I spent several hours talking to Ben and Jerri, tourists from Florida who turned out to be not rich at all. At issue was whether the Sunshine State was part of the South, a question on which I could, and did, take both sides.

I went home less hopeful about profiting off escapist-minded bourgeoisie, but bubbly with love for my chosen metropolis, sinking so determinedly into the mushy Louisiana earth, a lustrous and valiant spirit in the face of the mist-shrouded heavens. I wondered, rounding the corner to my apartment, what that dead man had been thinking about the last place he would ever see. If he'd had time to think of anything.

I WAS FILLING OUT a quarterly income tax estimate the next morning when the phone rang. I almost let the machine answer. Interesting option, looking back.

"This is Jack."

"Hello, Mr. Prine?" It was the kind of voice that makes you want to hear more.

"Yes?"

"I'm sorry to bother you but my name is Elle Meridian and I'm at the police station where an officer named Mallory has kindly given me your number."

It was a clear voice, almost like a TV reporter's. But softer. Southern, with an urban sharpness. It was full of sadness.

"Oh. Yeah. Patrolman Mallory."

"I'm Terrell's sister. Terrell Henry Meridian is the man you found. My name is Elle."

"I'm really sorry." I scribbled her name and his on a notepad.

"Thank you. I'm calling to ask if you would be kind enough to talk to me for just a few minutes, today if possible, before I have to go home and get things set up for the funeral."

I tried to piece it together as quickly as I could.

"Mr. Prine?"

"Sorry," I said, to make up for what must have been a long pause. "But I'm not really sure what I could tell you."

"You found him."

"I know. That's what I mean." I could hear my own impatience. Seriously, I had no shot at running a tourist agency.

"I'd rather meet you in person."

I tried for a much nicer tone. "Sure. I could see that."

"Is there a place easy for you?"

I suggested Napoleon's. It's in the Quarter but it's the kind of rendezvous you can easily duck if you get into a bad meeting. Exits had been something I had been trained to think about long ago and old habits die hard. I said

I would be there at six, but she asked for five, because she had a drive, and we ended up settling on four.

I HAD FORGOTTEN TO get her description but as soon as I saw her there was no doubt. A force radiated off her. Unless my gut was completely wrong it was primarily directed at me. She had short, light brown hair with small curls, a loose cotton dress, lavender, and a gold chain around her neck, which was smooth, strong, light caramel. Her small lips were bee-stung. What you might describe under different circumstances as kissable.

As for me, Patrolman Mallory's description had made it easy. I am pretty average of build and size, decent-looking enough to be on TV but no movie star and, now on the other side of forty, not likely to be. Also, a three-inch scar descends from my left ear to mid-jaw. On TV it looks rakish. It helps me remember what it feels like to almost have your head taken off in an alley in Seoul. All told, I was no problem to spot if you knew what you were looking for.

She told me as much when I walked over and introduced myself. She motioned to the rickety vacant chair across the old wooden table. Outside, on St. Louis Street, tourists passed by, some peering inside the open doors to see if they dared come in. Horse-drawn carriages clopped along on their routine route. Across the street was a bar I hated, touting itself as once having been the site of slave auctions.

We didn't drink much. Just a Pimm's Cup each, and they went down fast. I bit into the slice of cucumber and told her what I did, what I'd done. She asked if the scar was from the Army and I said yes. She said it was barely noticeable and I hoped so. She said she was a psychologist and guidance counselor at the University of Alabama, about four hours away in Tuscaloosa. We let the bios sink in a little. I noticed the afternoon light dancing across her almond-shaped, honey-brown eyes. There was quite a bit of awkward silence. Then she called the waiter and paid for our drinks. She said that she thought it would help with her grieving to see where her brother's body had been found. She said she wanted to get the vibes from the place in the presence of the man who had come across him all dead like that.

2

We decided to walk rather than grab a cab, passing at a steady pace along the narrow sidewalks and around the tourists in front of the shops on Chartres. In a few minutes we were at Jackson Square in front of the cathedral. A weary man with a gray beard and paisley fatigues was playing guitar on a bench. Around him was the usual skirmish line of hustlers and shills who wanted to read your fortune or paint your portrait. I guess I could've asked her a few questions, but the purpose of our foray dampened conversational openings.

At Esplanade, we turned up to Royal and then crossed over Elysian Fields. A few blocks farther was the street where I lived. I said so, but she wasn't listening. Her breathing was growing irregular and rapid. When we got to Franklin, I knew she was trembling because her arm brushed mine and it gave me a shock. It was the first evidence that she was barely holding herself together.

I stopped. "It's just two blocks more."

"Aren't you going to show me?"

"I just wanted to make sure you were okay."

"I'm fine."

We got to the street and turned the corner. Even though someone had cleaned up, the curb where he had bled out was stained.

"Oh, Young Henry." She broke from me to hurry to the obvious spot, bending down as she got closer like an airplane making a landing. She extended her right hand and touched the dark crimson patch. She picked up a pebble and rubbed it on the stain and then put the pebble in her small purse. She stroked the spot as if it were a stigmata and then stood up straight and backed away a couple of steps and stared at it.

I lingered several paces back. It was like going to a stranger's grave.

A delivery van passed. Elle didn't move. Usually they'll honk at you but this one didn't. Elle was saying something I couldn't make out. I assumed it was a prayer.

After an interval she crossed herself and turned back to me. She looked like a woman you'd see in medieval religious paintings. Suffering, with grace. Then her features steeled. "Tell me what you saw."

I took a few steps forward. It was hard to know how to put it. I didn't want to say more than I figured she could handle.

"Same as I told the cop. He was just lying there. Not moving."

"But what else?"

"I don't know if you want to know this."

"I wouldn't have asked."

"Yeah, okay."

There was a silence.

"So?"

"So the back of his head was pretty flat."

"Like he'd been hit."

"Yeah. I mean, I'm sure he'd been hit. How else would it get like that?"

"Did you see his face?"

"No."

"You didn't go around and look at his face?"

A warning light blinked in my mind. "I mean, I could see a little of it but it was mostly down against the sidewalk."

"Was there a lot of blood?"

"I don't know if you want to know all this—"

"Just tell me."

I thought back. "Not all that much really. Mostly just in his hair and on his shirt."

"No big pool of blood or anything like that?"

"No. Look, this isn't anything for you to think about."

"Let me worry about what to think about."

"I just thought it would make you feel bad."

She looked at me with a flat affect. "Then what else?"

"That was about all. I could see he was dead and I found a pay phone and called the police."

"And they came."

"Yeah."

"And then the police turned the body over and looked at it."

"Yeah. I mean, I didn't see all that. I was staying out of the way and answering questions for Mallory, that cop you got my name from."

"So they didn't say anything else to you."

"Not really. I left when they were done with me."

"There's not even a chalk mark."

I hadn't thought of that. "No."

"So as far as you know the cops just came because you said you'd found a dead body, and then they wrote it up and had Young Henry picked up; that's all there was to it."

"Well, yeah—"

She came up close.

"And what did you take before you called them?"

I drew back.

"You heard me. Did you take his money, or his wallet, maybe that silver neck chain he liked to wear? Something to write a story about?"

"Forget this." I put up my hands in a dismissive gesture and turned to walk away. I got maybe eight or nine slow steps.

"That was wrong. I shouldn't have said that."

I turned. She was standing straight, like a reed not bending in the wind. Her arms, down at her sides, ended in fists. They were shaking.

I went back.

"He was my baby brother. Young Henry. We played all out in the woods in the summers when my family stayed down in the Delta at Rosedale, you know, where the blues came from. And they definitely do." She seemed to choke on her breath. "We sneaked over the levee to the river—"

I had no reason to, but I took her in my arms. She let me, put her head against my shoulder, and cried.

It didn't last long. She pulled back, wiped her cheeks, and glanced around as though she didn't want anyone to witness. Then she looked into my eyes. I would simply say deeply, but it was more like she was the Hubble telescope and I was space, being probed.

"Okay. I'm okay." She sniffled slightly, as if doing so made her mad. "Thanks for what you did. It was a good thing."

"You don't have to explain."

She turned back to look at the place where I had found him. "I need to get back to Oxford. I have to set up the burial. I want to put him with our family. It was just me and him now."

"Look—I don't know you all that well, but if I can help, feel free to call. I'm not just saying that."

She pursed her lips and nodded. "Thanks."

She gave a last glance at the spot, then turned and started walking back toward the Quarter.

I caught up. "I need a way to get in touch."

She kept up her pace. "I've got your number, remember?"

"Oh, right—"

"It's better that way right now."

We went into single file on Royal to dodge some trash cans on the sidewalk and an elderly woman inching along in a walker.

"I can find my way." She plowed along.

"I don't mind." I moved up by her side again.

"I mean, I'd rather just be by myself, you know?"

We were at Elysian Fields. She stopped at the curb because of the traffic. When it cleared she could have gone on but instead she turned to face me. We were both hot from the walking and our body temperatures reflected off each other.

She touched my forearm with the slightest of pressure. "Really, you've been a big help."

A rusty Plymouth minivan with a broken muffler chugged by. Whatever I might have said, or wanted to say, was squelched by the din. Probably for the best. She smiled, removed her fingers from my arm.

We walked to the median in silence.

"I'm sorry," I said, as we waited again for cars in the other lanes to pass. She looked at me.

"I mean about your brother."

She nodded in a kind of acknowledgment and crossed over to the park. I stayed in the median, and watched until a stream of tourists from Frenchmen swallowed her from my view.

3

On Tuesday I did a little work and called Ray about another divorce surveillance. Ray wasn't there so I left a message and started working up a query for a profile of a young Nigerian carpenter I had met who had come into the country illegally but was now being blackmailed by a lawyer who was using him as a de facto slave on some housing contracts in Houma. Nobody involved was famous so I doubted I'd get a bite. But there was still enough journalist in me to try. Or maybe Ray would know a lawyer who could take the case.

Around four, a travel editor in Atlanta called, asking if I could put a rush on that Biloxi story. I said yes, because what else could you say? Later, I felt like cooking and whipped up a light meal of rotini with a splash of olive oil, parsley, red pepper, and fresh Parmesan, and a couple of glasses of Australian Shiraz, and went to bed early.

I didn't know if I'd ever hear from Elle again, and short of trying to get her phone number from the police I didn't even know how to call her. A rookie mistake. She had gotten to me.

Wednesday, I decided to go down into the Quarter and hang out at a coffee shop on Ursulines, around the corner from the old convent where the nuns had put their stamp on the city. I took my laptop, which had become such a constant companion that I was tempted to give it a nickname.

I got a *Times-Picayune* from a machine to which someone had chained a bike barely worth stealing. Inside, I considered the pastries behind the glass counter and asked the Vietnamese owner for some French coffee and a plain croissant. I settled in at a window table and had a quick scan of the paper. Yesterday there'd been nothing, but there it was now, deep in the metro section: "Body Found in Marigny."

Terrell H. Meridian was identified as a "frequent visitor to the city" but not a tourist. A police spokesman said there was "no apparent motive or suspect." The last graf gave the Crimestoppers number for anonymous tips, which they usually ran in all the minor cases. I knew the killers would never be found.

Across the street, a minivan pulled up. A half-dozen people climbed out and started looking around. They were German, probably on a package tour through Lufthansa, which often put up people at the little guesthouses along this block. A porter of sorts lurched out of Le Fleur, a hostel at which I had once stayed myself. I liked it because it wasn't fancy and overpriced but it wasn't a dump, either—the two general modes of Quarter lodging.

The tourists were chattering excitedly, and most of them gave up on the lone porter, picked up their own bags and disappeared inside. I knew that they would be down in the lobby presently, hashing out what to see next. Invariably they would decide that New Orleans was where people came to be somebody else, and they would hit one of the Bourbon Street bars for a pre-lunch drink, which would turn into many, and with jet-lag they'd be back in their rooms crashed out until the evening. Then they would go to Pat O'Brien's and it would start again.

Or maybe not. Maybe they would walk up to St. Louis Cathedral and look around Jackson Square, then up the levee to the river, and watch it flow along past the barges and the cruise ships. They might mosey on past the bend where the casinos perch like beached sharks, unable to really take a bite from the city but staying alive with nibbles.

Like me.

I heard a phone ring and gradually realized it was coming from my pocket. I'd only recently started carrying a cell phone. I didn't recognize the incoming number, but it was from somewhere in the city.

"Are you at work?"

"Is that you?" As if that voice could have been mistaken for any other.

"I didn't want to bother you if you were busy."

"I'm not."

"You can talk?"

"Yeah. I'm down here in the Quarter, actually."

"Oh."

"Gets me out of the house."

"Mmm."

A silence long enough for me to breathe.

"Jack, I wonder if I could ask you for one more favor."

"Of course you can."

"It's about Terrell—Young Henry. I need to go down to the funeral home later today."

"You're in town? I thought you were going to Oxford."

"It was easier to stay over to finish up the arrangements."

"Oh, right. Sure."

"Anyway, about the funeral home—"

"So where are you now?"

"At the moment I'm at a stop light on Broad Street. I have a lot to do."

"I was just going to suggest coffee, or lunch."

"That would be nice. I'll take a rain check."

"Done."

"What I was calling about, though, is that one of the things I had to do was go to the coroner's. They had the autopsy."

"That was fast."

"I didn't have to see the body again, though."

"Because you had already made the ID?"

"That's what the sergeant said. Taylor, I think his name was."

"What, they interviewed you?"

"It was okay. Mostly he wanted to go over the autopsy. He said it was routine. I was just wondering, as a reporter and investigator and all, does that sound right?"

"Like I said, it was fast, but if they had a slow day not too unusual."

"Really?"

"From what I know, anyway." A bar buddy named Ronnie once told me it could take all day on some bodies but the routine ones they could crank out. Ronnie was a waiter in a hotel on Royal but had worked in the coroner's office over on Tulane Avenue, using skills he'd learned as a mortician's assistant in the service. He'd quit, though, and now only wanted to be around live people, live music, live anything.

"He had cocaine in his blood."

I didn't know what to say so I left it alone.

"And it was like you said, a blow to the back of the head. They said it was wood. They found some splinters."

"That's all I could see. You know. When I came across his body."

"I know I was out of line back there."

"Forget it. So they're going to release the body?"

"They already have. The sergeant said it was okay, since I wanted to send the body to Oxford and bury him quickly. I told him my brother visited here a lot but needed to be laid to rest at home. He was a big help."

I would be too, I thought to myself. "Forensics doesn't need the body?"

"He said they're still investigating, but they're done with Young Henry's body. They said he was probably killed somewhere else and left there. He said that meant the search would be harder."

"You never know what any of that means."

"I think it means they might not look very hard for whoever killed a gay black man if it didn't even happen in their city."

"I wouldn't go there just yet."

"You're white."

"What?"

"I mean, you see these things differently."

"Maybe." I knew she was right but I didn't want to make her feel any worse than she did. I decided to change the subject. "Did they give you a report or anything?"

"I asked but he said the case was still open."

"It would have to be at this point."

"I sort of feel like a suspect."

"I doubt that."

"Then why couldn't I have a report?"

"Maybe they didn't have it worked up."

"I guess."

"Look, I know what you're saying. But some of those cops are okay. If you want, later on, I can make a call to a detective I know, just to see how things are going."

"Sure, if you think that would do anything. It's just that—you know."

"Absolutely."

"They did find one other thing."

"What, on his body?" I looked around the café. A couple of people seemed to be eavesdropping. I shot them a glare and they looked off, but I turned my head away, speaking a little softer.

"A napkin. In his pocket. From some club in the Quarter. Rio Blanche. You know it?"

I thought a moment. "Yeah. I don't really go there."

"Is it gay?"

"It is. But it's a hard-drinker kind of place. Depressing."

There was silence, then she said. "Young Henry didn't drink all that much."

"Well, maybe he liked it. You know how people find a place they like and just keep going there."

"The sergeant asked me if I thought it was . . . the way he put it was, 'a lovers' quarrel.'"

That was how I was afraid they'd peg it. "They just ask questions. However dumb they might sound. It's what they have to do." She probably knew I was lying.

"It wasn't that."

"Did you tell that to the cop?"

"I said I doubted that's what it was, a quarrel, that my brother didn't hang around with people who would get that violent."

"What did he say?"

"He said sometimes you don't know what people will do until you put together the pieces later."

"A cop said that?"

"Anyway, I didn't stay long. I hated being there."

"I understand."

"So I left. The sergeant said they'll call from time to time."

"I'm sure they will."

"So could you come meet me at the funeral home later this afternoon? It's called Orman Brothers. In Gentilly."

I watched some people passing outside on Ursulines. The eavesdroppers were talking to each other. "You know about funeral homes in New Orleans?"

"I have a friend that does. A priest."

"I see."

"It's where I go to church."

"When you're in town?"

"Yeah."

I thought on that.

"So you'll be there?"

"Tell me when."

"They said any time after two this afternoon."

"Sure. I can be there."

"I have to go over early to do some paperwork but mainly I'd like company after."

"Sure."

"With you seeing him and all, I feel like it's a connection. I guess that sounds stupid."

"There is."

"What?"

"A connection."

"I guess I wanted to call you."

"I wasn't sure after the other day."

"I wasn't, either. But you were there for me. A total stranger. Is that weird?"

"Not to me. I'm glad you thought enough of me to call. I'm sure you have other people."

"Yeah?"

"Yeah."

"I mean I do know some people in New Orleans but they're not really friends. More like from work."

"I can understand that. But I'm glad you called me."

A slight pause. "Jack?"

"I'm still here."

"When we're done I want to go have a drink. Maybe a couple."

"Definitely."

She told me the address for Orman's. We decided on 3 P.M. I worked a while longer at the coffee shop, then went to my apartment and did about thirty minutes on my treadmill. I had a quick sandwich even though I wasn't particularly hungry. I'd had low blood sugar since I was in the Army and had been warned to get protein more or less on schedule. I showered and made some coffee, and went over my checkbook. When it finally was time to go, I put on a freshly laundered white shirt and some dark trousers and went to meet a beautiful woman with a dead brother and a troubled mind.

Orman's was easy to find, converted from a stately, Spanish-style two-story with moss-draped oaks overhanging a circular driveway in front. I parked in a visitor space on the side next to a few other cars and a hearse and went up to the door. Knocking seemed kind of foolish so I just opened and went inside.

The foyer was large, sedate, furnished mostly with antiques, dark wooden colors. A middle-aged woman in a black business suit came out, introduced herself as Mrs. Sutter, an assistant, and told me Elle was still talking to Mr. Orman. She asked if I needed coffee, which I didn't, and showed me to a floral-patterned chair. I sat down and picked up a copy of *People* from an end table. I thumbed it without interest, looked for something else to read. *Southern Living, Ebony, Smithsonian.* I wondered about periodical choices in funeral homes, and then drifted into other thoughts, some taking me back to Dallas and the memorial service for Ben Lutz, a TV reporter friend who died at age thirty-one from a bee sting. Wife and kids. House with big oak trees. Chocolate Labs. Loved by all. I cried at his funeral and on the spot decided I wouldn't waste any more time with my life. Not long after that I got in the fight in the newsroom.

A door off the far side of the foyer opened and Elle came out, talking to a man in his forties dressed in a dark blue suit and a shirt so white it almost glowed around his neck. She shook his hand and said she'd call later and he disappeared back into the other room. He glanced at me and nodded but there was no need to say anything.

Elle took a breath and turned to me. She walked over, clutching some paperwork.

"Thanks, Jack."

"Sure."

"We can go. It's taken care of."

I took her arm, as though escorting her, but I could tell she didn't want that so I let go and we went outside.

"Where now?"

"You choose."

"Where's your car?"

"I took a cab. My car's back where I'm staying. You bring a ride?"

"That green Explorer."

She looked at it, then me. "It fits."

We got in, buckled up, and headed to a little bar on I liked on lower Decatur, the Urban Bayou. Nicer than Berto's and not too crowded in the early afternoon. I found a parking place on Esplanade right away.

On the way over she had sketched out the funeral home story. The body hadn't been ready for viewing but she had picked a casket, a medium-priced wooden model, silver and brown. It, and he, would be shipped to Oxford and the services would be in a couple of days. She'd been busy making calls and setting it all up since Monday. Breaking down into tears, as time permitted.

We settled into a table in a dark part of the bar. I ordered a bottle of Cabernet. It was on the second glass that she told me she had a timeshare in Mid-City, near the Fairgrounds. She apologized for misleading me about that, but said it was because we'd just met and a woman had to be careful about things like that. Another click went off in my head. I chalked it up to the chance and awkward nature of our entire mode of acquaintance.

She rounded out the picture a little more. Although her job was in Tuscaloosa, she needed a place in New Orleans because she had a year-long contract with Orleans Parish, working with abused women one or two weekends a month. Ironically, this was her week to have the timeshare.

She mostly came into town, counseled for double twelve-hour days, and left, so she didn't have much of a social life here. From what I could gather, not that much back in Alabama, either. When I tried to press, she demurred, something about "focusing on my own life this year." I told her more about what I did, and we joked a little, in a gallows way, about me having an exclusive on her story, but it had a bad aftertaste so we dropped it.

We went over the coroner's visit again and she told me a little more about her brother. We had been there maybe an hour when she excused herself and walked outside with her cell phone. She was gone for at least several songs on the famously eclectic jukebox: Patsy Cline, Tito Puente, Etta James, Olu Dara. When she came back she poured the rest of the bottle for us and seemed preoccupied. Then she said she wanted to go home.

I probably shouldn't have driven after all the vino, but it wasn't the first time I'd erred in that direction. Sometimes I got into situations and I just said the hell with it and did what I needed to do. On the other hand, I was working at keeping the outright stupid stuff to a minimum.

Her place was an upstairs garage apartment behind a larger bungalow, gray with blue trim, in the front. The garden between them was dense with bright, fragrant flowers, lush shrubs and towering magnolias. The inside was clean, hardwood floors, not much furniture, Pier I stuff mixed with Magazine Street boutique touches. I glanced into the bedroom. The oak-framed bed had a yellow duvet partly covering four pillows in white lace cases, a couple of cane and wicker chairs nearby, walnut dresser. Tasteful but impersonal. Like only strangers spent time there.

"I decided to have him cremated." She was in the kitchen. I heard a fridge door shut just before she came out holding a plastic bottle of spring water. "That's what I was doing on the phone."

It took a moment to register. "You're kidding. After all that?"

"It was what he wanted. I never should have gone for the burial."

"But I thought you already paid for it."

She walked into the living room and gave me the water. I drank it. My head was a little woozy and I figured hers must be, too. Still, I had expected an entirely different line of conversation.

"Mr. Orman was okay about it. He still gets a fee."

I put the bottle on an end table and moved close to her. "So, never mind Oxford?"

She moved back, slightly, but enough. I took a long drink.

"I'm still taking Young Henry home. Just differently. They'll send the ashes. Mr. Orman said he had a man heading that way so it wasn't an extra cost, or at least not that much. He's very nice to me. He knows the preacher in Oxford."

She glanced at some envelopes on the couch, like she still had business to attend. It was still early in the evening.

"Well, you know, maybe it's better."

"I don't know if it is or not but I don't want Young Henry going back the way you found him and with the way they cut him up over there in that basement. Even Mr. Orman said it would be better, a cremation. He's seen these before."

I began to feel uncomfortable, intrusive.

"I guess I'll go."

"I'm sorry. I wasn't going to bring it up tonight. I had a good time with you. It felt good to let go for a little while. It really did."

I wasn't expecting it but she came close and kissed me, lightly, on the cheek. Maybe it was just a courtesy, a thoughtful good night. But in her eyes dwelt the sadness. It was all that kept me from wanting to press her close for hours.

4

The Rio Blanche occupied a corner, open on both sides for anyone who wanted to go in. They did all day long, leaning against the weathered wooden counter or weaving on the vinyl-topped stools. Behind the bar, a long mirror was plastered with photos, music posters, beer signs, Hawaiian leis, jock straps, and dildos. At night the crowds came out onto the sidewalk, to the annoyance of the police and passersby, and the music got pretty loud. It was unusual but not rare to see a woman inside, or a straight guy. It was one of the best places in town for catfish po' boys.

When I walked in, around 5 P.M., the crowd was medium. I got the usual territorial looks, which basically said I wasn't invited—not because I wasn't gay, but because I wasn't a regular.

I found an empty two-top near the sidewalk entry and waited. I was pretty sure the server who came over was Elfego from the way Elle had described him: peroxided curly hair, pale, skinny, maybe late forties, usually wearing a guayabera. He had a triangle-shaped ring in his left ear. He was Spanish, she had said, not Mexican, and didn't like to be confused with what he considered a colonial nation.

He smiled a waiter's welcome and asked what I wanted. I ordered a Dos Equis. When he came back, I had placed a photo of Terrell on the table.

He glanced at it and said, "He looks younger."

"How old was he?"

"Now, as old as he's gonna get. In that, maybe twenty-six, twenty-five."

"It looks like he's on a farm or something," I said, shifting my body to look at it better. It was at least eight years out of date.

"Probably is." He pushed the photo back to me. "I don't want to look at that boy just now."

"Of course."

"You got a name or you just in the photography business?"

"Jack. I figured you probably knew. I guess you're Elfego."

"Why did Elle want you to talk to me?"

I looked at him closely. And he back at me. He seemed sincere. As sincere as you can look wearing lavender parachute pants and a bright green shirt speckled with red parrots. We knew we were in the same situation. The situation was Elle.

"I'm not sure why," I said. "I mean, obviously about her brother. They found a cocktail napkin from here in his clothes. Maybe the cops have already been here. She called me this morning and asked if I would come by. She's busy with the funeral stuff."

Elfego smiled slightly. "Or maybe the thought of coming here freaked her, you know? But whatever."

I shrugged. To be sure, I didn't really know why she asked me to see Elfego when she called me just after lunch, thanked me again for last night's "mental oasis," and asked, almost apologizing, if I could do her another favor. She had remembered her brother had some kind of friend who might have worked at the Rio Blanche. She said she wasn't sure and it had been a long time ago, and maybe it wasn't anything at all, but would I mind just checking it out, since I already knew where the bar was. She said she knew she was grasping but had to. She probably knew I would say yes, and I did.

He pretended to wipe condensation rings from the table. "Sí, handsome, the cops were here already. They asked me a couple of questions, and Quasimodo back there at the bar. We didn't know shit. They said they'd be back if they needed anything else. It took about ten valuable minutes of their time." He laughed outright.

I didn't know where this was supposed to go, so I just figured to keep probing out of habit.

"Elle said the detective told her he was seen here with a white guy, older."

"How do you know Elle, anyway?"

"I found Terrell's body. We got to know each other."

He nodded. We both knew she had filled him in. I guess he wanted to get in front of the conversation.

"Probably she wanted to know who was with him in here. Other than me."

"Were you and Terrell friends, or whatever?"

" 'Or whatever' for going on five years. Thanks for asking."

"I just meant, did you know him well?"

"I think I know what you meant."

"Sorry."

He fiddled with the photo again, and looked away.

"So I guess the funeral's going to be in Oxford."

"I guess so. Are you going?"

"Maybe. You gonna drink that beer?"

I looked at it but didn't pick it up. Some of the lads at a table in the corner were studying me, the stranger, pretty hard again.

"She thinks she knows it was Trey who came in here, but you can tell her I said it *definitely* was. I didn't want to say over the phone. She said to tell you what I saw exactly and to trust you. Me, I wouldn't."

I peeled at the label on the bottle. "She knows who this Trey is?"

"You better believe it."

"Who is he?"

Elfego thought about that. "You know much about Mississippi?"

"Does anybody?"

"About Elle's family?"

"Just the brother."

He rolled his eyes. "Nice. Anyway, 'this' Trey, he's the little niño of Tom Barnett, they called him Junior, some big businessman. But it was Junior's daddy, Big Tom, who made all the family money. Cotton and shipping, some shit like that. Anyway he was rich. They had a plantation outside Oxford from back when all those gringos were having slaves, like that. Rich white folks, you'd call them. Trey being the only child of Junior, who got killed driving his little plane into a mountain in Colorado, and mama already dead, he inherited all of it. Speaking of snow, our Trey got into the importing business, dealing some art, some powder. What they say." He stopped. "She says you're some kind of private eye or something."

"Not really. Sort of. But that's not why I'm helping her."

He examined me like a specimen. "Yeah. Maybe." He pulled back, crossed his arms. Then he leaned in. "Well Mister-Magnum-P. I.-Not-Really-Sort-Of. I don't really give a shit what you do. The reason I'm wasting my time talking to you about this is Elle asked me to." He paused. "And I could hear it in her voice."

"What?"

"You know what. I can see it in your face, too. What are you, teenagers? Hell, she's barely into mourning."

"What are you, her dad?"

He reached over and pinged my beer bottle with the ring on his fore-finger. Not an especially friendly gesture.

"Look, if you're going to be with Elle someday—you know, in about a hundred years—you should know a little about her brother's situation. And you should be good to her." He looked away.

I found something to study on the table.

Elfego put up a hand and waved it as if to end the digression. "Trey and Terrell were 'friends or whatever,' too, okay? From years back. They grew up together. Those two, and Elle. So like I said, Trey was in here with Terrell that night. They were actually sitting at this same table."

I was starting to get the drift. "I see."

"So you're listening. Good. That's good for Mister-P.-I.-Not-Really-Sort-Of."

"It's a gift."

"Maybe. Anyway, Trey got a call. Said he was going to look at a painting at some gallery down on Chartres. Left Terrell here alone. An hour or something." Elfego smiled. Big, Cheshire-cat kind. "That's how the napkin got in Terrell's shorts, you get it?"

"The police said it was in his pocket."

"Sure they did."

We looked at each other, then at the beer bottle.

"So you two got together. You and Terrell."

"Very good, Magnum. Together and together again. Right back around there in the office. Where you get to go if you know somebody here. Like me. Where you get a napkin wrapped around your dick."

I took a drink. He was taunting me, but his lover had been murdered just last weekend and he was talking about it with a stranger sent by a sister. He had to tell it to someone. And it sure wouldn't be the cops.

"Then, what, he came back? Trey?"

Elfego's lip curled. "Sí, señor. It got a little ugly."

"Trey knew? About you and Terrell? I mean about . . . while he was gone?"

"Claro. Hell yes. I told him. The prick."

"Damn."

"Terrell didn't like it much either but I said to him, little puta, you're going to fuck me don't expect me to keep it all to myself, querida."

I drank some of my beer. Elfego's face was red and his jaw taut. He took a breath and forced a smile.

"Anyway, that bourgeois bitch ought to of been proud being with me. I always was with him. We went all over this city, and down in Biloxi, and Mobile, Jackson, together. We were beautiful together. People watched us, because we were things of beauty. And then to waste it on that gringo Trey Barnett cocksucker, which he was—" He feigned spitting on the ground. "And right here in front of me. Sure, I'm gonna fuck my baby. And then you better believe I'm gonna tell that rich asshole he shows up with here exactly what we did."

"Elfego, you working here or what?" It was the guy behind the bar. He did sort of look like Quasimodo. Elfego shot him a finger, but slowly pushed back his chair and stood.

"So, next I know Young Henry is dead."

"I'm sorry."

"Yeah, well, what are you gonna do? You want another Dos?"

I PLANNED TO PHONE her about ten or so but she called me, from her cell. It was barely seven.

"Jack, how are you?"

"I'm good. I miss you."

"Same." It came out almost coquettish. Then some other quality. Strained, maybe. "Look, Jack. I'm just driving around now. In Tuscaloosa. I'm on some streets down by the UA campus."

"Roll Tide."

"Jack—" Instead of words I heard rapid, shallow breathing.

"Elle? Elle?"

Now a longer, deeper breath.

"I'm scared. I can't go home. I don't know what to do."

"Hang on." I had been watching a sitcom, or more accurately I had the TV on as background, a habit I had picked up from the newsroom. I muted the sound, then went over to the folded half-table in my kitchen. "What is it?"

"I was going home. I'd stopped at the Pak n' Sak for a couple of things and then was going down my street. It's not too far from downtown but it's quiet, just a lot of families and a few professors . . . Jack?"

"I'm here."

"There was someone at my house. I could see it when I was at the corner before my block. I could see a car parked in the driveway and the lights were on inside."

"You didn't leave them on."

"No."

"You mean you were being robbed?"

She didn't answer.

"Elle?"

"I pulled in behind a pickup on the street and watched. I watched about half an hour."

"They left?"

"No. But I did."

"They're still there?"

"I don't know."

"Call the police."

"I can't. Hang on." I heard the phone drop on the seat. "Sorry. I forgot my seat belt. I don't want to get stopped."

"You can't call the police?"

"No."

I walked into the living room, then into the kitchen and looked out into the garden. It looked nice in the approaching sunset. "I guess I don't understand."

"I'm sorry. I'm not trying to be vague." She didn't say anything for a moment or two. "I'm on University now, headed toward the mall. I think I'll go on and pick up the interstate. That should be okay."

"You're going to leave them there like that?"

"What can I do? I don't think they'll stay that long. If I don't show up."

"What?"

"I think I know who they are. I saw the plates on the car. It was a black Volvo, that fast-looking one. Mississippi."

I let that work in my head a minute.

"You're saying somebody came to your house looking for you. Somebody you know."

"That's what I'm saying."

"And you're afraid to go up and see who it is. Or call the police."

"Yeah. Yes. I am."

"Is there anyone else there you could call for help?"

"I have friends if that's what you mean."

"I just meant someone close by."

"I wanted to call you."

"I just meant, you know, you're in Tuscaloosa and I'm down here in

New Orleans. . . . And good."

"And there are some guys taking over my house. . . . And good."

I let the friendly volley settle. "Elle, what's going on?"

"It's complicated. It's hard to talk about over this phone. Hang on—" I heard a horn, muffled. "Damn, a pickup just ran through that light. Aren't you sorry you ever met me?"

"No."

I could hear the noise of the road from her end of the phone.

"I was going to call you anyway later to say I had talked to Elfego."

"Thanks," she finally said. "I appreciate that . . . a lot." Another pause. "So I don't have to explain calling you anymore."

"I didn't mean it that way."

We were silent again.

"So, Elfego . . ." I said.

"Elfego."

"We got together."

"At the bar."

"Rio Blanche, yeah."

"Did he tell you about Mississippi?"

I was walking around my living room, staring at familiar objects as though they were props in some movie in which I had been mistakenly cast. "He sure did."

"Such as?"

"Such as the guy who knew your brother, for one."

"Trey."

"Yeah."

"He told you about Trey and Terrell, then."

"They'd been there. Together, he said. By the way, he's a piece of work, Elfego."

"He's not so bad."

"I guess if you know him. Anyway, he said I should tell you they were at the Rio Blanche even though you already knew. For what it's worth, he was taking it hard."

"Hard?"

"Well, in that he was pretending he had it under control."

"Repression. Transference."

"What?"

"Shrink stuff. Counselor, I should say, but pretty much everybody calls us shrinks down here, so I just go with the flow." She paused, as if catching a memory. "You know, he doesn't want to deal. I talked to him on the phone. It was difficult. For both of us."

"What did he mean, you already knew about the Rio Blanche?"

"Because I did know, or sort of did. Elfego told me the same thing, about Trey being there. But I wanted to know if he'd tell you the same or change it around. I felt like he'd be more open with you, since you were a stranger but also someone connected to me, and sort of to Young Henry—"

"Hold on." I was back in the kitchen, and took a half-empty bottle of French house red from the counter. Or maybe it was half-full. I cradled the phone in my ear while I took out the cork and poured some into a drinking glass. I was trying to get my mind around this and it wasn't quite happening.

"Why didn't you mention that to me before? For that matter why didn't you tell the police? You told them your brother didn't know any violent people. Wasn't that what you said?" I took a drink of the red. Not bad, and only seven dollars a bottle.

"Okay. I understand. But don't be like that, not now. Please. I just . . . I just didn't know if I wanted to get into it all with you. You were so good to help me all you already did. And I just didn't want to go to the Rio Blanche, get into a lot of stuff with Elfego about him and Young Henry that maybe I wouldn't want to listen to right now. Can you understand that? You know? I'm sorry. Maybe I was wrong."

I felt bad for raising my voice. "I'm sorry. I didn't mean—"

"I sound like a basket case."

"Far from it."

"That's kind. Also a lie."

"Whatever kind of case you are, it seems like the best thing would be to call the cops right now about your house, to be safe. And what if it's just burglars?"

"It's not. Trust me."

"Call 911."

"Did Elfego tell you a lot about Trey?"

"Not that much. But that wasn't my question. Isn't this police stuff? Shouldn't you be calling them? Rather than driving around and talking?"

"I heard you. But I can't. It doesn't even matter. I know who's at my house."

"You mean Trey?"

"Or some of his low-life friends."

I took another sip and flashed back to her reactions in the Marigny. Anger in that sadness.

"I still wish you'd call the cops. It's the best way to handle it. Seriously."

She blurted out a quick laugh, probably from the tension. "Ordinarily I like that kind of perseverance in a man. But not right now."

"Uh-huh. Where are you now?"

"I'm just getting on I-20."

"So you're not headed for Oxford?"

"I don't know where I'm headed. I'm just driving."

"Let's think of a plan."

"Yeah, a plan. Be a man with a plan, Jack."

"How far to Birmingham? An hour?"

"About."

"Okay. Good."

Something came to me so I figured to just say it. "Here's an idea. Go on to Birmingham for the night. Instead of Oxford. It's not the way anyone would expect you to go. Find a decent motel. A place you can park in the back or in a garage."

Road noise again while she thought about it. "I go to Birmingham on business a lot. There's a Marriott down around Homewood."

"Would Trey know about it?"

"I go to different ones but he wouldn't know one way or another."

"Okay, go there and get a room. Get off the road."

"And?"

"And I'll drive up and stay with you. We'll go to Oxford tomorrow if you want and take care of the ashes and all that. It's really not all that far from Birmingham so you'd be most of the way there tonight."

She was thinking about it. I expected her to.

"Jack, it's a long drive for you."

"I could be there by one or two in the morning if I leave now. It's not like I could sleep."

"And you'd stay with me?"

I knew what she meant. "Nothing funny."

"I wasn't implying. . ."

"Just until you feel safe or we find out if this guy really is looking for you. Which, by the way, why would he be?"

"I'm sorry to be such trouble," she said after a moment. She didn't respond to the question about Trey.

"You're not trouble. Like I said."

"I know."

"So I'm coming."

"I mean I do know you're busy and you have a life that doesn't involve a crazy woman from Alabama. I don't mean to act like you have to drop everything for me."

"You're afraid. It's all over your voice."

"Maybe."

"Okay."

"Okay."

I could hear hard breathing again.

"I'm going to throw some things in a bag. I'll call you when I get closer."

"Jack?"

"Yeah?"

"I just hate to get off the phone."

"I do, too, but if we don't, I'll never get there."

"I know. I know."

"Turn on the radio. Listen to some music. You'll be fine. When you get to the motel order a pizza. Watch HBO. I'll call you when I get to Meridian or around there."

"Okay."

"All right."

"I feel better now."

"I do, too."

We said goodbye.

I finished the glass of wine. The bottle was tempting but I had a long drive and coffee from somewhere on the road was the only way to go. I packed up quickly. I own a police-style Remington 12-gauge and keep it in a closet. I don't particularly like guns anymore, but in this town you have to be practical. In Dallas I kept a Beretta, but one night, after too much drinking and too many bad thoughts, I held it in a way I shouldn't have, against my ear. Next day I dropped it into the Trinity River.

I zipped the shotgun and an unopened box of shells into a brown waterproof sheath. I carried it and my canvas duffel bag down the narrow walkway leading from my apartment past the garden and to the gate opening onto the street, where I had to park. My Explorer was an older model, not all that appealing to thieves, although, this being New Orleans, a stolen car figured in everyone's future. For some reason our block had been lucky on that score.

I stowed the gear in the back and threw an old Army poncho over it. Then I returned to the apartment to check that the timer light in the living room was set, the water was off on the leaky shower faucet, and so on. I unplugged my laptop. Almost as an afterthought, I grabbed some notepads. Some part of me hadn't decided whether this would become professional, too. As in something for Ray, or maybe some kind of story I could sell. I needed to talk to Elle about it more. Much more. But now she was scared and I just wanted to get there. I locked up and went back to the Explorer.

Before buckling in, I took a look around the street. Quiet, almost a storybook of stoops and French doors and pastels. Except for the rusty Chevy and the pile of junk outside one of the row houses a half-block away. Word was it was an eviction after a bad break-up.

Leaving the Marigny, I picked up Elysian Fields lakeside to the I-10 ramp and then glided up the highway with the city and all its lights and parties and people not involved in murders slipping behind me and unknown miles of darkness, fog, and deep Southern forest ahead.

And Elle.

5

The motel was on a residential exit just before getting into the city's southern suburbs, easy enough for me to find in the late night fog that draped the Appalachian foothills. It was almost 2 A.M. when she opened the door. She'd been sleeping in gym shorts and a baggy gray T-shirt and was only half-awake. I shut the door behind me and latched it. She hugged me and I hugged back, sort of woodenly, and then she sat on the edge of the king-size bed.

"Do you want to talk now?" she asked.

"Yeah, but I'm tired and you're asleep. Let's wait until morning."

She yawned and her head dropped toward her chest. I took that for a yes. I made a quick trip to the bathroom. Her overnight kit from New Orleans was on the sink but hadn't been opened. I looked pretty haggard in the harsh light of the motel mirror, so I splashed some water on my face before going back into the room. I took off my deck shoes and socks and lay on the bed near her, still in my jeans and a black T-shirt.

She was on her side, facing away. This is all I had been thinking about for hours. That and what might have made her so scared she couldn't go home and couldn't call the police. I looked over her shoulder. She was asleep.

I rolled back and let my head sink into a pillow. I drifted away into dreams I couldn't recall. That was good. It was the ones I could recall that were bad.

IN THE MORNING, SHE was awake, sitting in a chair near the window, looking out at the trees and hills of the little valley in which the motel sat. She had made coffee from the machine by the sink. I watched her a few minutes while I tried to wake up. The clock on the side dresser said nine-forty-five so we had slept pretty well.

When she heard me move, she turned and smiled.

"Good morning."

I tried not to look like I'd just woken up.

"Good morning."

"I needed that sleep. Thanks."

"It wasn't a bad drive. Not much traffic." I reached over to a glass of water I'd left on the bedside table and drank it all.

"I'm really glad you're here."

"Me, too."

"I hope you don't mind that kind of woman."

"What kind?"

"Complicated."

"I like complicated." I stood and stretched.

"I'm going to grab a shower," she said, glancing at the clock. "I didn't want to wake you up before." She went into the bathroom and turned on the water. The door didn't catch the latch and swung part way open. I heard the spray coursing over her body and tried not to think about it.

"What about the cars?" she called out.

"I was wondering about that. Maybe we could leave yours here somewhere unless you want to drive it to Oxford."

"No. And I don't want to go back to T-town, either." Splashing noises. "So we could take yours? I guess nobody would know it had anything to do with me."

"Right."

"I mean it would work out better that way. After last night."

"Yeah, it would. I know a place near the airport for long-term. I've used it before when I had to fly out of Birmingham. It'll be fine there. It's covered parking."

"Okay, I guess. I can come get it later."

"I'll bring you back here after the funeral."

"Okay. That's good. You don't mind?"

"I'd rather do it this way."

I heard the water turn off and the shower stall door slide open. A few minutes later the bathroom door opened all the way and she emerged through a bank of steam, a big white towel around her torso. Her hair wet and glistening. I pretended to sort through my bag for clothes.

"You should get dressed," she said. "Then we can go get breakfast."

"You clean up good."

Just the hint of a response in her face. "I have to change."

I went into the bathroom. I heard the plop of the towel onto the carpet and the clatter of hangers in the closet as she got her clothes.

When I came out, tucking a dark blue polo into the same jeans, she was sitting at the small pressed-wood table near the window. She had on faded jeans and a loose yellow cotton blouse. She didn't waste any time.

"Trey killed Young Henry."

I stuffed my dopp kit into my duffel bag, zipped it up, and walked over to the window. I peered out the side of the draw curtain into the parking lot, which wasn't very full, although it was a weekday. The sky was blue, almost cloudless.

"But I don't know what to do about it."

I let the curtain drop and looked at her. I wasn't sure how to respond.

She twirled a Styrofoam cup in her slender fingers. For the first time, I noticed her nail polish was light blue.

"I've known all along. Before I even got to New Orleans. First it was like a bad feeling I didn't want. But now I'm sure."

"From what Elfego said."

"More than that, but yeah."

I pulled back the chair from the other side of the table and sat across from her.

"It was the necklace. You know, I asked you about it? Trey gave him one and he always wore it. When I didn't see it, it just hit me that Trey had taken it back. I freaked. I can't say why. So I took it out on you."

"You were in shock."

"Not now."

She reached across the table and covered my right hand with her left. "There's something else." Her palm was warm.

"Young Henry stole something from Trey."

I looked away involuntarily.

She hesitated, as if trying to work out her thoughts.

"A painting, something from Mexico, or actually, Spain. A Spanish artist. It shows the Virgin Mary."

"The Virgin of Guadalupe?"

"It's about when she appeared to an Aztec peasant back after the Conquest. You know the story?"

"Yeah.

She seemed surprised. "You Catholic?"

"No. But I'm from Texas. She shows up, gives the Aztec some roses, he shows them to the Spanish priests, Mexico is converted." I must have ended that with a smirk because she responded with a frown.

"Anyway . . . this painting shows her with the flowers, some kind of nature scene behind her. I remember Young Henry saying it was a masterpiece and not that many people knew about it. He really went on about how much it impressed him. He taught art history, you know, in high school."

She stopped a moment, her thoughts gone back to her brother. "That was a couple of months ago. We got to where we didn't talk all that often lately." She stopped again. "He said he planned to take it because Trey owed him."

Her hand tightened around mine.

"Young Henry said it was worth millions, and he had a buyer in Houston lined up. A woman who owned an art gallery, I think. I thought maybe he was, you know, high. But now—" Her gaze shifted to the side just for a moment. "My brother did some art dealing on the side. Maybe Elfego mentioned that. Some of the time, anyway."

"Obviously Trey wants the painting back."

"Who wouldn't? It's worth millions."

"And you're sure your brother took it?"

"Same as I'm sure Trey killed him."

"That's why he was at your house. To see if you had it."

She nodded, sat back in her chair.

"But you don't have it."

"No, Jack. I don't have it."

"I didn't mean anything."

"You did. But never mind."

"Maybe I did."

She looked at me steadily. "That's why I want to go to Oxford. Besides the service for my brother. I think I can find out where Young Henry kept the painting."

"You have an idea where?"

"I do. But I need to see my Aunt Lenora. She and Young Henry were close, especially after our parents passed."

"Your mother's sister?"

"My father's."

I crossed my arms, trying to absorb it all.

"Let's say you find it. Then what?"

"Then I have it."

"If your brother actually had it himself."

Her eyes flashed. "I don't know, Jack. I'm just saying what I know."

"It's okay."

"What I think I know."

"I'm not saying—"

"I'm not crazy," she said, her voice down an octave.

"It's okay." This time it was me reached out to take her hand. Slowly, her face returned to normal.

"Look, let's go eat," I said, consciously changing the subject. "I think better when I'm not hungry. We can talk and go on up to Oxford after that." I didn't know what to do with all this and needed some time to let it work out in my head.

We got our bags and went outside to transfer whatever else she needed from her car over to the Explorer. I folded the rear seats down to make more room. Then I dropped off the card key at the office. She followed me up the interstates that looped the city to the Birmingham airport, and we left her Honda in a covered spot at the Drive-Fly-Park next to Denny's near the main exit.

We headed back toward town to catch the highway that would take us northwest to Jasper and then on to Oxford but first we pulled off at one of the downtown exits. She knew a little café on Second Avenue that had good breakfasts all day. I was starving and lightheaded.

I devoured my scrambled eggs, country bacon, grits, and biscuits and she picked at her fruit and oatmeal. We made small talk about the city, the weather, the news. People who didn't know us would have guessed we had just started dating and were floundering for things to say.

The morning was about gone, but she said it wouldn't do much good to get to Oxford before five because Aunt Lenora wouldn't be back yet from a doctor's appointment in Jackson. Elle said her aunt also had a house in Jackson, near Millsaps College where she sometimes taught a course on alternative religions in the women's studies department.

Elle said Lenora divided her time between the two towns but lately seemed to be in Jackson more and more and Oxford less and less. Also, she liked her doctor in Jackson but not the ones in Oxford. Aunt Lenora did healing work, Elle said, and sometimes clashed with the M.D. crowd. She didn't elaborate and by then we were outside, walking around downtown. It wasn't hot, and the air felt good.

We found ourselves at Kelly Ingram Park, outside the Civil Rights Museum. We stopped in front of the statue of Bull Connor's police dogs lunging at black protestors.

"Where were you then?" she asked.

"A little kid in a little town in Texas. I didn't know anything."

"They didn't have black people?"

"Well, yeah. They lived on one side of town and we lived on another. The Mexicans in another. But there weren't that many black folks."

"Let me guess who lived in the worst part of the town."

"I was a kid. That whole town is about gone with the oil bust. So where were you?"

"I was here. Or close to here."

"In Birmingham?"

"I was born here, but after the bombings. Then we moved to outside Oxford."

She touched the bronze sculpture, and looked around the rest of the park. A few white tourists. Some older black men on benches. Not far away were some dive bars, an auto sales lot, secondhand clothing shops.

"One of the girls killed in that church bombing, she was a relative on my mother's side."

"Really?"

"Really. I didn't know her, but Mama always told us about it. It was always like, there but for the grace of God . . ."

"Yeah."

We were walking again.

"I have to tell you about Trey."

"I know."

"If I tell you, it will be hard for you to keep out of it."

I shrugged. She smiled, then, shaking her head, peeled away toward a bench where the path curved. Before sitting down, she paused, eyeing me with her head cocked, like a hawk on a fence post.

"It's a long story."

I sat next to her, stretched out my legs. "You don't have to make it short."

She looked across the park, toward the museum. "We grew up together. My family moved to Oxford when I was little. My daddy got hired on doing maintenance for the university, but what he really knew about from college was growing cotton and peanuts, that kind of stuff. He sometimes taught a night class at a junior college near there, which was allowed because the students were mostly black." She paused but it didn't need expanding. "And he also did some consulting for the local farmers, because word got around he was good. That's how we got to know the Barnetts. We lived on a few acres south of town next to what was left of the old Barnett Plantation, and the manager was calling Daddy for help all the time. Mama helped a little when she had time, to make some extra money. The Barnetts never really did any of that work themselves. I don't think they knew much about crops or husbandry or the land at all." She paused. "Daddy always said that and I think he was right."

"Seems like he would know."

She drew a deep breath. Her body barely moved otherwise. "Young Henry and Trey started playing together when they were three or four, since we were so close and out there it didn't really seem to matter at that age. Then we all started hanging out by the time I was in the third or fourth grade, even though I was a couple of years older."

"Than both of them?"

"I was the Old Lady."

"The boss."

"For a while. Anyway, we stuck together for years in that way people do around here, pretty much into high school and then of course it started being a little weird. A couple of summers, Mr. Barnett, the one they call Junior, would have us go to Rosedale, where they had an old house in town and a small farm not too far from the river, for a few weeks. We had some relatives there, too. Not on the same side of town, of course."

She smiled oddly. "Actually it was fun. We had the run of the town and except for all the bugs and mosquitoes it was like a kid's paradise. Almost every day we were down at the grocery grabbing Yoo-hoos and hot tamales."

"For me it was the Dairy Queen."

She wiped a thin film of moisture from her forehead. "I think Junior just wanted Trey to have company so he wouldn't wind up hanging around with who knows who in Rosedale, which wasn't much of a town at all and really still isn't. Even Clarksdale was a big city in comparison. Cleveland was huge. For Mississippi, you know. Junior was always nice to us. His family had owned slaves but you wouldn't know it by the way he was. Mama always said that."

Across the park, a van pulled up in front of the museum and some people in suits got out.

"Later on we all went off to school. It was in the eighties. Trey went out to California, to Stanford, for a business degree, but then he came back and finished at Ole Miss. Terrell and I both went to Tuscaloosa." She watched the people walk into the museum. "I took a year off and transferred to Northwestern on scholarship. I got a psych degree. I really liked Chicago and thought about staying there, but you know, when the South is in you, you come back, sooner or later."

"What I hear."

"I wanted to stay near home, but not in Mississippi. The University of Alabama offered a good job working with marginal students so I signed up."

Two young teenage boys on bicycles cut by, talking loudly to each other about girls. I heard the words "fine" and "Janeeka" and "Sharon Lee." They looked at us and sort of smirked. One whistled. Elle waited until they were past.

"I started out counseling students on campus. But it didn't pay much and I got on with a new program, helping unwed moms, addicts, abuse victims.

Then the funding got cut to pay for their war and I went back to work at UA, but they let me do outside consulting to make some more money. There's always lots of work. That's how I got the contract in New Orleans."

She rubbed her palms up and down the sides of her thighs. "It's not just the abused moms. It's their kids, too. It's all passed along."

She was trying to decide what to leave out, maybe get to later. It was very quiet around us. She lowered her voice a little.

"Trey and his dad, Junior, never got along. Trey didn't care much for the cotton business and when Junior passed, he stopped trying. His mother had died of a stroke, they called it, years earlier and so he was the whole family all of a sudden. He changed a lot. He opened a gallery in New Orleans. I hear it does okay."

"He's an art dealer?"

"Sort of. Rumor is he got in deep with some gangs or maybe even the mafia out of Memphis or Texas. He was pretty much always owing big money to somebody or other. He gambled." She was rocking to and fro. "Basically, used his gallery to fence stolen art and launder money for his mob buddies. That's what I think got Young Henry killed, you understand? They had sort of hooked up again a few years back and I think Young Henry got in more than he wanted. I just don't know all of it."

"You think your aunt does?"

"She and Young Henry were always very close. Our parents are dead, too, like Trey's. Daddy of a stroke, only in his fifties, and Mama got bone cancer. It ate her up in a few months. We always thought it was chemicals in the fields. They died within a year of each other. Funny, isn't it. None of us with any parents left. And now . . ."

I touched the top of her hand. She didn't respond.

"But that was a dozen years ago, when they died. Anyway, Aunt Lenora pretty much became Young Henry's surrogate mom. I was more independent, I guess. She really loves him. Loved him. And he thought the world of her."

"I'm glad I'll get to meet her." It was just something to say.

"I guess Elfego told you about the other stuff." She pulled her hand away. "When I think back, I guess I could see that. Trey and Young Henry being gay. It never bothered me. But it did most of the family, except Lenora and

Mama. You can believe that. I think the day he went down to the Beauty Box in Tupelo to get his hair dyed was pretty much when it all started. Or that anyone knew about it." She smiled. "He was only in the eighth grade." Then her expression hardened. "Trey, that came on a little different."

I gently touched her shoulder but didn't linger.

She turned to look directly at me. Giving me the once-over. "People say Aunt Lenora has the second sight. Sometimes I think I do, too. I can see you don't believe me."

"That's not true."

"It's in your face."

"I don't want it to be."

She stood up, and I did, too. A mosquito was buzzing around my ear and she reached out to flick it away.

"It'll be okay," I said. "We'll figure something out." How, I had no idea.

She glanced at her watch, a little Seiko on a thin leather strap. Carrying a watch was something I had given up.

We walked back to the Explorer. Traffic was thick heading out of town, but it lightened in the country. I found a decent FM station playing Buddy Guy and Muddy Waters but we lost the signal in Jasper. It seemed to be all country or Christian from then on but I eventually picked up a public station playing classical. The NPR stations are linked across Mississippi so you can move from one reception zone to another and stay with the same program. Hard to say if that's a good or bad thing.

The highways through northern Alabama and Mississippi are not without beauty: rolling hills, thick rambling forests, working farms, small towns—bucolic to spare. Then there are the spots where poor people and their dwellings intrude on the fantasy, and history churns up the mirage. Not that I single out the South.

More than once, I looked in the mirror to see if we were being followed. It was pretty unlikely. I was a random addition to whatever drama existed between the Meridians and the Barnetts. I wanted to believe Elle's story about Trey, but I wasn't quite there yet. Maybe what I really wanted was for the story not to be true. If it was, it meant getting in deeper than I had anticipated.

Maybe what we both assumed that the police were thinking wasn't so far-fetched. Maybe her brother really just had been mugged outside some club or at someone's house after a stupid fight and dropped off on a back street. Cops had to play the odds on some cases, and this had to look like one where the murderer eventually would get coughed up, probably on some unrelated crime. Lovers' quarrel all the way, they had to figure it. Even in intelligence, where a million angles converge on every op and lies are but strands of the final agreed truth, the dust usually settles on the most obvious villainy. People just aren't that smart or that dependable.

Fact is, violent death in my adopted town was the urban equivalent of an occupational hazard. Maybe it came with being a city at the murky end of a great river. Bring what you will, roll-on-big-muddy sort of thing. I mean, it attracted me.

WE WERE BARELY INTO Mississippi when I noticed Elle slumped back in her seat, fast asleep. Snoring a little. Maybe she had been more exhausted than she let on. Her eyeballs were rolling under the lids like she'd already hit REM. Dreams putting on stage what she was doing her best to close down while awake. I had only seen her cry that once, back in the Marigny. I hated to wake her. But I had to after Tupelo at the cutoff to Oxford. I had no idea how to find Aunt Lenora.

When she shook off the grogginess she said to take the Lamar Street exit off Highway 6. We passed stately old neighborhoods, the way the town liked to think about itself. It was only about four o'clock but there was a little traffic, most of it coming from the Ole Miss campus as students got an early start on the weekend. It's not a big town and in no time we were past the courthouse and the boutiques that had grown up around it on the town square. I had never taken strongly to Oxford. I had a hard time thinking of Elle growing up anywhere near it.

Her aunt's house was just northeast of downtown. Terrell's apartment, or maybe it was a duplex, was off a loop on the northwest side. Elle didn't want to go there and given all that had happened I didn't, either. It would definitely be on Trey's radar. Lenora's might be, too, but whereas Elle didn't think there was anything at Terrell's that would help, talking to her aunt was a risk we had to take.

About a half mile past the square we turned right, down a hill and into a neighborhood of houses of varying levels of price and status. A couple of turns and we were on a street of small, modest bungalows.

"It's that one," she said, indicating a cream-colored brick with a green door, shallow screen porch on the front, surrounded by shrubs and flower beds. The yard needed mowing. The shingled roof needed work. A small gravel driveway ran along the left side to an empty carport. "She drives a Cadillac, would you believe? She says her clients want her to look prosperous."

I slowed to a stop on the other side of the street. We looked at the house.

"The healer thing."

"People have a lot of respect for her. She's been Aunt Lenora to more people than me for years and years."

"You come from an interesting family."

"I'll tell you all about it sometime."

"If we live that long."

She might have smiled. "So what do you think?" We looked at the house. It seemed quiet. Shades down. "Should we go in?"

"Or come back later."

"That's what you think?"

"Whatever we do, I don't think we should stay if she's not there. Do you have a key?"

"Under the watering can over on the side near that gate."

"I don't like it."

"Jack, I have to talk to her. We've already driven over here."

I did a quick recon of the street and saw nothing.

"What if she's not home?"

"Maybe there's a note or something."

I eased forward and turned in, all the way into the carport, which I noticed was leaning about twenty degrees to the left.

"There was a bad storm last summer. She never got it fixed."

I turned off the engine.

We both got out and walked to the front of the house. The door to the screened porch was open so I walked inside and waited at the door, still watching the street, while Elle went for the key. A calico cat darted across the lawn. The only furniture on the porch was a metal table and a clamshell chair. A broom in one corner.

Elle came back with a key and we were in.

THE AIR INSIDE WAS stuffy, but everything seemed normal, almost oddly so. Cozy, over-stuffed sofas, cherrywood tables, dozens of framed photos on just about every available surface, a lace-draped antique dining table, a TV and stereo in a prefab entertainment center. A big oil portrait of the Black Virgin dominated one wall, with votive candles and a clear goblet filled with sand and pebbles on a table underneath. Elle made her way to the two bedrooms in the back. She returned, looked at me and shrugged.

I went into the kitchen at the back, and then saw another room off to the right, probably a converted sleeping porch. A thick strand of painted wooden beads and seashells hung from the entry door. I parted the beads. Elle came up to me. "It's where she does her readings. You can look. It's okay."

The plywood walls were bare but for a poster of St. Michael, the archangel, and two framed prints: a snow leopard on a mountain and a Rousseau-like jungle scene. A table with votive candles, a bowl of water, a Bible, and a strand of beads took up the center of the room. Around it were a small couch and two matching armchairs. A shelf to one side was filled with books, photographs, a wooden sculpture of an African warrior, boxes of incense. A patchouli aroma permeated the room.

"So she does a lot of business here?"

"Some. More in Jackson. And she makes runs down to Laurel and Meridian—you know, our namesake."

We stopped talking at the same time. Outside, the sound of gravel popped under the tires of a car pulling up in front of the house. Stopping. Big engine idling.

"Shit," I said, more angry than I meant it to sound, as we hurried to the living room and the front window. The look she gave me was probably more frightened than she wished it to appear.

The blinds, yellowed but not dusty, were drawn. I raised my palm to her to stay to one side, and bent a slat just slightly. I saw a blue Suburban, darkened windows. I could make out a man at the steering wheel. Maybe another one in the passenger seat. I nodded to her and she came up to have a look, too.

"I would guess those are your friends from Tuscaloosa."

"What should we do?"

"I'd say go out the back."

"They'll still see us."

That was true. But I had been trained to always determine an exit.

"Look, in a minute or two, someone will come up to the front door." At my glance, she eased over to throw the dead bolt. "When he does, or if they both do, we go out the back. We can get in the car before they either get to us or back to the Suburban. They'll have to decide which move to make. That's our edge. We can make it while they hesitate."

She moved next to me. It was ridiculous that I noticed the sensation of her breasts against my arm. "What if we don't? What if one of them goes around back?"

"The way they just drove up like that, I doubt it. They don't even know anyone is here. They've never seen my car or even know I exist. Another edge we've got on them."

"I don't know."

I looked in her eyes. "Yeah. I don't, either."

I heard a door open on the SUV. I looked through the blind again. A white guy, medium build, dark black hair and a goatee, was coming out the driver's side, saying something to whoever was inside. I waited until he started for the porch.

"Trey?"

She looked quickly. "No. Anyway he wouldn't be with them."

"Go now."

In seconds, we were out the back door. As we ran through the grass toward the carport I could hear the front door being rattled.

We reached the Explorer just as I heard the crack of wood as the front door jamb splintered.

I cranked the engine, slammed it into reverse and peeled back. I was at the street by the time the dark-haired man had come through the house, rounded the yard, and reached the carport. I ground the gears and we lurched forward.

What I saw next, before flooring it, didn't register. The guy from whom we were fleeing was just walking up the driveway, watching us. He didn't even run to the Suburban. Whoever else was sitting inside the SUV never got out.

I sped down the block, still pretty empty since most people were at work, and turned several corners until I found a street that led back to Lamar, then turned right and just drove fast.

I went a half-mile or so before making a U-turn at a four-way. I took a loop road and then another turn that led into a residential area and a labyrinth of cottage-filled streets somewhere on the city's northwest side.

"Turn there," she said.

I went up a street named for Dr. King and then we were on another loop lined with HUD homes that had seen better days. I stopped in front of a brick house on a quiet stretch. Four black teenagers in baggy athletic gear and backwards hats walked by, giving us a look but judging us as little more than a curiosity.

It DIDN'T LOOK LIKE we had been followed. But it didn't make me feel better that we had gotten away so easily.

"This is crazy," I said, as much to myself as to her.

She watched the teenagers continue down the street.

"We need to get out of here, or call the police. Something."

"Calling the police won't do any good in this town," she said. "And where can we go?"

"We can get out of Oxford."

"I can't, Jack. The service for Young Henry is tomorrow. And I can't let my aunt come back to her house with those guys around."

"If she's coming back."

"Don't."

"I mean, why would she? If she knows what's going on."

"Stop saying it that way."

"I only meant—"

"She has to see her clients here. She has to come back. It's her business. I have to get in touch with her. Somehow. She doesn't have a cell. She doesn't like them."

"A friend you could call?"

"I don't want to start just calling around blind."

"Still—"

She exhaled heavily, slumping in the seat. "I don't know what I'm saying."

"Elle, that was a pretty hard-looking guy. They knew where to come. That or they'd been watching it all along. Maybe they knew what to look for. We were lucky."

"Trey knows my aunt wouldn't keep anything valuable at her house if it was trouble."

"Maybe. So why did they show up like that?"

She looked at me hard.

"They didn't even bother to chase us. Doesn't that strike you as unusual?"

Her nostrils flared.

Suddenly, I got it. "It *is* you they think knows where that painting is, isn't it? Not your aunt."

The hard face, harder.

"They're just going to follow you until you take them to it. They have all the time in the world."

She turned her face away. "No. Jesus Christ, Jack. I don't know anything."

"They think you do. Nothing else makes sense."

"Maybe he wants both of us. Me and my aunt. You know?"

My stomach knotted so hard I thought I had been punched. Somewhere in there, she was either lying or afraid to face up to the truth. Either way it was bad.

She balled her hands together and pressed them against her mouth. She took a few breaths, shook her head. Then she tucked a leg up on the seat and turned to me.

"I have to get word to her somehow. I just need to think. I just need a minute to think."

I put the Explorer in drive and started forward.

"Where are we going?"

"I don't know. I need to think, too."

She looked at the street behind us. Nothing. I kept driving. We passed a neighborhood police station. One of those old fifties-era black and white cruisers, the kind associated with police beatings, was parked in front.

"You're right. We do."

I was reading street signs, maybe with a hint of exasperation. We were on a wide street that ran around the back side of Ole Miss.

"Cut up through the campus. Students coming and going, one more car wouldn't get noticed."

"They're not following us."

"Anyway."

I braked down hard as a light changed. She jolted forward, almost hitting the dashboard.

"You don't have to take it out on me."

I looked at her with a raised eyebrow, but kept it to myself. Finally we got a green. I peeled off, jolting her back again. I didn't care.

We entered a street full of sorority houses and then on into the main part of the university. Thick trees draped in Spanish moss shaded the streets. Near the student union I turned left and passed alongside a big open park area, what they called the Grove, where three red-and white-striped pavilion party tents had been erected. I pulled the Explorer over at a row of parking spaces in front of the college's old observatory and backed in. In case we needed to leave fast.

I turned off the engine and looked across at Elle. "So?"

"I don't know."

We looked out at black workers carrying piles of metal folding chairs toward the tents. A group of coeds in shorts passed in front of us, talking loudly and carrying big plastic drink cups. It got pretty quiet. I finally spoke.

"Nothing is ever going to be the same for you now. You get that, don't you? I don't know what these guys want, but I do know that they aren't going to let you alone."

"I didn't want to get you into all this, Jack. Really."

"Really? I'd say just about the opposite."

The slap came so fast I took it full on. But I grabbed her wrist when she tried it again. Also her other wrist when she tried with that hand. Her eyes were hot and maybe mine were, too.

We held the position like we'd been sculpted in it, and I let go of her wrists. She slumped back in her seat. I did, too. We stared out the windshield at the ebb and flow of the campus grounds. Some kids walked by, looking in at us as though we were an exhibit.

"We can play them as much as they play us," I said.

"Yeah? Who are we playing?"

"We're not playing anymore."

Taylor Grocery is a down-home café in a rundown wooden tin-roofed building a short drive south of Oxford. It's a local favorite. I parked in the dirt lot in front, as it was a little early for the college kids except the early partiers who were already lolling about on the front porch. Elle had said it was a place in which Trey "wouldn't be caught dead." Not least, she said, because of a bad drunken scene he'd once caused, making him as persona non grata as a local rich boy can be.

Inside, we got a table almost right away, next to a wall covered with photos and grafitti from guests over the years. We both ordered the catfish. There wasn't even a smirk at an interracial couple. Mississippi had a past, but it had places like this, too.

A guitar, fiddle, and bass trio ambled onto the stage at a corner of the café and began picking out some easy Western swing. Outside, dusk was settling in and by the time we were finished, it had gone dark. I'm not sure if that made me feel safer, but I was with my girl. My girl whose brother was dead and whose childhood friend apparently was trying to kill her, too. My girl who had secrets. Some, I realized, from herself.

Over dinner, we discussed her friend, Colletta, who owned a small house a few miles down the road, the main reason we had come to Taylor. Elle stayed with Colletta from time to time on visits from Tuscaloosa and thought it would be safe. She didn't think Trey would know about it.

Elle said Colletta sold beauty products and was constantly on the road. She didn't answer her phone, but Elle said we could stay there anyway. I said it reminded me of dropping in at Aunt Lenora's. Elle said this would be different.

THE LIGHT GREEN, SHINGLE and wooden frame cottage was a mile or two farther south, past a couple of turns I probably could never find again, tucked against the edge of a forest line down a dirt lane. Exactly the kind of place you'd want to go if you wanted someone to come and kill you in the cover of night. But it was all we had.

I pulled up to one side, leaving the headlights on so Elle could see as she walked across scraggly country lawn to a small decorative rock display around a concrete bird bath. She bent down to turn over a large oval rock, looked back as though to say I told you so, and picked up the key. I cut off the lights.

We carried a couple of bags and my shotgun into the house. It was warm and stuffy until we turned on the air conditioner. The furnishings reminded me of Elle's place in New Orleans, although a little more rounded out. There were some big watercolors on the walls, mostly photorealism-style portraits of children and old people. Elle said Colletta wanted to be a painter.

I went back out to move the Explorer next to a tool shed at the rear of the house. I paused to admire a medium-sized vegetable garden full of tomatoes, squash, and green beans, but froze when I heard rustling in the tall grass beyond. A few seconds later, rabbits jumped out.

I wish I could say that we spent the rest of the evening in passionate lovemaking but in fact we found a few welcome beers in Colletta's fridge and drank them, sitting outside on her screen porch in the breeze while the inside of the house cooled down. Fatigue set in on top of the anxiety.

About ten, we decided on the plan for the night. We would sleep in four-hour shifts. She volunteered for the first watch and I let her. I pulled the Remington from the case, and loaded the magazine. Having grown up in the country, she knew about shooting. She settled on the porch to watch the approach and I stretched out in the front room on the sofa. To my surprise I drifted away.

It was just after two A.M. when I felt her rubbing my shoulder.

"The shotgun's on the porch. I didn't see anything." She stretched onto the couch where I'd been and her eyes were closed almost at once.

I went to the kitchen for a glass of water. The night air was chillier than I had expected and there was a light fog, but I could see well enough and I could hear anything coming for miles. I went to the porch, pretended to shoot a fast-turning dove, but then just sat with the shotgun across my lap.

I was surprised how wide awake I had become. I'd pulled all-night duty more than once and it was like that. I thought back to those days. At least this time I was guarding something I could understand a little better. On the other hand, in the streets of Seoul and Incheon I'd known pretty much what to expect in the way of an enemy.

About six, I could hear the sounds from the houses up the road coming to life for the new day. I went inside and, seeing Elle still asleep, figured I'd sit in the lounger over by the dining room and give her another half hour.

Two hours later I woke with a start, then got her up, too. The service for Terrell was at eleven. We needed to be on time.

The Merciful Witness Church was perched on the side of a thickly treed hill on a highway at the eastern edge of the city, encroached by gas stations, convenience stores, retail strips. It would suffer, at least scenically, in the coming years, but for now it was everything you could expect from a moderately prosperous suburban house of worship that didn't belong to white Mississippi. Red brick with green trim, it almost looked like a small, private Christian school. I guess it was.

We pulled into the asphalt parking lot in front just before eleven. Elle had asked Reverend Thompson to change plans and make it a private ceremony, although she didn't tell him why. It wasn't the church Elle had grown up in—she was a lapsed Catholic—but Terrell had gone there in recent years. He liked Reverend Thompson, who happened to be a second cousin of Mr. Orman at the funeral home in New Orleans. The two had expedited everything for Elle. I don't know the cost; she said she thought it was fair, considering.

A half-dozen vehicles in the lot, all Detroit sedans or pickups, indicated maybe a few teachers had come anyway, once they heard the news. Oxford might have gotten trendy, but it was still a small town that way. I gathered Terrell had been a popular teacher, although he'd been on a leave of absence for the current semester. Elle said he had been thinking of moving to Jackson, like his aunt. If Elle was correct, whatever he'd been doing in the meanwhile had gotten him killed.

"I should have invited everyone. Let it be a real service," Elle said as we sat for a moment in the Explorer.

"You did the right thing."

She shrugged and opened her door. She had changed into a black dress and black pumps at Colletta's. I hadn't thought to bring anything appropriate but had a dark blue camp shirt and black jeans. I hoped no one would look at my deck shoes.

I had barely locked the doors when I heard another vehicle pull up. Elle and I saw the sport model black Volvo at the same time.

"Go inside," she said.

"Not without you."

A strange look came over her face. Not mournful. She seemed to be deciding which direction to walk, but took a breath and we made our way up the sidewalk to the front door of the church.

No one got out of the Volvo.

Inside, the rush of cool air felt good. A dozen rows of pews lined each side of the modest sanctuary. A choir pit and organ were at the front near the pulpit on a small dais. A gilt-framed portrait of Jesus, classic pose, hung on a back wall with one of the black Virgin. Multicolored sun filters hung from the side windows. Next to the pulpit, vases of flowers covered a wooden table. Also a ceramic, bronze-colored urn with two horizontal black stripes. Elle saw it at once.

We walked up the aisle. Three women and a man, all black, sat near the front and turned to look at us. They nodded to Elle, who paused to shake their hands. She introduced me as her friend from New Orleans who had helped with arrangements. I didn't catch all the names but two were teachers, one was a parent, and the other a principal. The principal said they were all very sorry at the school and knew the ceremony was private but felt they should send just a small delegation. Elle thanked them and hugged each one.

We took a place in the left front pew. We were still a little early and the minister hadn't emerged. Elle kept looking at the urn.

I wondered if the two men in the Volvo would come in. I got my answer when the church door opened and light spilled inside. I turned but Elle didn't. One of the silhouetted figures was the goateed, dark-haired thug I had seen back at Lenora's. The other was Trey Barnett. Elle didn't need to tell me.

They took seats in the back right pew. A beat later, Elle stood, turned, and fixed them with a glare of cold hatred.

Trey nodded indifferently. He wore a black, double-breasted suit, maybe British-tailored. He was a good-looking man, medium-frame, light brown hair fairly short, a solid, rectangular face. His thin lips bore the trace of a smile. The thug was in a standard corporate business suit, dark blue, but betrayed by a black shirt and black tie. He looked like wiseguys I had seen in Dallas.

Elle sat back down. I took her hand. She pulled it away.

I didn't know what to say and was relieved to see the Reverend Thompson come in from a door near the choir pit. He was gray at the temples and wore heavy-framed, dark glasses. His robe was deep purple and he carried a Bible.

He came up to Elle right away and opened his arms. She stood and allowed him to embrace her.

"I am so sorry." His voice was deep, classic Southern preacher.

"Oh, Reverend."

He held her a moment longer. As they stood together, a woman in a green robe came in from the back and sat at the organ. She began playing a quiet hymn and the church was filled with music. It made it seem better.

Elle introduced me to the preacher and he told us what he would do. The service would be simple and she could say a few words if she wished.

We sat down. The reverend went to his pulpit, then seemed to change his mind and moved next to the table with the flowers and urn.

The music softened and stopped.

"Thank you for coming," he said, barely glancing at the two figures at the back. "This is an unhappy time, and yet one in which we are called to remember the ways of the Lord and how little we can understand them. No one could say that the loss of Brother Terrell Meridian in such a manner could be God's will, as you might say, but neither can we say that even in his passing was God's presence missing."

"Amen," one of the teachers said.

"Now, in our grief and sorrow, we struggle to find answers. I can only say that in time we might come to understand that which we cannot now. It is a small comfort if any at all, but I believe that just as the Lord is present in all that we do and experience, even in death so he is present as we struggle to find the light once again. And you know that we all have struggled to find that light so much here in this land of many sorrows and unexplained losses."

"Amen."

He paused. "At the request of the family, this service will be brief, but I call upon Terrell's older sister, Elle, who has kept ties to our community even as she has gone on in the world to her own calling, to say anything she might feel for her brother. Sister, please join me here."

Elle stood and walked slowly to take a place next to the minister. She looked at the table.

"Thank you all for being here," she said to the teachers, "and for the flowers. I know Young Henry would have been so happy—is so happy— now, seeing this." She touched the urn with her fingertips, then turned to the pews. "He was a fine, fine brother. He made us all proud. I am going to miss him terribly."

Just as it seemed she would begin sobbing, she straightened and glared at the men in the back.

"I know my brother is finding a place with the Lord, and that's good, Reverend . . .

"Amen."

Her jaw muscles seemed ready to burst her face. "But I swear he will have justice in his name here on this earth, too."

She took a very deep breath, exhaled, and nodded to the minister, then returned to her seat.

The organ began playing very softly, a hymn I didn't recognize.

"Let us pray," the reverend said.

We bowed our heads.

"Dear Lord and King of Kings, God Almighty please accept this young boy, who did so much in our community and for our children, please accept this boy O Jesus into your bosom, please accept this fine young man O Host of Hosts and keep him for eternity. And, Lord, protect those of us here now from the despair that comes at such a moment and make our sorrows run into rivers of joy for the path to Heaven that comes to all mortal flesh, no matter how it is taken from us.

"Bless especially the family and most of all the sister of our late brother, and guide her in the hard days ahead, and grant her spirit the power to prevail over the darkness. Now please protect and light the way for our lost brother, Terrell Henry Meridian, as he even now sits at your side. In the name of the Father, the Son, and the Holy Ghost, in Jesus's name we seek your mercy and glory everlasting, O Lord. Amen."

"Amen," from everyone, including me. Not sure about the two in the back.

The reverend motioned to Elle to come forward. She did. He embraced her for a long moment, then pulled back, looked at her directly, and took both her hands in his.

"Go with God and the spirit of Jesus Christ Almighty." He picked up the urn, placing a white lace coverlet over it, and offered it to her.

She took it, looked at it, then at the minister, and turned down the aisle.

I got up to escort her as we moved toward the foyer.

When we walked past Trey and the other man, Elle looked directly ahead, saying nothing. I looked right at him. I didn't have to put it into words.

Outside, the sun hit us in the face hard.

"We should go," I said, still holding her elbow.

"Yes. Go."

We went to the Explorer and put the urn behind the front seat so it wouldn't fall over. Trey and his friend walked up.

Trey held his right hand over his brow for shade. The other guy stayed back a couple of steps. Seemed to be watching me more than anything else.

"I'm sorry for your loss," Trey said. His voice was heavier than I had expected, and clearly of the bourgeois South. "We had some good times back in the day."

Elle turned to stand directly in front of him.

"Go to hell."

I expected her to hit him and sure enough, she did. It was as if he expected it, too, and he didn't even try to deflect it. Afterward, he touched the redness along his left cheek. "You've gotten stronger."

She hit him again, this time a sharp slap to the nose, and might have done more but I stepped up behind and held her arms. She didn't struggle.

"I guess that runs in the family." He had that smirk again and I wanted to punch him, too, but we were pushing our luck. The dark-haired guy was hovering in a boxed-off stance as if waiting for a signal. I knew he was carrying.

"Who's your friend here?" Trey asked.

"Nobody you'd want to know."

"You talk for yourself?" he said to me, looking over her shoulder. A trickle of blood came down from a nostril and he wiped it away.

"Why don't you just leave?"

His brown eyes didn't flinch, but if they were a window to his soul, it was not a happy place. His glance shifted back to his pal, then to me again. Then to her. "Where you going now, darling? I was thinking we could have a coffee or maybe a drink. You know, like a wake. Talk about back in the day. Talk about where the hell your brother stashed what he stole from me."

"Go to hell."

"You said that already."

"Then go there."

She moved a little in my arms. I released her.

"Let's go, Jack. Let's get out of here."

She adjusted her shoulders and smoothed her dress, then walked to the open passenger door at the Explorer and waited. As though nothing had happened.

I had to think how I would now get past Trey and friend. I wasn't much of a brawler but knew how to handle myself from military days. If it came to that. Which I didn't want. So I just walked away to my side of the car as if nothing had happened.

Trey looked at me hard, then at his gunslinger, and shook his head slightly. He was giving me—or more accurately Elle—a pass. Except he wasn't the type.

I opened my door. Elle and I looked at each other across the roof.

"You go do your crying now," Trey called out. "Let it all out, big sister. We'll get together later on. Maybe visit Lenora."

"Forget him," I said across the roof, loudly enough. Too loud, considering they were letting us walk away and a wiseass retort could be a serious mood-breaker.

She got my point.

Trey dabbed at a corner of his mouth and in the same motion put on some expensive-looking sunglasses. "The guy they'll be forgetting about is you, what is it, Jack? Hack? Kack?"

I let it go.

"I'll look you up in the book. We'll get a beer next time I'm in town," he said as I opened my door.

"Bastard motherfucker," Elle said as she got in, looking out at him. First time I'd heard her curse like that. She slammed her door shut and turned to me. "Now do you believe me?"

I cranked the engine and backed up, not really looking to see if anyone was standing behind me.

"One hundred percent."

I put it in drive and we left the church parking lot just as the double door opened and the school folks came out, talking to Reverend Thompson. He looked in our direction, and then at Trey.

We went down the hill to the potholed street that led back to the highway. I turned west, as if headed to Oxford again, but then after two exits got off and went east again. Maybe they knew we were headed back to Birmingham but maybe not.

The Volvo had followed us west a little, then turned off. As he had back in the parking lot, Trey might have been giving Elle a pass. But it was just more rope.

I thought it was best to take a roundabout route to Birmingham, where we vaguely thought to get Elle's car, and then—we didn't have that much of a plan yet. Maybe back to New Orleans. Maybe together. Maybe not. Past Pontotoc, I turned down a moderately busy two-lane state highway that runs through farm-laden hills and the strange phenomenon of rural sprawl alongside the Tombigbee National Forest west of the Natchez Parkway.

I was actually thinking about lunch. All I'd had was toast and coffee at Colletta's. Elle said she couldn't eat, but passed me a water bottle. I drank it all. Outside, the sunny weather was disappearing fast as a thick gray cloud line closed in from the west. I hadn't really been following the news, much less the weather, but we were in for something.

The encounter at the church had left me with a feeling other than the expected emotion, fear. It was like the rush I got back in TV land when I was about to find the clue needed to make a story fit together. Less pleasant to admit was that it was also like the adrenalin spike I'd felt when my team had reeled in some North Korean agents slipping into the Incheon harbor. Or that time in Costa Rica. I pushed away the memories. It wasn't like that. And I wasn't the one doing the hunting this time, either.

In contrast, Elle seemed almost deflated. She slumped against the side window, saying little. She found the NPR station again but it was news instead of music. She tried tuning something else and then gave up.

I thought she was going to sleep again, but then I heard fitful breathing. "Oh, Jack, oh, Jack, oh, Jack . . ."

It came on fast. She burst into convulsive sobs—primal cries of pain, long, aching vowels with no kinds of words around them, just straight out of her gut and soul. She kicked at the dash, then pounded it with her fists, shaking her head violently.

I slowed down and looked for a place to pull over but after each hill there was always another prefab house or mini-mart or church or retail strip or video store. New South, indeed.

I reached over to comfort her but she swatted my hand away. Her face was drenched with tears and her mouth and nose were shiny with saliva and mucus. She collapsed forward in the seat, almost motionless, crying in a way that broke my heart.

Torturous miles went by. Finally I saw a red-dirt turnout to the left past a clump of trees leading up a small hill. I braked down hard and pulled across the highway, bouncing in over a broken-up asphalt apron, spewing gravel and dust. The lane curved up into the trees right away but then widened, almost enough for two pickups to pass each other. Then it curved a couple more times until we came to a broad turning area. A sign said, "Green Valley Covenant's Promise, 1/2 mile." An arrow pointed up a small rise.

I eased past the sign, then turned on the wide arc of the curve so the Explorer would face out toward the highway. I pulled to the far right, almost into the thick brush, then turned off the engine and got out. I hoped it was a time of day when nobody would be seeking the Lord's advice.

I went around to Elle's door and opened it. She looked at me like I was a stranger, like she didn't even know where she was.

I reached across to undo her seat belt. She didn't move.

"I'm so sorry," I said. "I'm so sorry."

Her face turned to me but I don't know what she saw.

"Let's rest here. It's quiet. It would be better out of the car for you."

Gradually her reddened eyes seemed to come into focus. She nodded a little, smoothed at her dress. She eased out of her seat, holding the door for support as she got out. We took a few steps. Her knees buckled but then she stayed up.

I helped her over to a little ridge of earth under the trees where a patch of weeds had been beaten down, maybe by utility crews who used the place for lunch, working on the power lines down the road. She sat down, drawing up her legs and resting her head against her knees in an upright fetal position.

I got some water for her but she didn't want any.

"He was my brother."

"Yes."

"He was my baby brother."

"He was."

"They killed him like that."

"They did."

"Young Henry."

I reached for her arm but she shook it off.

"Oh, Jack." She began weeping again, not hard, like before, but in steady sobs. She rocked to and fro.

I touched her shoulder and she didn't flinch so I sat next to her. I reached around to lightly massage her neck. A breeze whirred through the trees. It had been quiet when we stopped—but now a chorus of birds erupted. I heard a rustle in the underbrush and the birds flapped away. Flopping and flailing noises followed. A huge gray cat moved off past a cluster of leaves.

THEN CAME ANOTHER KIND of sound. Faint, then easy to recognize: tires crunching on gravel. The laboring of a big engine coming up a hill. Then it was in view, and although it was impossible, there it was. The dark blue Suburban pulled to a stop at the curve just down from this one, maybe fifty yards away.

No way I had seen them following. But I had been looking for the black Volvo. They were good. I could hear the SUV shift into park, the engine idling high, as if the air conditioner had kicked in.

"We need to leave." I pressed my fingers hard into Elle's forearm.

She looked up at me, and then, following my gaze, at the latest intruder. Her throat was raw from the sobbing and it was hard for her to talk.

"Just get in the car. Don't look at them."

I started the engine and waited to figure the next move. I couldn't get around the SUV, and if I backed up, where would that lead?

The Suburban flashed its lights, twice, and eased up towards us. Elle and I exchanged quick looks.

But the big SUV just rolled up the trail slowly, stopping directly in front, blocking the lane. I realized they were toying with us again.

After a few moments, the driver lowered his window and waved his arm outside, making a peace sign with his fingers. The Suburban moved forward again. I waited for the moment I could gun it and get around, but the SUV glided on, at a crawl. The arm and peace sign from the open window belonged to a black man, forty-ish, with the fashionable narrow trace of a beard along his jaw line. Close-cropped hair. One of those faces clean like a scaled fish. I could barely make out the passenger, but it looked a lot like the goateed guy who had been with Trey.

As he passed, scaled fish puckered up as though blowing a kiss. Then he laughed, turned to the passenger, and the tinted window slid up with a smooth electric movement. They peeled away, spewing gravel, up around the curve that led on to the country church.

I hit the accelerator. At the bottom we jolted onto the highway so hard we banged our heads on the roof. A welder's truck veered around us doing at least ninety, laying on the horn. We headed south.

"It was him, from the church, wasn't it?"

"And somebody new."

"Why—?"

"Who the fuck knows. More of that crap Trey was pulling."

"Whatever he wants, he isn't getting it."

"He wants you."

"So?"

I pushed it up past seventy, always watching the rearview. Elle turned frequently to give the road behind us a good scan. We never saw anything. But we felt it, like the storm-scented air.

I knew I had to keep changing our route. I dropped off the highway when I spotted an exit for a road connecting to the Natchez Trace Parkway. It led all the way down to Jackson, but hardly a main thoroughfare thanks to its fifty mph speed limit.

We crossed an earthen dam at a small reservoir and instead of getting onto the Parkway directly, I picked up a county road, then doubled back north, instead of south. In a few miles we were back on the state road and after that found an exit onto the Parkway. It was confusing and I meant it to be.

The Parkway followed an old Indian trail, slicing through thickets of moss-covered trees, hillsides buried in kudzu, sporadic farmland. I liked it because it had only a few entry and exit points. Anyone still following would be easy to spot.

I kept heading south. We passed no cars and met only two or three heading north. Maybe a Saturday afternoon was just slow in general. Add to that the weather, which seemed to get worse by the minute, winds bowing the treetops and scattering brush.

The Trace, already primordial green-black, turned even darker.

"We could go to Rosedale," she said, looking out her window. "We could get off this road and go there, instead of Jackson or Birmingham or Tuscaloosa."

"Rosedale?"

"I know people. They'll take care of us. Trey can't get to us there. We can figure out what to do. You know?"

"Rosedale."

"I don't want to go to Jackson now."

"What about Lenora?"

"Someone in Rosedale can help me find her."

"We don't have to go anywhere. I mean, we can go anywhere."

"I just don't know."

Calculations raced through my brain. "It's okay. Rosedale will be good."

"Good. That's good."

I watched for an exit back to the state highway we'd have to take to get to the Delta, but the first thing we spotted was a marker for restrooms at the Witch Dance trailhead. We both needed a pit stop.

I pulled off at the roadside easement and stopped next to litter barrels above a small stone path leading down to the public facilities. An RV with Oregon plates was parked just in front of us. I was trying to look inside it through the back window when an elderly man and woman came up the path. They waved at us, half-smiled, got back in their vehicle and drove off.

We were alone. A larger, secluded parking area was down the hill below the johns. I drove down and we got out. A wooden park information sign at the edge of the parking area depicted a map of the area and trails and explained that this was where witches and spirits allegedly danced. It said that on the spots where they danced, no vegetation grew even today. Visitors were invited to look around for barren patches.

"The government shouldn't pay for stuff like this," Elle said, pausing en route to the women's. "It isn't even history. It's barely even hearsay."

I glanced up at what sky I could see through the thick pine canopy.

"I wish Aunt Lenora were here. This is the sort of thing that makes her crazy, making fun of spirits. And, come on, Jack, *women*? Who do you think the 'witches' were?"

A crackle of thunder sounded, then a couple more. I couldn't see the lightning but it must have been far away.

"We need to keep moving."

Elle looked up at the sky, too.

"Maybe it's the witches."

She gave me a look and we went to take care of business. When we came out, she took another disapproving look at the wording on the sign. She turned to me and swept one hand across her torso. "I need to get out of this dress. But I'm not changing in a park outhouse."

"You look fine."

"On the outside."

She smiled for the first time in a while. I did, too.

"I think there's an RV clearing," I said, pointing farther down the park trail. "At least according to this sign. You can change there. I need to look at the map, anyway."

"I know how to get to Rosedale."

"I know. But I hate being lost.

"I thought men never needed directions," she said, starting toward the Explorer.

"I got over that."

We drove down the gravel loop around an S curve and sure enough it widened into a large turning circle that would accommodate RVs, boat trailers and the other accoutrements of vacation. It was completely empty.

I parked and got out. I popped the rear hatch and pushed away the tarp covering our stuff. She pulled out fresh clothes and I dug into a plastic storage box where I kept the maps and a first aid kit. I pushed a box of shotgun shells and the Remington, still loaded, to one side.

The wind was really whipping through now and I figured we had maybe ten minutes before getting pelted. Might even be a tornado. I didn't feel the need to change my clothes but slipped off my deck shoes and put on a pair of sneakers.

Elle changed over next to a concrete picnic table. "You're taking all day," she called out, tucking a black T-shirt into her jeans.

That's when we heard it. Again. Up along the Trace. Again, I didn't want to believe it. Again, I had to. The Suburban. The air conditioner kicking in. I didn't even have to see it.

Elle knew, too.

I couldn't figure how they had followed us, but it didn't matter. Gravel from the loop road scrunched as the SUV came down slowly. By the time it reached the parking area in front of the restrooms, I could see it through the trees. I don't know if they knew exactly where we were yet, and it was our one advantage.

Lightning flashed off to the west, followed by a horrendous thunderclap.

"Hurry," I called to Elle.

She was almost to the Explorer when the Suburban reached the entry to the RV circle. It stopped, facing us dead-on. I could hear the engine rev as the transmission shifted into park.

Luckily, I hadn't closed the rear hatch. As stealthily as possible, I reached for the shotgun, pulling it back by the stock. They hadn't come any closer, but they weren't going to play cat and mouse with us forever.

"Over here," I said to Elle, who was still about twenty feet away. "Around back with me."

Still watching the Suburban, I bent down slightly for the box of shells. I grabbed three and stuffed them into my pocket.

Elle watched.

"Jack?"

"If you have to, run into the woods. Stay there."

A lightning bolt lit up the woods like a flare. The strike afterwards was deafening.

The passenger's door on the SUV opened. Goatee guy stepped out. He took a drag from a cigarette, flicked it to the asphalt lot, and moved forward. He didn't have his wiseguy suit coat or tie on anymore. He might have been smiling.

In hindsight, maybe there was another play. Maybe it's always that way.

I clicked off the safety with my thumb, held the shotgun down against my right leg, and walked around the left side of the Explorer directly at him. Goatee got about five more steps before he put it together.

I shot him in one leg, then fired again at the other.

He staggered backward and collapsed, almost like he was sitting down in a funny kind of way. Then he slumped onto his back, screaming. I could see his legs tremble and spasm. "Shit, Delmore, motherfucker shot me."

Already the driver's door was flying open. The black man jumped onto the running board. He held a pistol, muzzle upward, like someone trained in how to use it.

I turned at once and fired. He ducked. Then, after a beat, he dropped like a stone.

Another flash and bang from the skies, a thousand times louder than the gunfire.

Elle had taken cover behind the Explorer. I dug out fresh shells from my pocket, stuck them into the magazine and moved forward.

Goatee was moaning and trying without success to sit up. I didn't see any kind of weapon on him, so I eased around the front of the Suburban to check on the driver. He was lying motionless on the asphalt, bleeding heavily from a gash across his brow and nose. A Colt .45, the sidearm I favored over the newer Beretta 9mm, lay about a foot from his left hand.

I didn't think he was dead but I didn't want to get any closer. I needed to keep goatee in my field of vision. But I got close enough to kick the pistol away with my foot.

Meanwhile goatee had gotten up on one elbow. He was looking at his tattered suit pants and legs, and at me. "Fuck you. Stupid son of a bitch. Are you fucking crazy?"

I returned to him. He was in plenty bad shape, but I hadn't been close enough to do him lethal harm without a heavier shot load and must have missed any arteries because the bleeding wasn't severe. I considered finishing him off with a round to the head, but Elle was there and she had seen enough.

I shifted my attention back to Delmore. He still hadn't moved. I also wanted to get a look into the Suburban, engine still idling and doors wide open. I stepped up on the running board on the passenger side, reached across the seat until I could grab the keys and turned off the motor.

A Glock lay on the floorboard. I knew the goatee prick had to be carrying something. Was he too arrogant to take it with him when he had walked up to us? I put it, and the keys, on the bucket seat. Then I hopped out.

"You'd be better off shooting yourself in the head with it right now," he yelled amid the groans. "Shit."

I walked over and held the muzzle to his face a long moment. He glared. I had to give him points for attitude.

I went back to the Suburban and threw the keys into the thick brush. I put the Glock in my jeans waist.

"Jack," she said.

She was pointing to the trail road down from the highway. A medium-sized RV, its lights on because of the impending storm, labored down the gravel to the restroom lot.

I lowered the shotgun along my leg to mask it as best I could, kind of a stupid gesture. If they could see me, they could see the two guys on the ground. But we were partly hidden by a stand of trees and it was almost dark as night. It was all the camouflage I had.

Fat drops of rain began to splat.

"Stay there. Act like you're getting something from the trunk."

She made an effort, but mostly was watching our visitors.

The RV stopped and a door on one side opened. A middle-aged woman in bulging halter top and shorts emerged, holding something over her head to protect her coif. She raced to the women's toilet. I was sure they hadn't noticed us.

I began easing back to the Explorer, keeping my eyes on the two men and on the unwelcome RV.

"You're dead, motherfucker," goatee hissed, his voice almost too weak to hear. "Fuck, now this." Rain splatter was hitting his wounds. I'm sure it was painful.

I was back to the Explorer when I saw the woman running back to the RV. She got in quickly. The brake lights flashed as the driver shifted into gear and drove out and back up to the highway.

I took another look at goatee, who was trying to crawl back to the Suburban, but without much luck. No problem for us. I decided to check Delmore one more time.

When I did, I could see what had happened.

The driver's door was blistered with pellet holes, but more importantly, the upper corner was covered with blood and bits of flesh. Looking closely at Delmore's splayed-out torso, I could see he had no gunshot wounds.

It wasn't my blast that had taken him down, it was the sharp edge of Detroit metal. He'd slammed into the door when he ducked.

I had a moment of hurt pride. I had missed him, and I was damn near sniper-qualified. I never have understood why my mind works that way. In other circumstances, I might have laughed.

I picked up the .45 and tucked it into the other side of my jeans. Delmore was breathing, but out so cold he probably had a concussion.

I glanced back at Elle, who stood by the passenger door of the Explorer. I must have looked quite the gunslinger.

"We need to go, Jack."

"I'm coming."

I was about halfway there when a cell phone chirped from inside the Suburban.

I looked at Elle. She turned up one hand as if to say WTF.

The chirping stopped before I could get to it. I smashed the phone on the asphalt and threw it into the brush where I'd hurled the keys. Then I stowed the weapons in the Explorer and covered everything with the tarp. I was completely soaked.

"Shouldn't you get those?" Elle called out, gesturing toward the lot.

"Shit." I trotted out to police up the red shell casings, then got in the car, shivering. I wiped the rain from my face and took a couple of deep breaths.

Elle was bone-drenched, too. Her expression, reflecting mine, told me anything I needed to know.

I cranked the engine, turned on the wipers. I glanced at both of the hoods as we drove past them. Maybe they would drown like turkeys in the rain. Die of their wounds. I didn't care.

Back at the easement, I paused momentarily, looking down the hill through the trees. From the road, it would have been pretty difficult to see what had happened.

I pulled onto the Trace.

Elle looked back at where we had been. "Jesus, Jack."

"You know they would have killed us."

"Jesus, you just blew their shit away."

"They had guns."

"I'm not saying that."

"This was the third time, four counting the church."

"I know. I know."

"I know."

"They'll come after us. Trey will. He'll never stop."

"They were already after us. Or at least you."

"I know."

I realized I was driving way too fast for a hard rain and slick roads. I slowed to fifty. "Now we can't call the police, either."

Elle looked out through the sheets of rain. Side gusts of wind threw branches and leaves across the pavement, almost as a tornado would. I slowed even more and clicked the wipers to top speed.

"Rosedale," she said. She slumped back against her seat and took a long breath. "It could be that's where Aunt Lenora is anyway."

Lightning attacked the forest. Insane thunder. It was so humbling it broke the tension just a little. "Nobody finds Lenora if she doesn't want to be found," she said. "And Trey's afraid of her."

I must have looked skeptical.

"You'll see."

I looked at her closely. "Are you okay?

"What about you?"

"I'm okay."

"You just shot two men."

"One, anyway."

Suddenly her body bolted forward. "Oh my god! The ashes!" She punched open the buckle on her safety belt and turned around in her seat, kneeling so she could reach the storage space behind. I glanced back. She was wedging Terrell's urn tighter between the seat rest and one of our bags. "It's okay," she said. "It's fine."

She buckled back up and stared out at the yellow stripes on the gleaming asphalt ahead. I drove into the deluge.

We moved across the middle of the state toward the Delta in random zigs, zags, double-backs, and back roads—textbook evasion. I wasn't wildly happy about Rosedale, but the more we talked it through, it seemed the only safe place where we could get in touch with Lenora, whose phone remained unanswered in Oxford. She was the only person, other than Trey, likely to know what Terrell had been up to and where the missing painting might be. If we couldn't find her, I wasn't sure what we'd do.

The storm kept moving on to the southeast, so the more we drove west, the more the clouds dissipated behind us. Before long all that was left of the monsoon was a verdant lushness of land steaming after a hard rain.

At Cleveland, we turned off U.S. 61, what they sometimes called the Blues Highway, to pick up Mississippi 8 for Rosedale. I was starting to feel the familiar wave of a low blood sugar hunger-headache. Elle wasn't hungry but needed a pit stop.

Just at the western edge of Cleveland a couple of pickups sat outside a ramshackle burger and blues joint. I pulled to one side of the building, although it didn't really hide the Explorer. If somehow they were still on us, it wouldn't matter much anyway. Before we went in, Elle put on sunglasses and borrowed one of my caps. She said it was better than showing her face, still puffy from grief.

I pulled my own cap down low on my forehead. The place was fairly empty because it was already too late for lunch and too early for the dinner crowd. We took a table to one side, under old soda pop signs and other leftovers from estate sales. It looked more like a roadhouse bar than café, with a band stage at the far end. But it was dark and that was good. A busty young waitress in jeans and T-shirt with a "Holly" name tag came. She was friendly, but also the kind whose thoughts tended to focus on plans for the evening rather than on customers, even a biracial couple doubtless wanting to look anonymous. And that was good, too.

I ordered the grilled chicken burger with fries and ice tea, unsweet. Elle didn't look up so I suggested the same thing and she nodded—"but a Diet Coke instead of tea." The waitress went back to call the order through the window slot behind the bar. Elle and I headed for the restrooms.

I tried to clean up at the sink. But while throwing away the paper towels, I glanced down and noticed what I hoped no one else had: dried blood on both my shoes and some on my black jeans. I wetted more towels and dabbed it off. Maybe goatee guy had shaken some of it on me when he was kicking up his tattered legs. I had stopped once for gas on the way here but it was a self-serve and I used my credit card so no one would have given me a close look.

I beat Elle back to the booth. She slid into her seat, looked across the formica-topped table and sighed: "Here I am, in the Delta, black tee, shades, ball cap. With a white man."

Holly brought the order right away. Elle picked at hers, but it wasn't from being dainty. I could tell she could barely get anything down.

I wonder if she saw the thinness of our defenses as starkly as I did. Or were we moving in a direction that had to be right because it was the only one? Difficult to take stock of the chain of karma: mine had started with nothing more than a routine stroll for coffee in the Marigny and then morphed to shooting two thugs on a rural Mississippi highway and hightailing it into the alluvial plains of Deep Dixie. And no idea—none—where or how we would ever get out of this. Or if. We finished up and left a big tip.

The road to Rosedale was dead straight as it rolled past fields of cotton, soybeans, rice. Farmworker shacks still dotted the former Dockery plantation that had generated the blues. The fields were even flatter than those along the coastal plains of south Texas. Flat enough to see the sun beat down without pity all day long in every direction. Flat enough to grow anything with a seed. Flat enough to absorb whatever evil, or good, was sufficient unto any number of days.

Elle began to look in her purse for an address book with half-forgotten numbers. She said most of her contacts were on her computer at home in Tuscaloosa. As soon as she said it we both got the same bad feeling. The computer at home: i.e., where the thugs had been. But they would've needed a password, she said, and some hacking skills not usually associated with cheap Southern hoods. I could only hope.

After we let that stew a few moments, like remembering you'd gone on a long trip and left the gas on, she shrugged it off and concentrated on immediate concerns. She said her cousin, Artula, on her father's side, lived just north of Rosedale, although she wasn't sure exactly where. Elle said we'd be welcome because they had been close as children and because that's the way people around there were.

She finally found an address and a number and called on her cell but the number was no longer in service. She tried Artula's married name, Johnson, if she was still married, but couldn't get a listing for that, either. So we were just going to show up and take our chances. Worst case, we'd find a motel.

I kept driving.

A few miles from Rosedale, a bright yellow crop duster buzzed down near the highway. It made a steep, banking turn and went back at the field, trailing white fumes. For some reason it made me feel more vulnerable than I had all day. Just like that, things can drop out of the sky to kill you.

I stopped at the junction of Highway 1, what's called the Great River Road, then turned right toward a smattering of buildings. Rosedale was bigger than I had expected, which isn't saying much. Maybe the commercial port to the south of town and whatever accrued from being the county seat made it more than a road speck.

All I really knew of Rosedale was from a line from Robert Johnson's "Crossroads." I had danced with prostitutes in bars in Incheon and Seoul many nights to Eric Clapton's version. On nights we could get away from black ops and keep it all together for another week or two. Given the way keeping it together had played out for me, hard to believe, even now, I had ever volunteered for intelligence. A bird colonel I once liked told me G-2 was "combat chess"— abstract mind games using real people. Good training for whenever my four years were up. I bought in. Then they assigned me to a liaison unit with the spooks.

I turned right at the river road, toward the town. We passed empty buildings and a few others, like the White Front Café, a venerable hot tamale place, trying to hang on. The main square was dominated by the county courthouse. I remembered an odd factoid that I had once come across, that for some reason Bolivar County, one of the nation's poorest, had two county seats. The other was back in Cleveland. I had never taken the trouble to find out why but assumed it was another barely explainable quirkiness of Delta history.

Rising up above the courthouse and the town and its kudzu-draped water tower to the west was the levee. On the other side of that, a long stretch of flat, fecund soil feeding dense forests and bounteous crop fields leading to the river's edge. So long as it stayed in its banks. It seemed a strange way to live: because of and in spite of a great waterway so fearsome that protective mounds of earth more than a mile away could be breached as though they were nothing.

On one end of the courthouse lawn, a group of black women had set up a church rummage sale under a blue and white striped awning.

"Pull over. I want to ask them where this address is."

Elle rolled down her window as we neared tables filled with secondhand clothes, rows of used furniture, garden tools, and lawn mowers. Another table was loaded with plates of cookies and pies. Next to it, soda pop cans floated in melted ice in a huge tub. You could tell it had rained earlier in the day by a few puddles.

I stopped near the cookie table. Elle leaned out her window. "Hey, y'all. Say, I wonder could someone help me with a question?"

A shapely woman in a floral print dress stepped over. She was about Elle's age, maybe younger.

"You lost?"

"Not exactly. We're trying to find a cousin of mine, and I'm not sure where Memphis Place might be."

The woman looked at Elle closely, and at me, then tilted her head upward as though thinking it over. She turned to the ladies behind her. "Memphis Place? The one up in the New Place?"

"Not over there," said one of the women, also in a print floral. "Just up the highway past where that trailer park is."

"Where Brother Tyne and them live?"

"You know, maybe halfway."

"Oh, yeah, where Sampson's used to be."

"That's right. Memphis Place. Right in there, just off the highway."

The first woman turned back to Elle. "Who you looking for, though?"

"Her name is Artula. Johnson, I think. Used to be Meridian."

The woman looked back at the others, then at Elle again. She leaned in closer. "I know you? Behind those dark glasses?"

Elle glanced at me, then at the woman, and took off her shades.

"Sister, you okay in there?" But she was looking at me again.

"I'm fine. I am."

"Ellie? Ellie Meridian from Oxford? That you?"

They studied each other.

"You used to come down here with your brother sometimes. Stayed in town and out south past the park, on the way to the lake. With some white folks part of the time."

"I wish I could say who you are."

"Claudia. Claudia Pettit. You know me. They call me Cici."

Elle looked at me again, just the hint of a smile. I cut off the engine.

"Cici? Cici Pettit? Well of course I remember you. I'm sorry it took a minute. We went into Cleveland a couple of times for ice cream and parties at the church."

"We did, girl, we did. But say, your eyes all red. Are you really okay?"

"I am. But, Young Henry, I have to tell you, he's passed. We were just at the services up in Oxford."

"No! T. Henry? He couldn't be that old."

"It was an accident."

Cici reached through the window and touched Elle's cheek. "I'm so sorry."

"We're just here going back to Alabama. It's where I live now. I just wanted to drive by and see this place where, you know—"

"Sure, Ellie. I heard T. Henry was a schoolteacher up there somewhere. It's been a while."

"It has."

"You? What do you do in Alabama?"

"I'm sort of a counselor. What about you?"

"I'm still here. I teach at the school. Second grade. Went to Delta State and I guess I just never got away."

"Married?"

Cici laughed and glanced back at her friends. "Married with children, as they say. That's pretty much the way it is around here. You?"

"Not yet."

"Well, park this truck and come over and let's talk. This is no way to catch up."

"I need to get up to Tula's first. We can come back later on."

"That'd be fine. You be sure and do that, though. But we about to close up at six."

"We will."

I cranked the engine.

"Say, you know your aunt come through here time to time. They call her Sister Lenora here. You know we don't like that hoodoo around the church." Then she winked. "But people say she's good."

Elle's body tensed up. "You've seen Aunt Lenora?"

"Couple of months back, I guess. She comes in and sets up not too far from where you're going. She stays maybe a week, or just a few days. Does some readings over in the New Place, that nasty old subdivision off there—" She waved her arm back around to her right. "Or whatever she does."

"But she's not here now?"

Cici looked in at me again. "Not that I know of."

A dirt brown pickup with one dented white fender cruised by, turned in at the corner, and parked. An elderly man got out and dropped the tailgate.

"Claudia," said the grandmotherly woman, "Brother Carver come with some more ice and sodas. We got to help him unload."

"Coming right up." Then, to Elle. "We're getting ready for the people come through late afternoon. Some of those tourists looking for the blues clubs up in Clarksdale drive around down here sometime. We get some politicians now, too, with the election coming. You remember how all that was."

Cici leaned in and she and Elle exchanged a quick kiss.

"See you later on," Elle said. Cici walked over toward the pickup. She stopped, turned as if to say something, but didn't, and went back to her friends.

"We can go," said Elle.

"You know where it is?"

"Yeah."

"I guess you know everyone in Rosedale."

"Not really. Town's grown. But some I do know, that's for sure." She breathed heavily. "That was good to see Cici. She was a good friend to me and Young Henry."

"She'd changed that much you didn't recognize her?"

"It's been at least twenty years since I was here, except just driving through one other time. I just didn't see it right away."

"I guess she thought you looked about the same."

"Except my bloodshot eyes and my face swollen up like the moon."

Elle left the window down as she waved to the others at the tent. I began to ease down the street.

It didn't take long to hit the northern edge of town and then it was just more cotton fields and thick stands of trees and the levee off toward the river.

I had barely gotten back up to sixty when Elle told me to slow down. We passed a few small clumps of houses and shacks, and then there was a small sign on the right that said "Small Engine Repair" by a little dirt lane.

"That's it. That's Memphis Place."

"I guess they were thinking big."

She flicked a sharp look my way. "Just drive up slowly so I can see the numbers." Three clapboard houses and a big double-wide lined one side of the lane, punctuated at the end by a clapboard shed with a tractor inside. Off to the other side was a half-acre lot with a ranch-style brick house dead center under a grove of oaks. Almost like in the suburbs, if there were such a thing in the Delta.

"That's it."

I turned into the gravel driveway. At one side a black mailbox stood like a sentry, held up by a long silver stretch of industrial pipe. Atop the box a stylized black and red rooster was fashioned out of metal.

I stopped the Explorer in front of the house. The front door was bright yellow.

"Are you sure about this?"

"This is the place."

"You see anyone home?"

"There's a car over there."

"So you just want to go up and knock."

"You have another idea?"

"No, that's pretty much it."

"Wait here."

She got out. She checked herself in the side mirror but I knew she didn't really care, or felt that there was only so much she could do. She took off her sunglasses, which I thought was a good idea since wearing shades to meet people you haven't seen in over a decade to ask them for a place to hide out from trained killers probably isn't the best move.

She went to the door and knocked.

Nothing.

She knocked again. Nothing. She was turning to leave when the door opened. The small child who peeped around the edge seemed surprised. Whoever he thought he would find, it wasn't the woman he beheld. But who was she? Almost at once came a muffled shout from inside, followed by the appearance of a very thin woman in a blue T-shirt and jeans, holding a baby clad only in a diaper.

Elle stepped back a couple of feet.

"Artula Johnson? Is that you?"

"Who wants to know?"

"Tula? It's me. Elle. Elle Meridian. Ellie."

The woman with the baby looked Elle over, in detail, and then opened the door wider and came outside. The boy, maybe three or four, scurried out, too, more curious than ever.

"It is you, I swear."

Elle came forward and they attempted a hug around the children.

"I tried to call but the number was disconnected."

"I changed it a while back. Good lord, girl, oh my good lord. It is you. Now come on in, now. We got bad mosquitoes here."

They went inside and the door closed.

In a minute or two, it opened again and Artula waved me inside.

The house was more spacious than it looked from the outside: four bedrooms, living room with conversation pit and fireplace, kitchen with all the accoutrements, wall-to-wall beige carpet throughout. Artula was doing well.

Elle introduced me as a friend from New Orleans. Artula took my hand and said the girl in her arms was Vanessa, now thirteen months. The boy was Byron Jr., but everyone just called him Junior. Elle hugged the boy and cooed over Vanessa and then Junior went back to a cartoon show on a big Sony TV at the far side of the living room. We followed Artula to the conversation pit and sat on an L-shaped, plaid fabric couch. Artula put her daughter into a portable playpen and settled into a leather Lazy-Boy.

She asked us if we wanted anything to drink but we both said no, that we had stopped at a joint back in Cleveland. Artula said she knew the place and it was good, but she hadn't been there in a while, that she didn't get out that often these days.

She and Elle made small talk about the past, but it was pretty obvious Artula wasn't as well as she let on. She got to it right away, keeping her voice low so Junior wouldn't hear. Cancer of the kidneys, she said. For about a year. Maybe in remission but the doctors couldn't be sure. Elle apologized for not knowing. Artula said she hadn't really told a lot of people, even family.

"How is Byron taking it? Here I am in your house and I forgot to even ask where he is. Is he out of town?"

Artula looked away. "I thought maybe you knew. He passed, back before Vanessa was born."

Elle's face had lost most of its puffiness, but fell again, in part because of the news and in part because I think she was shamed at knowing so little about someone with whom she had been close as a girl.

"It was an accident, over by the port. He fell off a construction beam he was checking out because they thought it had a crack. Byron was what they call a project manager. A black man in charge of all those white folks." To me: "He had an engineering degree." Back to Elle: "His head hit the dock, and he dropped into the river. It was two days before his body washed up. It was pretty bad."

"I'm so sorry," said Elle.

I nodded but you can't say anything meaningful to that kind of news as a stranger. I looked over at the TV. Junior was watching *Lion King*.

"We had a small service here but he was buried up in Blytheville, where he had come up."

"And you found out about the cancer after all that?"

"Can you believe?"

"It doesn't rain but it storms."

"Amen to that."

Artula glanced toward her children. "I think your parents both passed right about the same time didn't they?"

Elle leaned in to her cousin. "They did. They sure did. But, Tula, you're still here."

"Thing is, we're pretty okay other than that," Artula said, catching Elle's head-to-toe inspection, shrugging. "B. had the insurance with Conocor, and I'm still on his health policy another two years." She looked off quickly. "After that we'll have to see. Of course Mama would take care of—" She glanced at the children. "She lives down in Mobile but that would be okay. You know, if it comes to that. Anyway, we may need to be closer to a big hospital than we are here."

Elle took Artula's hand. "They have a lot of new medicine now. It's not like it used to be."

"I know. The doctor says if I make it three years I'll die an old lady."

They both laughed.

"You're so strong, Tula. You've always been."

Vanessa started fussing and Artula walked over to give her a juice bottle.

"Well, never a dull moment," she said, coming back to the couch. "But, girl, you haven't said, what brings you here to this old puddle in the road? With that face?"

Elle ran her fingers through her hair self-consciously, until her cousin reached over and smoothed her cheek the way you would a child's. "Girl, you are still about the most beautiful thing in this whole state."

Elle thanked her, glanced at me. I shrugged as if to say, why not tell her?

For the next ten minutes, she did. But only about Terrell's death and the memorial service. Nothing about Witch Dance and Trey. Later, Elle told me it wasn't about lack of trust, but not wanting to add to Artula's load.

"Jack, you must think we a couple of freaks," Artula said, lightly stroking Elle's cheek.

"Nothing like that."

"He's been solid," Elle said.

Artula patted her cousin on the shoulder and excused herself to make a sandwich plate for Junior and something for Vanessa.

Elle and I used the time to bring in our things from the Explorer. I decided to leave the weapons. Covering them again with the tarp, I had the flash of a view from on high, something looking down on me doing what I was doing. I reached back in for the Colt and pushed it into my duffel. You never know.

"We can only stay tonight," Elle said, as we walked back to the house.

I made a quick visual recon. "She's glad to see you."

"Yeah. Better late . . . I guess."

We stowed our things in the spare bedroom. I offered to take the couch but Elle said for me to use the bed; she wanted to stay up and talk to her cousin after the children went to sleep.

I had a beer and watched CNN while Elle and Artula gave Vanessa a bath so she'd be clean for church in the morning and put her to bed and then got Junior showered and settled in for the night. Not all that much had happened in the world in the past few days that I could tell, at least from the TV. Back in New Orleans, before all this, I kept up with events as part of my job; odd how unimportant and distant it all seemed.

When Elle and Artula had finished with the kids, they came out and we talked a little about the Big Easy. Artula had been there with her husband. They had splurged at Commander's Palace. She said B. loved her cooking best, though. I had another beer, while they started their catch-up, and about ten I realized I was yawning.

I went to the bedroom, but when my head hit the pillow, my mind came alive. I was back at Witch Dance, and goatee guy was on the ground in front of me. I could hear Elle and Artula talking like teenagers. Finally I didn't know anything until the sun woke me.

ARTULA WAS IN THE kitchen, getting breakfast for Vanessa. The coffee was brewed, and she'd set out mugs for her guests. I filled mine while Artula fussed over the baby. It was probably the first time in far too long that a man had been here in the morning.

Elle shuffled in about the time I was getting a refill. She wore an old softball jersey and baggy shorts. Her face looked quiet again; the sleep had helped even though I think they had been up late. Elle hugged Artula and got coffee. After a sip, she leaned down to kiss Vanessa, then did the same to me, on the cheek.

I opened the sliding glass door leading to the back yard and strolled out onto the wooden deck. The fenced yard must have been fifty yards deep, freshly mowed and surrounded by trees. The air was unusually cool from yesterday's storms. I let the Delta sink in around me. The bugs weren't all that bad, although the cans of spray and mosquito coils on the edge of the deck indicated normality was otherwise.

Elle followed me out and we walked about halfway towards a prefab storage shed in the far back corner. Past that all I could see were cotton fields and surviving stands of trees.

"Sleep okay?"

"Right through the nightmares. You?"

"Same." She walked off a few steps and turned. "Vanessa wants to go to church later. I said I would think about it."

I gave her a look that must have been sharp.

"What?"

"Nothing." I drank coffee and looked out at the cotton fields. "I mean we didn't come here to socialize."

"I didn't say we'd go."

"No."

"No."

I got over it. "So, Tula. She's okay? You must have talked a lot after all this time."

She studied me, one eyebrow raised. "It was like we couldn't stop."

Conversation lapsed. We could hear big tractor-trailer rigs out on the highway, the way sound carries early in the morning. TV coming from one of the houses down the lane. We walked to the back fence.

"There's something you should know," she said, running her hand across the top of the chain link. "About Byron."

I touched her hand lightly and she smiled a trace.

"She's still taking it hard."

"It's more than that."

I let go of her hand and finished my coffee. She held her mug to her lips a moment without drinking.

"I think you should know. I mean, I want you to know. It wasn't an accident, at the river. He jumped. Sort of."

"Sort of?"

She looked back at the house. "It was what he thought he needed to do. He had it figured out. He knew the current would drag him down, ruin any autopsy. He didn't think they'd even find his body."

"He killed himself."

"Yeah."

"All this from last night."

"She needed to talk. You know. It's what I do for other people. My job."

"You didn't go into any more of our thing—"

Her eyes flashed. "Come on, Jack."

I looked away. "So anyway . . ."

She let it hang there. "So anyway . . . there was Tula and Byron Jr. and the baby, Vanessa, to come in eight months. They needed his insurance."

"I thought they had a good marriage. I don't . . ."

". . . All that. They loved each other. He was a good provider. All that."

She looked up toward the morning sun, not even shielding her eyes. "Except he also . . . he also had HIV."

The light showed crinkles of pain in the corners of her eyes.

"They were going to church. He just sat down on the bed, holding his tie, one shoe off and one shoe on, and told her."

"Jesus."

A flight of birds swooped low over us, then settled on a power line. Just as quickly, they flew away. "It was some woman up in Memphis. Tula said he cried and hit his forehead through a wall. Then they didn't talk for a long time."

The humidity was coming back. I felt sweat forming on my neck.

"Tula said she told him, at first, she told him she didn't care if he killed himself." She looked at me, squinting now. "But you know she did. A lot."

"I'm sorry."

"And now Tula is HIV positive." She took a deep breath, looked back at the house again. "Vanessa, too. Tula tells people she has cancer because, you know, it doesn't freak them out."

"But she told you."

"I'm the only one other than her mother and her doctor and a case worker. She said it was killing her to keep it in. She doesn't know I'm telling you. Keep it that way until we've gone."

I nodded.

She threw the rest of her coffee onto the grass. Just missing my shoes.

"One other person knows. Lenora. She's been helping Tula with spirit work."

I averted my eyes.

"Doesn't need your approval."

"I haven't been around those ways like you have."

"Be around this way. Tula has a number I can call."

"Lenora's number?"

"Kind of makes hearing that little story all worthwhile, huh?"

"What?"

"I know what you're thinking."

"I'm just thinking about how we live through this."

"How Tula gets through it, too, Jack."

"Come on."

Artula waved from the deck, beckoning us back. "Y'all want breakfast? Ellie, you still want to come to church with me?"

We passed the square, the back side of town, and an abandoned, rusty hulk of a cottonseed pressing plant that looked like an apocalyptic movie set. We got to the levee and followed a trail to the top, where we'd be able to see the best way to get down the other side. To scatter Terrell's ashes at the river's edge.

Soon we were threading a maze of fields and thickets of trees that had survived the clear-cutting that carved out Delta agriculture over the last century and a half. Every acre was anointed in blood and grisly death, whether from heat stroke, logging accidents, or the natural dangers of snakes, alligators, and bears. I became disoriented but Elle knew exactly which fork to take and what dead end to avoid.

We had left Artula and the children at the house. At first she wanted to join us, but she felt she had to take the children to Sunday school and church. She said it was important for her to attend every Sunday. She said she had to thank God for another week; that was one of the deals she had made with Him to get through this.

So we'd come on our own. Elle wanted to find the "beach" along the riverbank where she and her cousins, and sometimes Trey, had played as kids. It was on private land, but Artula said the owners lived in Atlanta, and not all that many people knew about it. She said especially on a Sunday morning we probably wouldn't encounter anyone.

I was glad we had come alone. We needed time to regroup. Getting to Rosedale was only supposed to be a breather, and a way to find Lenora. But we had become distracted. Denial might also be a term. If I was supposed to be the man with a plan, I had come up short. Bad people were literally hunting for Elle, and for what she might be able to get for them. And now they were also looking for the guy who'd been shooting up the hired hands.

The dirt lane veered this way and that. After three or four miles, it headed directly toward the water. The trees got taller and thicker. I went over a small rise and there it was: frothing, full-bore, hard-churning, rain-swollen. The mighty Mississippi, the Amazon of America. The sight was so sudden, so vast, so immediate, I had to catch my breath.

We drove parallel to the bank for another half-mile or so. The muddy tide surged right up against the trees, ebbing and flowing through low, marshy scrub. I didn't see any place where you could easily walk to the edge to scatter someone's ashes.

"That's it," she said, almost in a whisper.

I would never have imagined something so serene in such a wild place. A sandy beach, fifty yards wide, sheltered from the powerful currents in the main channel by a half-moon cove cutting into the bank. It wasn't a complete secret. The rutted trail that led down to the beach was littered with beer cans and fast-food wrappers.

"Here?"

"Here. Stop. We're getting out."

She took the urn from the back seat and we walked to the water. The hydraulic roar, the thickness of the air, the intensity of the colors made it all seem unreal.

She held the urn against her chest. "I'm going to pray now and say a few words. You don't have to be here but I would appreciate if you'd stay by me."

"I'm here."

She bent down to wedge the urn upright on the sand, then knelt before it. I did the same.

She extended her right arm and with her index finger drew a circle with intersecting lines and one squiggly line encircling all that, like a snake biting its own tail.

She closed her eyes and prayed, her lips barely moving. Then she crossed herself and stood.

"May God be with you, Terrell Henry Meridian."

We stood and she handed me the urn. She slipped off her black canvas sandals and held out her arms, palms up. She nodded, indicating that I should pour the ashes into her cupped hands. I unscrewed the top and did. She stepped barefoot into the waves, up to her knees, then allowed the ashes to sprinkle from her fingers. They lingered on the surface, sank, and were borne away by the current.

She looked at me and I knew she wanted the urn.

I kicked off my shoes and waded out to her.

"Goodbye, Young Henry. This is the home of all our people and all our life and it runs from now until forever. Bless you, bless you. . . ." She watched as the remainder of the ashes floated away.

Her eyes were moist but she looked at me with a smile.

AFTERWARDS, WE SAT ON a grassy spot above the beach. The river's chorus unfolded: birds in the trees, the thunder of waves, distant noise from busy farms, the blat-blast of a horn from a barge making its way downstream for Vicksburg or Natchez or New Orleans. Same as Terrell's ashes.

"What you drew back there. It looked Haitian."

"Lenora taught us how to do those. They're called vévres. It's a way to pray to African gods."

"You believe in that?"

"I believe what can it hurt?"

I nodded. "What about your brother? Believing."

"I think he did. Maybe more, being around her."

"Your aunt."

"It's what she does. She's very devout."

I watched the barge.

"Do you believe me?"

"That your aunt believes in voudou? Sure. I was asking about you."

"I said."

"Can't hurt?"

"Jack, I was raised Catholic. I got away from the church but I still believe in God. You don't? You told me you studied Zen."

"I know. But it feels different."

"You should believe in something."

"Something and nothing are the same, the Buddhists say."

"Let's just sit here."

"Let's just sit here."

She stretched her legs, wiggled her bare toes. "I saved some of the ashes."

"What?"

"I put a handful in my pocket. I'll give them to Lenora. She'll make a special offering."

I picked up a small rock and threw it into the river.

We fell into another silence, listening to nature's chorus.

I stretched, too. "Any ideas?"

She bent double, her head between her legs, like a gymnast.

"About?"

"You know."

She leaned back on the ground.

"It's hard to think right now."

"Still."

"Yeah."

She sat up, then got to her feet. "Can we go back? I know we need to talk but I think I'm ready to leave."

I caught her face in profile. She had just buried her brother. She was the last of her family. "Sure. You want to just drive around?"

"Yeah, let's do that."

We put on our shoes. Elle carefully emptied the ashes from her pocket back into the urn, then stowed it behind the seat again. I cranked the engine.

In a way, I wanted to stay. It was another world. It was the Delta. But we had to leave.

I backed around as best I could without getting stuck in the muck, then drove back toward the levee and Rosedale.

WE'D BARELY GOTTEN STARTED through the cotton fields when we came to a tricked-out black Dodge Ram pickup blocking our path on the narrow lane.

At first, I thought it was a worker or maybe a foreman from the big farm on which we were trespassing. I had a story worked out about getting a little lost, trying to find our way back to the Great River Road State Park, which was just to the north. But it wasn't that kind of thing.

The pickup stood idling in the middle of a curve around a cotton field so that we couldn't get around. The driver turned off the engine and climbed out of the cab. He was a youngish guy, burly, wearing a dark blue ball cap. Staring at us.

Now that I had a better look, I pegged him even younger. Frat boy type but more rural. He was holding a beer can. Unless he'd had one for breakfast, likely he'd been out all Saturday night and just coming home.

"Can you get around him?"

I looked at the drainage ditches on either side of the lane. "I don't think so. I don't suppose you know him."

Her look didn't need words.

"I guess not."

He stopped alongside the front fender of his truck and pointed to me with his beer-can hand. "Say, what y'all doing down here on private prop'ty? An' blockin' my way?"

I got out of the Explorer.

"Just tell him we're lost," she said as I closed the door.

"Y'all not from around here, are you?" He started walking toward me.

I waited. "Look, if you could just move over a little we could both get by. We just need to get back to Rosedale." I reworked my fake story. "We need to get to church. We're visiting some friends."

He closed about half the distance to me. "You don't have no friends here."

"Hey, man, can we just get by? Both of us go on our way?"

He pulled his cap lower.

"That's a nigger with you, ain't it, son?"

I rolled my eyes, took a breath.

"Ain't it?"

"Look, we need to get by." I heard the growl in my own voice. He was now only a few yards away from me.

"I said, what are you doin' on this road? Fucker."

"Move your fucking truck."

"Yankee asshole."

Putting it all in slow motion, my mind was trying to take in the whole incredible cliché of the thing even as I was working out violent possibilities.

Then I heard Elle's door open and slam shut.

"You got a problem?" she walked up to us.

"Goddam, girl. Ain't you something! You want to party?"

Elle gave him a classic sizing-up, and shook her head. "He's just a drunken fool." Then, directly to him: "We need you to move your truck. This is an access road. You don't own it."

"It ain't access for you."

"We just want to get around you. Okay?"

I had begun easing toward the back of the Explorer. Elle saw me.

"Jack, no. He's just an idiot."

"What was that?" he said, his words full of drunken saliva.

"I was talking to him. I said you're acting like a fool. Now move that truck a little and let us get on to church."

I kept moving.

Her tone shifted. "Where you going this time of morning all drunk, anyway?"

"What . . . bidness is that of yours?" He seemed startled at being scolded.

"I'm just saying this is Sunday church time and you don't need to be like this. What's your name?" Her voice sharpened.

"I ain't givin' you no name."

"It's just as well, then, so you don't embarrass your family."

He took a step forward, but tripped and fell down, first on his knees, then his ass. "Shit."

"You're way too drunk to drive anyway."

"I was just goin' to fish." It came out in more of a slurred muddle than ever, so he had to repeat it.

"Well, then, go." She looked at me, maybe winked but I wasn't sure. By now I had opened the hatch. The Remington was loaded and ready.

He got up slowly, wobbly. Whatever was in Elle's voice had taken command of the morning. The boy stumbled back to the pickup and opened the door. "You jus' get on, then," he called out.

Elle turned to me. "Let's go."

I closed the hatch.

No sooner had we gotten back in the Explorer than we heard gears grinding. The Ram lurched backward, almost into the ditch.

I backed up, too, to get more room. Then the pickup started forward, fishtailing slightly, and hung onto the other side of the trail.

I drove forward, right wheels half into the ditch. When I saw the young bubba was at least moving in a straight direction I gunned it and we were past him, maybe a forearm's distance from a sideswipe.

He kept going. I saw his brake lights as he got to the next curve.

"Probably drive right into the river," I said. I could feel my fingers dig into the steering wheel.

"I expect he'll be passed out before much longer."

I looked across at her. "That was pretty good back there."

"Well, you know, in theory I'm supposed to be able to read people and get in control."

"You didn't mind what he said?"

"What, calling me a nigger?"

"Well, yeah."

"Of course I did. But that wasn't the point, was it?"

"Meaning?"

"Meaning not much point grabbing for a gun to make our lives even more complicated just because a redneck calls me a name."

I drove a half-mile before I knew what to say. Then I stopped, put it in park, and shifted in my seat to face her.

"It set me off."

"I could see that."

She studied my face closely. "What are you saying?"

"I'm saying something is weird in my head now."

She looked at me "Look, we haven't even had time to think about the fact that we're in Mississippi, a black woman and a white man going around like it was the most normal thing in the world." She paused. "That little moron back there—there's going to be more of that. You know that."

"I know."

"If somebody says something I can't handle, I'll let you know."

"I know." She leaned across to kiss me on the cheek. I kissed her back but it wasn't good, just a thing that had no meaning. I settled back against the seat and took a couple of breaths. I felt like some monster was swimming around in the deep of my mind but for now all I could feel were the thick, cold pulses of its waves.

"This is no good. We brought your brother's ashes here and that was right but—"

"You think I don't think about what else is going on, too?"

"Then what do we do?"

"I have to talk to my aunt."

"If you can even find her. And what will she be able to really tell you?"

"She'll know why Young Henry is dead. That's a start."

"All we've got is 'starts.'"

She didn't answer.

I drove on. When we got to the highway, I headed north, but instead of turning in at the lane to Artula's house, I kept going. No real reason.

We rehashed the bubba incident and she told me more about her brother and Artula and Rosedale back in the day. I talked about living in Dallas, down in Oak Cliff, the southern half of the city split among blacks, whites, and browns and utterly distinct from what festered in the downtown skyscrapers and Republican suburbs.

We agreed that we were both glad we had moved on. But we couldn't get a fix on what we had moved on to. We were almost to the bridge across the river to Helena, Arkansas, before I turned back, the morning eaten up.

Artula and the kids were already home from church. She was still in her dark blue dress suit, Vanessa still on one arm. Junior, still wearing his blue slacks and a white shirt, ran up to hug Elle. We slipped off our mud-spattered shoes.

"How did it go at the river?"

"It was good. I feel like he's home."

"That's good, Ellie. I'm so glad."

Elle didn't elaborate and Artula was too preoccupied to delve. Elle picked up Junior and went to the kitchen to get some apple juice. He ran right back to the TV, giving me the once-over on the way. Artula put Vanessa in her playpen.

"By the way, if you were looking to lay low here, I guess you'll be thinking that over some more," Artula called out. "You know these small towns."

Elle was taking a plastic pitcher of iced tea from the fridge.

"Cici Pettit and the people from the church sale were all talking about you," Artula said, coming back into the kitchen. "So Cici flat out asked me if you were staying over, which she already knew you were, and I couldn't just lie. Anyway, you're supposed to call her."

I was in the kitchen by then, too. Elle reached for two glasses from the cabinet. She filled one and gave it to me. "Baptist grapevine, sure enough. I guess some things never change." Her voice was even. Too even.

Artula frowned defensively. "Everybody heard you'd done so well for yourself and they just proud of you, you know?"

Elle poured a glass for herself. Extremely slowly. "I guess maybe I should have gone with you after all. I could have brought this one, as well."

Artula looked me over, then back at her cousin.

"I'm just saying what people say."

"I know. It's okay."

"Never mind me," I said.

We laughed, more or less, that being the only option.

"I got to change, girl, and them, too," Artula said, her voice taking on a deliberate brightness. She walked toward the hall, but stopped. "Hold on."

On a table across the living room, a light was blinking on her answering machine. "Never saw that when I came in." She went over and clicked the play button.

There was one message: "Tula, hey, girl, it's Lenora. How are you? Look, I'm over here in Clarksdale but I'll be down there by this evening and I'll come by then. Keep it to yourself, please, ma'am, if you don't mind. Love you, darlin'. Hey to your little ones." Slight pause. "Hey to your cousin if she's still around."

12

It was a vague and purposeless afternoon, consumed by waiting for Lenora, and what might be information that could save our lives. Elle and I went to a grocery and bought a dozen bags of food as a way of thanks for our stay. She and Artula talked a little more, and Cici came by and they all sat in the living room and visited.

I went out for a drive. Rosedale didn't take long, so I cruised on to the industrial port south of town, where Byron had taken the noble way out, if you wanted to look at it that way. En route, I noticed for the first time that Rosedale had a municipal park and golf course. It seemed out of place. Like myself.

I stopped in at a convenience store for a Dr Pepper and a pack of sunflower seeds, then went back to the square and parked. I didn't want to go back to that house. Not because I wasn't any part of the conversation going on there, but because it reminded me how much we needed to keep moving. I was losing faith that Lenora would even know anything useful, but Elle was convinced. I got out of the Explorer, ambled over to a shaded bench and sat there like a tourist. A couple of people walked by, said hello, kept going.

A sharp flash of sun broke through the clouds and I pulled down the brim of my Saints ball cap. Just like that, I was back in Incheon. It was hot then, too, late July. A pack of drunken off-duty MPs had gang-beaten one of my deep-cover informants in a nearby ville. I had worked with Mr. Lee for months and liked him, and it wasn't easy running agents with contacts north of the DMZ. I couldn't file a charge against the MPs through anything like "normal" channels, given my line of work, but I couldn't let the killing go unanswered, either. So I got two of the hard guys in my small intel unit and we caught three of the MPs outside a bar after curfew. We left them in an alley, worked over but alive. It was as wrong as anything I'd ever done. But also right. I don't know if it was about revenge. I don't know what it was.

Something changed in me after that and it never got right. Or maybe something inside cracked open and came to the surface. What was eating at me now was the possibility of the latter. The brawl in the Dallas news-room, the Beretta in the Trinity, the leap into this situation, the way I felt at Witch Dance. Connect the dots. Any surprise I was willing to shoot that kid back in the field?

A city police car pulled past and I snapped back to the present. The young white cop gave me a cursory look-over and parked at the station a block away. I was of no further interest. Maybe I did look like a tourist.

"AUNT LENORA, THIS IS the man who is helping me about Young Henry."

"That you left the message about on my voicemail."

"I'm glad you got it."

"Hello, Jack." Her grip was firm, indicating a core power that would have seemed more appropriate from a grizzled Shaolin monk. She had ar-rived about nine, just after Artula put the kids to bed. She was petite, almost cloud-like in a light yellow shift with green trim, lots of golden jewelry. Her body seemed to match her voice. She was probably twenty years older than Elle, darker and stronger, with sharper features. Maybe that's what Elle's father had looked like.

The three of them exchanged hugs and brief condolences about Terrell, but in a measured way that I'm sure came from having a stranger in the house. Then Artula led them to the bedroom so that Lenora could have a look at the sleeping children. I went into the living room and settled back into the La-Z-Boy with the beer I'd been nursing while passing time watching TV. I channel-surfed mindlessly and settled on Larry King interviewing a celebrity.

Artula led her guests into the kitchen and got each a glass of wine. She couldn't drink, from the medicine, and had an iced tea. I worked on my beer. They continued to talk, quietly, catching up on family business other than murder. Probably sizing me up, too. Larry was asking about the burdens of being famous. I clicked over to a rival news channel. It was all war and politics. I was surrounded by words, none with meaning.

Presently Elle and Lenora joined me. Elle gave me a passing peck on the cheek. Her aunt scrutinized me like a stray dog somebody had brought home.

Artula was baking and stayed in the kitchen. She turned on the radio and sang along with a blues and gospel station. "Another beer, Jack?" she called out.

"Thanks, I'm good."

Elle and Lenora settled into the sofa.

"So the service, it was good?"

"It was good. Reverend Johnson gave a good service."

"You had him cremated."

"We put his ashes in the river this morning. Except a little I saved for you."

She fluffed a pillow behind her back for support. "That's a good thing." She glanced at Artula, humming and lost in the pleasure of taking care of company. In a lowered voice, to Elle: "And the other? That you wanted to talk about?"

Elle leaned close. "You didn't go to your house, did you?"

"Not after I heard that message from you."

"There's more since then. Trey came to the service."

Lenora's body stiffened.

"And he's been to my house in Tuscaloosa, too."

Lenora looked away, taking it in. It took her a few moments.

I went over to squeeze in next to Elle. I leaned toward Lenora. "You also need to know he sent a couple of his crew after us yesterday."

"Trey did?"

"I shot them."

She looked at me as though she'd just seen me for the first time.

I tried to keep my voice low. "I didn't kill them."

"We didn't have any choice," Elle said.

Lenora continued to stare at me. Through me. "This is bad."

"You could say that."

"Y'all doing okay in there? More wine, Elle?"

"Okay for now. You just bake that cake. We're going to be hungry."

"Bakin' and shakin'. Shakin' and bakin'." She turned up the music.

Elle shot me a look, then turned to her aunt. "There's more to tell you. Later." She tilted her head toward Artula. "I don't want her involved."

"No."

"It's just that we don't know where to go with this. I thought maybe you might know something. Anything."

Lenora shook her head, as if she were trying to sort things out. "There's so much."

"Start with that painting. We know Young Henry stole it."

I added, "More to the point, so does Trey."

Elle's look told me to watch my mouth. But I wasn't in the mood. Nor did we have the time.

I could see that Lenora understood my directness. She crossed her arms, leaning forward in thought, trying to retrieve a series of memories that only now seemed to fit together. "He told me they'd had a fight. He took it to get even. I tried to tell him not to go that way, but by the time we talked he'd already done it. What he wanted was for me to help him find a way to hide it." She glanced back to reassure herself that Artula wasn't hearing us over the radio and kitchen noise.

"So you hid it?" I asked.

"He was real impatient, you know, like all men tend to be." A warning scowl that had nothing to do with Trey and everything to do with Elle and me crossed her face. "And I think he was doing the coke again, and he wouldn't listen to any of my cautions. I'd never really seen him like that. I called him a couple of days later. This was only a month or so ago. All he'd tell me was that he'd taken care of it."

"Uh-huh. He always talked like that when he was hiding something."

"So I said, 'How?' And he said not to worry, he was going to meet with Trey and 'deal with it.'"

"'Deal with it.' He talked like that, too."

"After that he didn't bring it up, at least with me. You know, he was taking a break from teaching last semester and so he was always gone. Never at home much."

"He talked to me about the painting, how much it was worth and all. But not about the fight," Elle said.

"He was strung out, you understand? I asked him to sit for a reading, maybe the spirits could find out the truth. But he wouldn't. It was like, you know, he didn't want to know."

She stopped. Her eyes were misting. Maybe bottling it up ran in the family. Elle took her hand. "It's okay, auntie. I know you miss him. I do, too."

"You know, sometimes being Sister Lenora to my people is hard, when I feel all like this inside."

Elle held her aunt and stroked her back. Then she stood, and kissed her on the forehead. "I'm going to bring you something. I'll be right back." En route to the bedroom, she walked through the kitchen, tasted the cake batter, praised it to her cousin who was still dancing to the music.

Lenora stared down at the shag carpet, wiped her eyes again and breathed out. When she looked up, it was back to her harder self. "You've been good to her but you got yourself into something, didn't you?"

"I did."

"You regret it?"

"I don't regret meeting Elle."

"That's not what I said."

"No."

"I can see it in you. You have a heavy spirit on you."

I shrugged.

"No maybe about it, honey. I don't know much about you, yet. But I know that."

Elle returned with Terrell's urn and handed it gently to Lenora.

"These are saved from what we put in the river this morning."

Lenora opened the top, looked inside, closed it.

"And there's this." Elle gave her aunt an envelope. Inside was a folded-up tissue. Lenora unwrapped it to find a small pebble.

"That's from where Jack found Young Henry's body in New Orleans. That's Young Henry's blood."

Elle glanced at me as if to say there would always be some things I didn't know.

Lenora looked at the stained pebble a long time, then folded it back into the tissue and returned it to the envelope. "This will be good."

"Aunt Lenora, what are you going to do? You can't go home now."

"I don't know. I can just stay down in Jackson or even over in Birmingham for now. And get out on the road like this. Maybe it's time to get out of Oxford anyway. You know how it's gotten."

Elle nodded. "I don't think you should go back there. Ever. Trey or no Trey."

Lenora smiled. "Well, I don't see that boy living to retirement years."

I had the same reaction. Lenora caught it. "So what are you thinking?"

I said, "I'm thinking let's get Trey what he wants, and let the law take care of the rest. Which means I'm thinking I still don't know where that painting is and I need to."

Elle sat up straight. "He can't get away with it. I won't let him."

It came out loud and strident. Artula stopped her singing to look our way. "Got one in the oven. Cake, I mean."

"You best mean that, girl," Lenora called out. She turned the urn slowly in her hands.

"Do you believe Trey really thinks you know where the painting is?" I asked. "You personally?"

"He knows I don't." She looked at the urn, then at me. "You know I put down a goat on his spirit last year. Not for him, but for Terrell, to try to protect him from Trey. Trey knows that, too."

"But he was at your house."

"No, sir. Trey wasn't there. It was those two men worked for him."

"Yeah, but . . ."

"That's different."

"It is," Elle said.

I sat back. "So it really is just Elle he wants."

"I've been telling you," Elle said.

"He knows you won't give up until you find the painting. He'll let you do all the work," I said.

"It's bad," said Lenora.

"And then he won't want you anymore."

"It's been that way with Trey all his life."

"It is bad," I said.

"It's bad," Lenora said again.

Artula came into the room, wiping her hands on a towel. "Hope y'all love chocolate as much as I do."

13

It was a waxing moon, but the sky was bright, and the profusion of stars here, so far from the big cities, amplified the effect in ways urban dwellers like me tend to forget. After we sampled the cake, Artula went to bed, exhausted, to sleep with her children. Elle and I waited outside on the deck for Lenora. Bug spray and a strong northwest breeze kept the mosquitoes at tolerable limits.

Lenora wanted to offer something for Terrell's spirit and was in her room preparing. She wanted to use the pebble from the Marigny gutter to get a "second sight" into what Terrell had been thinking, or what might have happened that night.

I didn't know what to think, so I tried not to.

Presently, she came outside, carrying a large straw bag. We followed her to some plastic yard chairs under an oak at the side of the yard. We sat and she took out a white cloth about twice the size of a large napkin. She spread it on the grass. Digging into her bag, she pulled out the tissue Elle had given her, unwrapped it, and placed the blood-stained pebble on the cloth.

She said a few words from what I assumed was an African language, and then took out three small vials. She opened two and sprinkled the pebble with scented liquids. She knelt and asked Elle and me to join her and close our eyes and say a silent prayer for Terrell's spirit. Elle took my hand and gripped it tightly.

"Elegba, Ochosi, Ogun, Oshun, Olodumare, spirits of our ancestors, praise all, praise the Lord, praise all the mighty spirits here and for all time . . . ." She repeated this several times, rocking gently on her knees. Then she opened the third vial. "This is Henry," she said to Elle, "from the urn." She sprinkled ashes over the pebble, then closed the top and put it back in her bag.

"Please help this young brother and fine young man find his peace and his path. Help us find him now, accept this from us."

She reached into the bag again and took out what seemed to be a stuffed sock. It concealed a dazed, gray pigeon. I guess she traveled with all her spiritual supplies.

"Obatala, Elegba, Ochosi, Ogun. . .Obatala, Elegba, Oshosi, Ogun . . . Ashé, Ashé . . ."

With a deft motion she twisted off the bird's head, dropped it to the grass, and let blood from the neck drip across the pebble and ashes, holding the body tight until the wings stopped flapping.

She pitched the body next to the head, chanted more African words, and finally tilted her head backwards, up to the sky. She remained like that a couple of minutes. Then looked at us with a strange smile on her face.

I didn't know what to make of it, but she was in a trance.

I held Elle's hand.

Barely aware that we were also present, Lenora pulled a half-pint of rum from her bag, took a swig, and then spewed it onto the cloth and its contents. She recited more incantations, and reached out to pick up the pebble. She touched it to her mouth, then held it tightly in a balled-up fist. She was silent. At one point, her body jolted and her head shook.

Then she opened her hands, dropped the pebble onto the cloth, and sat back on the grass, her legs crossed. She looked at Elle, then, briefly, at me. She took a long breath. She seemed to have returned to us. Then she reached forward to pick up the pebble and bits of ash. She put the bird's body and head onto the cloth and wrapped it up. She put the pebble back inside the tissue and put it in her bag.

We stood. She handed me the cloth.

"This needs to be gone."

I looked at Elle. She nodded that it was okay.

"Anywhere?"

"There's a soybean field across that back alley. That will be fine."

I climbed over the wire fence at the end of the yard, crossed a narrow lane, and hurled the bundle as far as I could into the field.

When I got back to the yard, Elle and Lenora were sitting in the chairs. Lenora had re-packed her bag. There was a finger-stripe of blood on her cheek.

I TOOK THE COUCH now, with Lenora and Elle in the guest room on the twin beds. That whole side of the house was shrouded in itself. I felt like I was out on the perimeter. I had brought my duffel out of the bedroom on the pretext I would need a change of clothes, but mostly I wanted the Colt nearby. Being in the front of the house meant I'd hear anything, and I knew I'd wake up. I should have slept there last night, too. Trey's goons now wouldn't want to harm us until we came up with the painting, which was almost certainly stashed in New Orleans, but thugs aren't always rational and I had shot two of them.

I was already awake when the early strands of dawn danced through the house, just ahead of cries from the baby. I slipped into the guest shower, then put on my old jeans and a fresh blue polo shirt.

When I got to the kitchen Artula was holding Vanessa, talking and cooing. "Sorry if she woke you."

I smiled. "I was already awake."

"Coffee's made."

"You're an early bird," I said.

"I have a baby. I do this every day."

She put Vanessa in a chair-swing and gave her a sippy-cup of milk. I poured myself a mug of the coffee and leaned against the stove. I watched the widow at the routine of her new life. What she hoped would be a life that wouldn't be cut short.

"I guess we'll be leaving today."

When she finally looked at me, her eyes, as haunting as Elle's, were glistening. "I know all about that."

"Elle told you. About everything." I must have looked annoyed.

"We're family. We're friends. You know."

I went over to touch Vanessa's cheek. It made her smile. "So you also know the best thing is to get back to New Orleans," I said.

"That's what Ellie thinks, too."

"And we don't need to be here, either. Baptist grapevine, Elle calls it. Trey will find out."

"Trey Barnett is nothing to us here."

"Well, he has some hard boys that might make that different."

Artula studied her baby.

"I think we'll be moving soon anyway ourselves. You know, the treatments and all. Lenora is going to read me today but I'm pretty sure what she'll say."

I heard a stirring from one of the bedrooms and a bathroom door shut.

"I know all that will work out. If you treat it in time and all." We both knew I sounded like a Hallmark card.

"More coffee?"

"Thanks."

She took my mug. "You take milk?"

"A little. I can get it." I opened the fridge and took out a nearly empty gallon jug.

"Can't believe I ran out. Go ahead and finish it." She wrote "milk" on a magnetic note pad on the fridge door. "So, you know about everything about Byron and all?"

I poured the rest of the milk. "I know."

"See, it works both ways. Ellie talking."

"I guess."

"She just needs people now. Same as me."

I put the empty container in the trash.

"I had to tell her. I had to talk to someone I could trust, you know."

"I understand."

"People here are very old school, you might say. About all that AIDS and HIV."

"You and Elle found each other again, though."

"Something good out of all the bad."

"Yeah."

Elle came into the kitchen. She hugged Artula, a small peck on the lips for me, a kiss on the forehead for Vanessa.

That moment, that sliver of a moment, was the life some part of me wanted. It was not the one I expected to get.

Presently Lenora joined us, dressed for the day in a plum-colored pants suit. She was strikingly beautiful. The Meridian family wasn't short of impressive genes. When Junior came in and asked for cereal, I volunteered to run down to the corner grocery for milk, and while I was at it a loaf of bread and maybe some bananas.

I was about halfway to Rosedale when I noticed the brown sedan following me.

No question it was a tail. For all I knew it had been out there all night waiting for us to leave. I got to the four-way stop in town and thought about zooming east to Cleveland just to see how far Trey's boys would go—figuring that's who it was—but I knew they would go as far as it took. I also considered playing wounded mother bird to their prowling cat to lure them away from Elle. But even if they were morons, they'd know enough to drop me and go back to her. The only play was to draw them out and find out who they were, what they knew. Or make a stand. And hope there wasn't a back-up team. So far there hadn't been but that was before Witch Dance. For the life of me, I couldn't see how they had followed us. I'd been very careful, and Elle had been sure Rosedale would never cross Trey's mind.

I made a quick right on the two-lane asphalt road leading toward the Great River Road State Park, alongside the Mississippi. I had passed it yesterday driving around. If things were going to get rough, and I had to face them down, doing so at the park wouldn't endanger everyone back at the house. No matter what, I couldn't go back to Artula's running from thugs. Since I had foolishly left for the grocery without taking my cell, I didn't have a way to call and warn them, either. What I did have were the shotgun and Glock. That and a hunch. I figured that an early weekday morning at a lesser-known park on the banks of the Mississippi Delta wouldn't be that busy.

The sedan, a late model Plymouth, kept a discreet if irrelevant distance, since nobody was being fooled. From what I could tell through the rearview mirror there was only one guy in the car. White, it looked like, heavy-set.

But it was hard to see much more than a silhouette.

At the park entrance, I stopped to throw in a couple bucks admittance fee at the unattended honesty box. The tail did the same. I slowed; he slowed. I sped up; he sped up.

I drove on down a tree-lined asphalt two-lane, across a little bridge where an elderly black woman carrying a cane fishing pole and wearing a cone-shaped straw bonnet was making her way down to the edge of a pond. The road curved on through deeper woods until I was into a broad, open plain, some kind of day-use public recreation and picnic area. Nobody was around.

The big draw of the park was its wooden observation tower, whose height lured a trickle of tourists for the panoramic view of the river and the Delta. I drove by, thought about pulling up into the gravel parking lot and maybe bolt back out again. But I noticed that the narrow park lane we now were on continued past tree-lined fields and a grassy area downriver. I decided to keep going. He followed.

Just past the first curve I came to a recreation area with a softball field, but right away that led to a wide turning circle with beat-down grass tire trails, basically a dead-end. I had no choice but to make the circle. He could have blocked me. Instead, he kept his distance.

I was tired of games, the same way I felt back at Witch Dance. I drove very slowly back to the observation tower and parked under the big shade tree. I opened my door, stood for a moment at the side of the Explorer. The sedan sat idling at the parking lot entry. I stared, no response. I went around back, opened the hatch, and pulled the Glock from my bag. I tucked it in my jeans and covered it with my T-shirt. I don't know if the guy saw me and I wasn't sure if I cared. But I grabbed a water bottle and took a big swig as I closed the hatch door, as if that were the reason I'd opened it. I walked toward the tower.

The Plymouth pulled in and parked. Nobody got out.

Crossing a long open space bothered me, but I figured the tower and its steep, narrow stairwell at least gave me the upper hand. Not ideal, but if the issue had to be forced, I needed something.

I worked my way up the wooden planks. Just before I reached the top, I heard the sedan's door open and shut.

Because of the high angle, I couldn't see anyone approaching from directly underneath, but I knew it was only a matter of time. Early morning fog draped the river and the land was all soft pastels in the diffuse light, of somewhat lesser aesthetic impact on me than it might have been under other circumstances.

I listened to the creaks and cracks in the stairway planks of a steady ascension. Another of those recurring dissociative interludes in which I seemed to be watching a movie about myself. I heard heavy breathing cutting through the morning stillness. In less than a minute his head appeared through the stairwell opening at one corner of the viewing platform. When he emerged fully, I almost had to smile.

If this were a movie, he would have come straight from central casting. A big guy, craggy Irish face, black hair laced with scarlet, and gray, just like the well-trimmed beard. Blue and yellow Hawaiian shirt. Not fat so much as sturdy, like maybe he'd been a football lineman. Way over six feet. He wasn't holding a gun in his hand, but I had little doubt he had one.

I kept my own tucked in. He'd been following me steadily and patiently. Back at Witch Dance, I knew I had to make the first move, and fast. It didn't feel the same here. I was sure that if he had wanted to hurt me, I would already be feeling it and one or the other of us would be dead.

He stopped a couple feet in front of me.

"How you doing?" He wiped his brow, and made the kinds of mental calculations I guessed he had computed on many occasions in the past.

I nodded but didn't speak. He looked at me hard, wanting to establish dominance. I'd had the same training. Ready for anything. Initiate nothing.

"Whatever you're thinking of doing right now, don't," he said. It wasn't a movie-Mafia voice, although whiskey-coated. It sounded more like Tennessee, maybe by way of East Texas.

I adjusted my stance. "I'm not thinking of anything. Except why you're up here."

He glanced off toward the river. "Damn. Never seen the Old Man from a perch like this before."

He took in the view just long enough to say he was in control.

"What you doing mixed up in all this anyway? A white boy?"

"I don't even know what I'm mixed up in."

In a flash he was within an arm's length.

"You have something I need to get."

"Turns out I don't have it—"

I tried to step back while I was talking, but I was late and sloppy. I barely saw the ham-sized hand until the back of it slammed into my right cheek, dropping me to one knee. I got up, my eyes watering.

"I don't care for smart-ass, son."

I nursed my jaw and tried to back away.

"Don't," he said, noticing my hand moving toward the top of my jeans. "It don't need to go there." With one hand he pulled back the tail of his shirt. An automatic tucked into a waist holster. "You can put it on the ground, you can make it out of here."

His other hand was blocking mine. He could have played it differently. In any case, it wasn't like I had a chance. I pulled up my T-shirt and eased out the Glock.

"Careful."

I put it on the deck, and faced him.

"I don't have any painting, if that's why you're here. Unless you came for the view."

He seemed to be considering another physical incentive. "But you know somebody does."

"I don't." I could see why he liked to get close, fast. He had at least six inches and sixty pounds on me. Guys that big didn't need to use guns, especially the pros.

"You a strange one, ain't you?" He seemed to be working something out in his head. "So try again. How you involved in this? If you're a bodyguard . . . well, that's pretty fuckin' sad."

My mouth was having a little trouble working, I realized, maybe from the blood inside it. I touched at it with my fingers. "I'm helping a friend bury her brother."

"What, that fag stole the painting?"

"I don't know anything about that."

Another swat, more like a cupped palm this time, hitting me in front of the left ear. I almost went over the rail backwards but held on.

"Can't seem to get your attention." He waved his hand in the air. "Damn, that's a hard head."

I looked down toward the Glock. He picked up the look, pushed the gun away with one foot, as though it bored him to do so.

"You can take a punch. Just keep it at that, son." He was up in my face again. "Look, here's the thing. All I want is that painting. Not you. Not her. Nothing else. I know where you stayed last night. I didn't go in. I could have. You understand? Let's just concentrate on business, what say?"

I shook my head a few times, to stay alert. "You've been following us?"

"Me? Hell, no. I'm on business up in Tunica. I got a call to come down here to the boonies."

"A call?"

"You know, a junkie. He wanted to get out of some trouble and said there was a white man and some hot black piece come into Rosedale, getting everyone talking up at the church or wherever, maybe in some kind of trouble. Junkies are like that. Most of it's crap but I happened to know there's been some trouble, definitely. Damn, here comes the sun."

We both shaded our eyes as it came out of low clouds. I couldn't shake the fog in my head or the ringing in my ear, but tried not to show it.

"So you found us that way?"

"It's what I get paid to do, son. But back to your problem. Reason I'm here is to collect that piece of property. You give it to me and we're done. That easy enough for you to follow?"

"I follow. I just don't have it. She doesn't, either. I don't know why Trey thinks we do."

"Trey Barnett?"

I came back to life a little hearing that faint note of surprise. Clouds covered the sun again.

"Forget him. All those damn fags."

"I don't get it—no, wait—" I put up a hand defensively.

He waved it down with his own. "It's too hot. Humid as a fuckin' dish rag, too. I figure you're lying again, I'll let you know."

"I mean, you aren't working for Trey?"

His right arm drew back and I steadied myself. But he dropped it to his side. He looked off at the river. "Jesus Christ." He shook his head, studied me again. "You have any clue at all?"

I looked once again at the useless Glock. I hoped my eardrum was okay. In retrospect, climbing the tower hadn't been my smartest move. Maybe I should have just shot him in the head in the stairwell. But, hell, I hadn't been in the game for damn near twenty years. And this was a game with its own rules. "Tell me what you want to know."

"The painting, man. That not sinking in?" His face turned dark red.

I steadied myself against the railing. "We've been trying to find it, so you guys would stop trying to kill us. But, look, here I am. Do I look like I know what I'm doing?"

That got a throat rumble that sounded like a laugh. But it was better than a punch.

"Who the hell are you, anyway?"

"My name's Prine. Jack. I live in New Orleans, I'm a writer. Sort of. I met a pretty girl. People started chasing us. I'm just making this up as we go . . ."

The anger passed from his face. It was replaced by something akin to bemusement.

"You don't have any idea who I am, do you?"

"Other than one of Trey's guys, no."

He shook his head. "Writer, huh? Sort of? Hmm. Well, Shakespeare, a rose ain't a rose out here and I ain't workin' for that rich boy scum. So don't call me that again."

I nodded with what I hoped was conviction.

"I work for some other people. This Barnett prick owes them a lot of money. He has a piece of art worth a few million that'll pay it off. He was gonna give it to us but somehow hasn't been able to." He wiped his forehead again. "Turns out you're the reason, at least so he tells my boss."

"That he doesn't have the painting?"

"That's his story. And then there's that business back there on the Natchez Trace. What kind of guy are you?"

"What business?"

This time it was in the stomach, leg-kick. Big guy was agile. I collapsed onto my knees. I don't know how long it was before I could breathe steadily.

"You might be an okay guy for all I know but that's not my job to pass that kind of judgment. You follow? Stand up."

I did, slowly. I coughed up some blood. My ribs were on fire.

"You get that painting for me, you and that woman. It'll save me some extra work and you a lot of pain."

"I'm telling you I don't know."

"It's the only shot you got, Shakespeare."

Against the railing again, I was leaning. Or was that how my German grandmother used to talk? "How much time?"

He thought for a moment. "I'd say 72 hours. That'll be Thursday. No, wait, I got something in Houston. You get a break. We'll say Saturday."

"I don't even know where to start."

"Seems to me you already are started. So let's say Saturday. Noon."

"High noon?"

It was a light swat this time, but I got the point.

I spat out some blood. "How would I get in touch?"

"That's the easy part. The hard part is showing up with something."

"If I can't find it?"

He shrugged. "I just gave you two extra days."

"And if I do? Then our business with you is all done. Elle, too."

"I could give a shit after that."

"You'd let us walk away."

"You can walk to China for all I care once I get delivery."

I thought on that.

"What about Trey?"

"I wouldn't worry about him."

His eyes told me he was telling the truth.

"Take this." He pulled a piece of paper from his pocket and wrote a number on it and gave it to me. "Don't lose it. Call when you have something."

"'Big Red?' That's who I ask for?"

"Ain't nobody else gonna have that number."

"No."

"So we'll have proper introductions later. Have some tea and cookies and all that good shit."

"What if I just give it to Trey? He always seems to be able to find me anyway. You can get it from him."

The big man's eyes narrowed. "Under no fucking circumstances. You gonna bring that up again?"

My head needed to be less foggy. It needed not to be hit again. "Trey who?"

"I'm going to leave now. You probably ought to get busy."

"You're not giving me much time."

"Can't help you, hoss. Saturday's a hard date. Noon."

"Why not just throw in the weekend?"

"Weekends are for fishin', the boss ain't got anything for me to do. And you know what happens if I do have to work the whole weekend? Having to find you and all that shit 'cause you're late, when I ought to be down in the Gulf?"

"I have an idea."

"Nothing personal. But that's the way it would have to be."

He started to back away, then stopped.

"Only thing is, back there the other day when you were doing all that fancy work with the shotgun on the Trace. You remember that, no?"

"I remember."

"Those were Barnett's boys. At least one of 'em was, the brother. The other, Reggie, he's with us. Works with Barnett off and on, but mostly he's one of our boys. You can't just shoot him. We can't let you. It was pretty impressive, though. They're pros. You was in the military, maybe?"

"Army."

"Over in Iraq?"

"Korea, couple of other places. I was out before all that."

"Me, too. 'Nam, though. Right at the end. And a little after."

He pulled up the right sleeve on his shirt to show me a black horsehead tattoo. First Cav. We exchanged a weird look of recognition that all vets know means something and doesn't.

"They won't let you get away with it, though. Shooting up the help."

"I thought you wanted me to find that painting."

"Yeah, because that's the real business. But you know, there's penalties in this game when you break the rules. You broke some. You sit in the box."

This time it was a right fist, hard to the chest, and another to the stomach. I dropped like a sack of cats. It was easier just to lie back on the wooden floor rather than go to all the effort to actually sit up.

He stood above me. I think he was smiling. "Thing is, nobody likes that little bastard Reggie, that you shot up. Most of us wish you'd blown his head off instead of just making him limp around for a while, whining about how you ambushed him and Delmore, who by the way got a pretty good concussion. We like Delmore, though. Good thing you didn't shoot him, too."

"I thought they were going to kill us."

"Hell, you were probably right. That's how stupid Reggie is. But I'm not."

I coughed and raised to one elbow.

"So that's the fine for Reggie."

He walked to the stairwell and started down. From a few flights below, I heard him call out, "Good luck. I'm counting on you."

I lay back, watching the sun brighten the morning and drive away the mist and clouds. I realized there were no mosquitoes up here. That was good. It was all good, wasn't that the deal? And then the night came, and stars, and sleep.

It took me a few moments to recognize Lenora's face, but then I saw Elle's beside hers, and gradually heard their voices. They were talking about me, but I couldn't tune in. I blinked a few times and the wooziness dissipated into clarity, the kind that comes when you wake up with a hangover. All the soft light gone harsh. You liked it better where you were. For a fraction of a second, watching the faces over me, taking in my position on the top of a tower overlooking the Mississippi, I had a strange sense that something . . . how to put it? Maybe I liked it? Couldn't be. I was drunk on pain.

"Maybe we shouldn't move him." It was Elle, bent low over me. Now I was awake, I could see her face, and her eyes. Definitely that girl was in love with me.

"Jack. Jack. Can you feel anything broken?" It was Lenora's voice. "Can you move your feet?"

I raised a leg and tapped it on the deck. Then, with Elle's warm breath coursing over my face, I slowly got onto one elbow. I shook my head, which hurt. With her help I scooted back enough to lean against the railing.

I said, "I think I'm okay," which is what people always say when they're not.

Lenora and Elle continued to inspect me like some kind of specimen.

"I think nothing's busted up, especially," Lenora said.

Elle touched my face, lightly. "Any of that hurt?"

I drew back a little. "It stings."

"But nothing broken."

I ran my tongue around the inside of my mouth. Tasted the blood. Looking down, I saw more on my shirt. "I don't think so." I touched my nose. I couldn't feel any crackle. That was lucky. I tried to change my position and winced in pain.

"It's my ribs, mostly."

Lenora looked at Elle.

"I got kicked."

Elle touched my side. "It's hard to tell with ribs."

They exchanged looks.

"You didn't come back home," Elle said.

"No."

"I had a bad feeling. Lenora and I came out to see where you were. The clerk at the store said they'd seen you come through, then head up to the park. You know, people here notice everything."

I nodded.

"Then another car behind you."

"Yeah." I moved my body slightly and felt better.

"Can you get up? We should go to the doctor. We can go to Tula's after, or we can go into Cleveland."

"I think I'm okay. Give me a minute."

"It was Trey," Elle said. Not a question.

"I don't think so." I dabbed at my mouth.

"We need to get down from here," Lenora said to Elle. "Before anyone else comes along."

"If he can move."

"And this," Lenora said. She held the Glock in one hand. I had forgotten about it. Definitely he was a pro. You don't handle any more heat than you need for the job.

"It goes in the back of the car." I pushed myself up a little more.

"What happened here?" Lenora said.

"I don't know. Things seem to happen without warning lately."

I tried to stand.

"Take my arm," said Lenora.

I reached out for it. Then another wave of woozy came in and I may have blacked out. Probably did.

"You okay, honey?" Lenora asked, her hand wedged up under my arm, strong as a car jack. "Lost you there for a little while."

"No. No. I'm okay. It was standing up like that."

"Oh, Jack. Damn." Elle holding me up from the other side.

"Yeah."

"Can you get down the stairs?" Lenora asked. She tucked the Glock back into my jeans. It was hot from the sun.

"I can walk." I moved forward, holding my hand over the gun so it wouldn't pop out. The pain that came then was sluggish and sharp, from my abdomen to my rib cage. I felt my chest but nothing seemed sharp or bulging. Maybe it was just a bad bruise. Hell, the guy was a Ph.D. in beatings. A surgeon.

"Just go slow," Lenora said.

When we started, I tried to count each of the wooden planks to help me concentrate, but after the first flight I just focused on one step at a time, not thinking about the bottom. Very Zen of me, I said to myself, which of course it isn't if you have to say it. And I thought about that, too—anything, really, to make it down. I was sitting cross-legged on a zafu in a monastery in Japan. I was wondering if this was how Mr. Lee had felt when the MPs beat him up. Or before he died. I wasn't going to die. I was very definite about that. Lenora was in front, Elle a step behind, in case I fell. Twice I almost did.

When we had cleared the stairs, I looked back up at the tower.

"Ranger hasn't come down here, thank God," Lenora said, escorting me on. "We don't need a lot of questions."

"It's early and off-season," Elle said. "He might not even be home."

"Let's put him in my car. You drive his Explorer. Jack, do you have your keys?"

"In my pocket."

Elle dug them out.

We were at the rear door of the El Dorado, and then the door was open and I was inside. The seats were leather, soft. Lying down seemed the wrong thing to do. Sitting didn't hurt. I sat.

Lenora pushed the door shut and went around to get in. I saw Elle get in the Explorer, start it up. Lenora backed out and then we were all on the road heading out of the park. I think I may have dropped off again because the next I knew we were in front of a small brick office building and I was being helped out of the car. It was a little hazy for a few minutes but the doctor, a young black guy, was looking in my eyes and variously poking around and then wrapping a brown bandage around my chest.

Once again, it was like I was watching this happen to someone else. I remember taking a pill of some sort and thanking the doctor and being led back to the car and then I remember being tucked into bed by the new love of my life, the Black Madonna, the Aphrodite of Pain, the incomparable Helen of the Delta, who ministered to my wounds even in this time of great distress and I'm pretty sure pressed her lips against mine before I was asleep again.

15

I woke up that afternoon in the guest bedroom. I did my best to brief Elle and Lenora on what had happened at the viewing tower, as coherently as possible under the Vicodin, and fell back asleep for another hour. My abdomen hadn't been that sore since I'd broken a rib ten years ago falling off a broken railing at a mean-street South Dallas apartment complex where I was doing a story. Whatever the diagnosis, I knew that it would get worse before it got better.

But I needed to get up and made myself put my feet on the floor. That's when I realized they had taken off my clothes and all I was wearing were my blue boxers. I'm sure it was a very compelling sight. I felt the bandage along my rib cage and saw how my stomach and sides were red and raw. I already knew my face was swollen. But I didn't think I'd lost any teeth.

"We cut off your shirt. We couldn't get your arms up. The jeans were pretty easy."

Elle glanced at her cousin, who smiled like a teenager who'd just pantsed a boy. "How do you feel now?"

"My mouth is full of cotton and my body got hit by a truck. Otherwise good. What time is it?"

"Five, nearly."

I thought that through and realized the drugginess was going to be with me longer than I wanted.

"Did we go to a doctor?"

"Doctor Porter. He's Tula's ob/gyn."

"He did all this?"

Artula bent down to look into my eyes. "How many of me do you see?"

"How many of you are there?"

She looked at Elle. "I've seen worse. Byron took a few falls working construction time to time."

"He'll be fine." It was Lenora.

"Jack," said Elle, "can you stand?"

"I think so." I pushed myself upright. A little dizzy but not that bad.

"I'll get some coffee," Artula said.

Elle helped me get stable. She brushed my swollen cheeks with her index finger, the way you'd put the final touch on a fine piece of crystal. "I was so scared for you."

"I think that guy, Big Red, wasn't going to hurt me much more than he did. Which was enough."

I touched my ribs.

"Doctor Porter said he didn't think they're broken. More like deep bruising. We have to see if you cough up any blood in the next 24 hours. Your nose was broken, though. He popped it back. You're not supposed to touch it."

Which I did, immediately.

"Jack."

"Damn."

"It could have been a lot worse."

"Yeah."

I pressed my fingers against my chest again. I figured the doc was right.

They helped me get into the living room and to the La-Z-Boy. Artula brought coffee and I drank most of it right away. Then she brought over some water and I drank a lot of that, too.

"How much did I tell you?"

"I think we got it," Elle said, sitting near me on the couch. "The Big Red guy wants the painting. Just like everyone else in the world."

"By Saturday noon."

"You said."

"It wasn't Trey's buddies this time."

"No."

I looked into her brown eyes. "This guy was mafia."

"That's who Trey owes money to. He has a gambling jones."

"Big one. Young Henry talked about it," Lenora said.

I leaned back. "So that's where we are." I looked across the room. Funny, the meds, how they created a calmness in the eye of the storm that allowed you to consider just how much shit was flying around you and how much you needed to duck it but allowed you just that fine frame of clarity to consider it all very objectively.

"There's more," Elle said.

She looked at Lenora again. "You were mumbling a lot after we got you off the tower, about having no time and the Saturday thing and so my aunt decided I needed to know some things. So she told me."

"I was going to tell you anyway," Lenora began, "but now, even on some of what I'm not sure of, I know it's better that you know . . . than that you don't."

"I'd always rather know."

"You would. Others, sometimes they don't. In my experience, sometimes it's not always for the best, knowing all that truth."

Elle got up and sat on the arm of my chair, stroked me softly on the back of my neck. "Tell him. It's okay."

Lenora took Elle's place on the couch. She seemed to be studying me to see if I was alert. "I already told you Terrell Henry went down to New Orleans to meet Trey. We talked about that."

"I remember. I'm okay."

"But I know why. Now."

Elle was smiling at me. A sad smile. Only the drugs kept me from thinking of it as heartbreaking. Though it was.

"This gets back into the family, and it's hard for Elle. Hard to hear the second time just as much as the first."

I tried to get her to look at me, but she wouldn't. Kept stroking my neck, as though I were a baby.

"The painting," Lenora continued, "Henry had it all right. Took it from Trey's place in Birmingham. It never was in Oxford."

"We know that. Just tell him."

Lenora pursed her lips.

"It's okay," Elle said. "Jack, you need to know this."

Lenora swallowed. Her eyes darted to a corner of the room and then back, like she had made a decision. "They had had a big fight, Trey and Terrell. But not about the painting so much. It was mostly about her."

Elle stopped stroking but took my hand in hers.

"A long time ago, this was all different around here," Lenora said, her hands clenched in her lap. "Not so many people, and not so many kinds. Black folks, mainly, and the whites who owned most everything. Then the black folks started getting some education, traveled a little, came back, got into some business. That's what Elle's daddy did, and her mama, too. They were unusual people in Mississippi, or Alabama, where they started out. They were noticed. The white folks took to them and saw them as kind of,

I don't know, civilizing influences on us Negroes, they said in those days. I don't use the other word."

Elle shifted a little.

"I'm just saying that people bonded together in unusual ways, especially out in the country, and Oxford was definitely country in those days." She paused. "And so it wasn't unheard of for a white man and black woman—sometimes the other way but that was very dangerous—to find something together. It wasn't anything anyone admitted and it happened all the time. I guess it's been that way in the South all along."

I looked up at Elle, my hand resting on her leg as she sat on the armrest of the La-Z-Boy. It started coming to me where this was going. I was glad the Vicodin was giving it a soft focus glow, some grainy documentary.

"Elle's mother, Pearl, and Junior Barnett, they were around each other a lot and both were most handsome and beautiful people, especially Pearl. It wasn't some kind of sleazy thing. That man loved Elle's mama. And he loved Pearl's daughter, too."

Elle held up her hand for Lenora to stop. She wanted to be the one to say it. She looked down directly at me.

"Trey is my half-brother."

As my bloodshot eyes met hers, I tried to convey, wordlessly, the only sentiment that came up: compassion, for lack of a better word. What could I say, that I was sorry? For that matter, what could she say? She took my hand again, pressed it against her leg.

"No one ever knew," Lenora continued. "It was right after they moved to Oxford and Abe Henry and Pearl weren't getting along so well. Pearl felt like she'd been dragged out into the sticks and, well, she was a real beauty and one of the things about them moving was that she would help with some office work for Junior. So they got to be friends, in that way it happens down here. And then they had what you'd call an affair. It didn't last long. I think Junior thought it was going to ruin Pearl's marriage and he couldn't marry her. Like that."

LENORA PAUSED, HER HANDS working together like she was washing them. Elle let go of mine, stood, walked around to the other side of the coffee table, then sat on the couch, alone.

Lenora noted the distance, then continued. "But then . . . Pearl was pregnant. It worked out that the timing was that it could have been Abe's child. But Pearl knew it wasn't. We were very close. She was the sister I never had. We shared everything. I swore never to tell, because what good would it do anyone? Abe Henry was a fine man, my brother was, and a father sent by the Lord to this child. It never would've mattered."

I looked across at Elle, who was looking right back. I turned to Lenora. "So how did Trey find out?"

"That's where the fight started. You know, that boy always owes lots of money. But sometimes people owe him."

Artula came back into the room and sat near Lenora. I could tell she knew all this, too. It was like being in a house with someone with a cold. Everyone gets it.

"There was a lawyer, I think from Tupelo, not a very good lawyer, got into Trey for some coke or gambling money and couldn't pay. His name was Fredericks. Trey was going to have him killed or hurt pretty bad. But Fredericks, I think they called him Chick, turned a deal. Told Trey he had something that could pay off his debts. Anyway, that's what Terrell told me happened."

"That's how we know all this," Elle said.

"That's how. And his spirit spoke to me last night."

"It did," Elle said.

"Praise the spirits," Artula added.

"Amen."

"So the lawyer told him he had seen a special will, made out by Junior."

"About Elle."

"About Elle. A lot about Elle. It said Junior was her father and that on Elle's thirty-fifth birthday she gets half the Barnett inheritance, which is in trust. With Junior and his wife both dying young, there was a big nasty fight about the will. Trey wanted it all, of course, both halves, and right away. But he couldn't because the estate was tied up. Junior had put in a provision preventing anyone from saying why. It's all kept by lawyers in Jackson. Basically, Trey gets his half when he turns forty. By then, of course,

Elle would be way past thirty-five, since she's two years older than Trey. So the best he'd be able to get would be his half."

"When is your birthday?"

"November eleventh. Veterans Day. How about that?"

"And you'll be—"

"Exactly."

"I don't know why Junior set it up that way," Lenora said, "but the point was that Trey got the farm and some of the physical stuff when Junior passed, but not the bank accounts, which was the main part. At first it pissed him off, but what he told Terrell was that it was just something his dad had done so he wouldn't blow through the money when he was young."

"Which he would."

"Of course. All this time, he's been living on the idea he'd have about $30 million in trust instead of just fifteen. So he figured he could handle any debts, eventually."

"If the mob gives that kind of credit."

"Which they don't."

"Let me see if I get this," I said, as much to myself as anyone. "Trey gets into a lot of debt, and then, trying to raise money from a crooked lawyer, finds out about a secret will. And his newly discovered half-sister. So he freaks."

"He freaks," said Elle.

"He freaks and he goes to Terrell," Lenora added. "Confronts him about it all. He tells him he has to get Elle's original birth certificate—the one Junior and Pearl hid away. He thought without that, the will couldn't be enforced for Elle. Maybe the lawyer told him that."

"No will, no money for Elle."

"Exactly."

"Young Henry went crazy on him," Elle said.

Lenora nodded. "Terrell said they got into the biggest fight they ever had, yelling and even punching each other. Terrell called me about it. I never told him I knew all along about Elle, but I had no idea about the will. No one did but Junior, I guess, and that lawyer. Maybe the firm in Jackson."

She looked at Elle. "So then Terrell realized Trey would never let it rest. That's when he went to Birmingham and took the painting. It was some kind of black market deal Trey had gotten for drugs and he was going to send it to an underground auction in Houston or Mexico and use the money to pay off the mob. So Terrell took it."

Even with the pain pill, I could feel the dimensions widening, deepening.

"It was after that he called me to tell me what he'd done and ask me if I knew about the birth certificate. Who might have it. I just said I didn't know." Lenora's brow furrowed in deep thought and she seemed to be weighing something. "Then I didn't hear from Terrell for a while. One day he called to say he was going to New Orleans to meet Trey and sort it all out."

"And that's where I came in."

"That's when you found him."

Junior ran in and jumped up into his mother's arms. "I'm going to give them a bath," she said, holding him up in the air until he giggled. "Vanessa's probably about to pitch a fit to get out of her playpen, too."

Artula tucked the boy under an arm and headed for the hall, pausing once to look back over her shoulder.

I touched my nose so the pain would keep me in focus. "So, one more time—Terrell telling you all this, he never let on where he was keeping the painting? Or that birth certificate? They were connected? We're running out of time."

Lenora looked away toward the back yard. It had been hard on her, having to admit she had been covering up a family scandal, even if it was obvious it had been done only to protect Elle and also Pearl's reputation all these years.

"All I know is Terrell said it was somewhere safe in the city. But where . . ." she looked at me, then Elle, and shook her head . . . "I truly wish I knew. I truly do."

I SHIFTED IN MY chair. I wasn't sure if we now knew more than we did, or less. And it took a beating just to get this latest tidbit.

Lenora slumped forward, unguarded, a woman undone by remorse. But then her head came up and there was a kind of light in her eyes, like bottled fireflies. She looked at Elle. "I do know this. Terrell Henry died trying to help you. Now he's a trapped spirit"—she turned briefly to me—"what we call 'bound up.' He was taken before his work on this earth was done. But he wants to help more. I know that." She paused, smoothed her slacks along her thighs, willing herself back to business. "I have to do some more work tonight to see if I can get to him." She looked at me dead-on.

It was impressive, but I probably didn't respond with the right measure of enthusiasm. Seventy-two hours to put together a lot of loose ends and we were going to have a séance.

Meanwhile something was going on with Elle. She stood up suddenly, as if energized by whatever had passed through her aunt.

"I understand how you feel, Jack. Imagine how I do."

"I'm sorry it came out like this." My neck muscles felt on fire.

"Nothing for you to be sorry about." She turned to Lenora. "What you said, him dying trying to help. It just came to me."

Lenora smiled.

Elle was around the coffee table in three strides. She knelt down in front of me, her body liquid gold against my legs, so that her eyes could be level with mine. She was stone beautiful and utterly unnerving.

"The silver neck chain with the little square locket. The one I couldn't find that day you showed me where his body had been. I thought you took it." She shook her head, smiling like some mad inventor. "It wasn't you. Young Henry gave it to someone else. To do something for him. To—"

"Elfego."

"Elfego."

We were going back to the Rio Blanche.

16

But not just then. I got up to go to the bathroom and a sharp pain stopped me after about three steps. I waited for it to go away and then proceeded, much more slowly. By the time I was able to urinate, and happy to see only a little blood, I knew I was in no condition to drive, or probably even to sit in a car for hours.

I washed my hands and looked into the mirror—there was a little frog sticker on the lower right corner. The break in my nose was barely noticeable, beyond the swelling. Like my ribs, just a lot of temporary pain. As for the rest of my countenance, it was woeful enough to ride with Sancho Panza. Bruises on both cheeks and darkening under both eyes. I looked like a cheap club palooka.

I had to keep my mind on the temporary misery of my body—what did the Buddhists say, that all suffering can be overcome? I would have to work on that. I would have to work on a lot of things, and most likely I'd still come back as a mosquito.

Ideally, I could lay up for a week and nurse my wounds and let Elle minister to me and make me feel like an injured war hero. But we were pretty far from the ideal. And we were pretty far from New Orleans, where we had to be, somehow, before Trey put together the same part of the puzzle we had. If he got the painting before we did, no telling what Big Red would do. I was not inclined to rely on his compassionate nature or tolerance of excuses.

Then my knees crumbled a little, and I was slumped on the bathroom floor, light-headed and half-sick at the same time.

I sat there a few minutes. Elle peeped in, then pushed the door all the way. "Tula, can somebody come help?"

This by way of saying that's how we spent another night in Rosedale. I awoke at dawn, from the light and from the noise of some kind of tractor or big machine in the nearby fields. I was in my shorts again, but this time my head was clearer. I still felt the pain but not the overwhelming nausea. The other twin bed was rumpled and I think Elle had been there for part of the time I was zonked.

I got up, dressed myself slowly. Artula had made coffee, as usual. I poured a mug and walked into the back yard. Feathers had blown around the spot where Lenora had been the previous night, beseeching her African gods. On a large serving tray completely incongruous in the morning sun were some bowls of something—water, maybe, or blood.

I went back inside just as Elle and Lenora came in from the front door. I realized they had been up for a while, packing.

"How are you feeling today, honey?" As always, Lenora was impeccably outfitted, this time in dark green pants suit and form-fitting tan blouse.

Elle kissed me, gently. "You look better. You tossed and turned last night for a while but then you settled down."

"I feel better."

She tried a playful cuff on my chin but I had to wince.

She nibbled at a cinnamon roll Artula had baked. "Feel like traveling?"

"I know. We should have left yesterday."

She touched my cheek softly, "No, no, that's not what I mean. It was better that you slept. But we have to get out of the house."

"I'm not arguing."

"I can drive." I tried to stand up straighter. "Maybe at first."

"You're not driving at all," Lenora said, laughing. "You could barely sit behind the wheel, and if you could you'd fall asleep with all those pills inside you."

She and Elle shared an eye-rolling at my expense.

I grabbed the rest of the cinnamon roll and went back to the bedroom. Elle had packed my duffel bag, the Glock right on top. I took a Vicodin from my pill bottle, partly for the immediate pain and partly because I knew how the road would be.

Elle came in. "Lenora's going to stay with Tula tonight. You know, we have our troubles, but that girl has the kind that aren't going away."

"Ours are?"

"They might. But they don't live inside our bodies, ready to kill us."

"No." Actually I wasn't so sure what was living inside my body.

She picked up the duffel and carried it to the front door. I wolfed down the roll but didn't want to trouble Artula for anything else. At the slightest hint she'd be frying bacon and scrambling eggs. I liked that woman. A lot.

It was like Elle said. We had troubles. Some we had made for ourselves and some we were willingly taking on. But Artula's burden was heavier and beyond reason. It was the kind of thing that gave me problems with karma, same as it would have about God's will had I still been a Methodist. Artula was a good woman; braver than any of us. I was in no position to know all the answers, or all the vectors of fate in this life or any previous. Ignorance didn't make me feel better.

I took my duffel to the truck, and Elle came along with her own bag. I arranged things in the back of the Explorer to be sure I could get to the sundry weapons I had accumulated if need arose. It seemed sort of nuts to be thinking about another firefight, but that's where it was for us now. Still, I hoped that Big Red's intervention meant Trey was taking a back seat now as far as following us, and leaving it to the mob boys. Or more likely that's what they had told him to do.

But it was a no-brainer that Trey would be on us sooner or later. Either Elle would inherit a fortune very soon, or she wouldn't make it to her next birthday.

They all came outside to see us off. Hugs and kisses all around. Several times. Everyone seemed ready to cry.

"We'll stay in touch from now on, Tula. Always."

"I miss you already. It was so good to see you again."

We got into the Explorer, me in the passenger seat. Elle cranked the ignition, pulled around the little circle of the drive. They all waved and went back into the house.

We took the lane back to the Great River Road, then south, to whatever awaited.

THE HIGHWAY WAS UNCOMFORTABLE but not gruesome. The Vicodin helped. What a great drug. Put Valium to shame, really. I made a mental note to go buy a lot of it. You weren't supposed to use it with alcohol but I figured what the hell, it would go great with a no-bullshit Cabernet. I was very glad not to be driving.

Elle tuned in a blues station out of Greenville or maybe Cleveland. The highway was deserted, cutting down toward Vicksburg through the Delta's contradictions of lush, rich bottomland and world-class poverty and racism.

We pulled into a one-room fried chicken and tamale joint in the hamlet of Benoit, where I got an egg and bacon soft taco and a half-dozen hot tamales, of which I ate three. Elle had an egg and potato taco. We carried out to-go cups of coffee. With the food and caffeine, I started to get slightly more lucid, but still registered somewhere between woozy and ditz. From now on, unless the pain was severe a half-tab of Vicodin would have to do.

It didn't look as though anyone was tailing us. Nor did they need to. For the next 72 hours, we were as safe as gold in a Swiss bank. All our pursuers were united in one objective: pressuring us to come up with the goods. We were their hounds, hunting down the quarry. But we wouldn't get pats on the head when we delivered. I guess that made us more in the nature of pawns. Either way, we were the only ones who really understood how problematic the quest would be.

The big river was on our right, to the west; the Great State of Mississippi extended to the east. When the River Road ran out, we'd have to decide which route to take to New Orleans and for that matter where we would stay if we didn't go to my place. For all I knew, Trey by now knew where I lived.

She was quiet, the way she had been after we first met. I didn't know what to say yet about her and Trey and I guessed she was a long way from bringing it up herself. She was related to a man I might have to kill to stay alive.

I might have been wrong about the medication easing up. A rolling wave of both nausea and serenity passed through me. I drifted in and out of a reverie of sitting in an SUV driving through the Delta, to floating around through the entire universe. I started to daydream, if that's the right term; I would say meditate but you can't really do that on drugs, New Age versions of enlightenment notwithstanding. But this daydream was okay, and it took me back to a place I needed to find. Because the place I was in now was off the charts.

I let my head lean against the seat back and closed my eyes. She reached over with her free hand to lightly caress my chest. My woman, taking care of me. Life was good. The rhythm of the road was soothing. In that spirit, I thought it wise to reexamine things, a kind of pain-and-pills autobiographical précis. It flashed out into a nice little daydream manuscript, all right there on my mental Powerbook, the Apple of my third eye.

"Jack . . . Jack . . ." I gradually heard a voice and felt hands pushing against my arm. "Jack, are you okay?"

The dream in my head stopped. I opened my eyes and shook my head.

"You were shaking and mumbling something. My name, I think."

I tried to get my mouth to work. If I had been mumbling, it must have been pretty unintelligible. I reached down to the floor for a water bottle and took a drink.

"I'm okay. Sorry. I didn't mean to drift away."

"I just thought you were having a nightmare."

I looked at a road sign, which said we were coming into Onward, a wide spot in the road consisting mostly of a convenience store and gas station.

"I'm going to stop," Elle said.

"Good. I need to get out."

We filled up, took care of business. I wasn't pissing blood, a small favor for which I was immensely grateful.

I walked back to the Explorer to wait for Elle. The air was almost sweet, heavy with the river. My gaze wandered to a big wooden sign at the edge of the parking lot. I walked over. It was tourist information, like at Witch Dance. But not about witches. It said that near this spot, Teddy Roosevelt had refused to kill a captured bear while on a hunting trip, and that's how a "Teddy Bear" got its name.

Elle came up. I was so zoned out it startled me. We drove away, me wondering what would the bear would have done if it had the gun.

At Vicksburg I was hungry again so we stopped for lunch. Elle was quiet, looking off in a private distance as we ate. I thanked her for driving since I was still cruising in and out of real time. She said she had it covered, to just rest because the city still lay ahead and I would need my strength. Good woman, I kept thinking. This is a good woman.

It occurred to me I hadn't checked my answering machine at home in days. I did so from my cell as we walked back to the Explorer. I had a dozen messages, four from editors, four from Ray Oubre, two from a couple of occasional drinking pals from the Times-Pic, one a hang-up, and one from Art Becker. He said he was calling because someone had been around looking at the property and had knocked on the door asking for me. He said the man was a white guy, late thirties, well-dressed, said he was a friend but didn't leave a name.

It wasn't that hard to track me down in New Orleans. Being reachable was a big part of my business. Still. I told Elle about Art's visitor as we drove away.

"Trey, right?"

I said that was the way I figured it.

She'd checked her voicemail, too, and said no one had called except for someone at the university asking if there was anything she needed and when she thought she might be back.

I briefly nodded off as we drove on, cutting over to Natchez to cross the big river on its western bank. It wouldn't be the fastest way down to New Orleans, but even though we had little at this point to fear from being followed, taking a minor state highway rather than the main drags was a good way to spot a tail. Elle agreed, lost in her own thoughts. We chose a route that would take us down through Baton Rouge and into New Orleans on Highway 61, which I always used when I was at LSU.

About ten miles from Natchez she wheeled to the side of the road, came to a crunching stop in the apron gravel. Without a word, she flung open her door, got out, and ran around the front to the shoulder on the passenger side. I was opening my door to see what was wrong when she doubled up and her body began to heave in spasms.

A procession of 18-wheelers, SUVs and panel trucks shot by like phantoms. When I touched her back to see I could help, she shrugged me off, angrily. I went back to the car for a napkin from our last stop. I hurried back and gave it to her to wipe her mouth, then went back to find a bottle of water.

She leaned against the front fender, then sat on the bumper, spat out the foam in her mouth, and drained the bottle. She threw it far into the weeds, litter be damned, and walked back around the front of the Explorer, climbed back inside. I barely had time to get in and buckle up before she peeled up the shoulder and rammed into the traffic, hitting eighty-five before she decided to slow down.

Still, she didn't talk. Instead, turned up the radio. We were now in junk broadcast land and it took some intervention on my part to find something at least tolerable.

We were through Natchez, across the high bridge over the river, and into Louisiana before she said anything. I had seen this before and should have seen it this time, too. And maybe would have without the fog of pain-killers. She'd been too in control, too calm. Too bottled up.

Who knew if that was the best or worst way to deal? Especially with what she was facing. But she was my girl and that was her way.

She talked now, talked for long miles, uncorking the bottle. We slid down the edge of Louisiana on a bumpy state highway spotted with towns whose chief industries seemed to be gas stations, washaterias and drive-through daiquiri stands. I mostly listened, event though it was hard to take in all at once.

It came out too fast, too fragmented, to consider as some kind of rational discourse. Something only approachable in the abstract, in the aftermath, like piecing together the chronology of a bad car wreck right in front of you that happens in real time but has to be recollected in the more limited terms of human apprehension.

She put personal history together, tore it apart—the most awful thing a person can do to herself. It's the kind of horror that shrinks get paid to unravel. Which Elle was. So maybe she had a special talent for it. But she had no shrink for herself. Just me, to hear the things that no person should have to say.

The story of a life built on a lie.

It had blindsided her. It had taken her entire family. And now it wanted her.

As fast as it had started, the confessional stopped. Not like it was over. More like it had hit a wall. Another wall. Presently her breathing calmed, her grip on the steering wheel eased and the blood returned to her cheeks and fingers. There was nothing I could say, and I didn't. Then for a moment she seemed to drift into something else, almost like what I had seen in Lenora. Words came from her mouth, but I wondered if I had really heard them: "Now I know who you are, and me never seeing it. Me, your sister with the second sight."

A nasty rainstorm put her full attention back on the road—the weather dogging us again. Big drops hit the roof so hard it sounded like hail. I offered to drive but she waved me off. I theorized that as a shrink, she had to have known she couldn't function through what was sure to come without emotional release. Talking to me wasn't any kind of sharing. It was making a scar. It was the kind of thing you would only do if you had to survive. Or to punish.

17

The highway dumped into another outside Simmesport, in the old plantation country where blacks outnumbered whites in huge numbers and had suffered proportional repressions. In some places, the faces were as bright and happy as at a Caribbean market; in others there was a density of alienation that could not be penetrated by mere human sight.

She had not cried while nailing down her newfound history, as she had over her brother's death. It wasn't really a crying kind of thing now.

I found a classical station on the radio, a Beethoven violin concerto.

"I like that," she said, finally.

"We're quite a pair."

"Did you take another Vicodin?"

"I'm trying not to."

"You can if you want. No need to suffer."

"I know. But I need to be clear."

"Well, yeah."

"It's a lot to take in, all that."

"I guess I was really going on."

"Not really."

A short, explosive sound like a laugh came out.

We drove a few miles in silence. "It's the first time any of this started to make sense," I said.

"What?"

"I mean how it blew up with Trey and your brother. It makes more sense now."

"Jesus, Jack."

"What?"

"What sense does it make that Young Henry is dead? Does it help you to think there was some kind of rational reason? Does that make it okay?" Her face filled with blood again. Her teeth flashed.

"I didn't mean that."

"Then what, what 'sense'?"

I leaned back against the headrest. "Nothing. I said it wrong. I've just been trying, you know, to figure things out."

She took a few deep breaths, and her fingers went up along the wheel, as if to signal a truce. "I know. Forget it."

"We can't take this out on each other."

"I should know that more than you. It's what I get paid to know."

"Nobody gets paid to know this."

"If they did, we'd be rich."

We both smiled, wanly. No cash-out for us.

"I mean, do you have any idea what happens after we get this painting, if we can get it? Does that mean Trey leaves us alone? Does that mean he gets away with murdering my brother? I mean, murdering . . . his own brother. If you wanted to see it that way." She paused. "And I do."

I saw the speedometer moving up past eighty again. I reached across to touch her arm, from comfort. I might have been touching a steel girder.

"I just mean that things are going to play out. Trey isn't going to get away with anything."

She faintly smiled again, but more like a cobra. I realized she must have been wondering if her new pal, her rib-sore road warrior, would bail. And I didn't blame her. Human relations very abruptly had become dramatically unglued in her life. But she was now the love of my life and I would never leave her.

So I told her that. She reached across with her free hand, took mine, and placed it on her breast, over her heart.

WE WERE IN BATON Rouge by early afternoon. I wanted to eat again, so we exited near LSU and found a Vietnamese place near the campus. The town had transformed over the years into a congestion of shopping malls and suburbs and not much of what I remembered. I asked her to drive past my old place off 19th Street, in what was once a very poor black neighborhood where white college kids were tolerated. Elle wondered why I hadn't lived elsewhere and one truth was that it had been cheap and the other truth was that eventually I got to like it.

We got back on Highway 61 and in no time were on the outskirts of New Orleans, coming in past the airport. Cars plied the crowded streets in the customary manner, a combination of aggression and disregard for traffic laws. Twice we were almost cut off by smoke-belching wrecks, once by a sleek bronze Infiniti. At stoplights, people waiting for buses in the hot sun seemed to peer into the windows, looking us over.

Our first task was to find a place to hole up. We had come to where Airline turns into Tulane Avenue, and the seedy motels stretch out like some hard part of LA. I couldn't see spending my last days there, if that's what it came to. I told her I knew of a little place Uptown, a private house with a back unit rented off-the-books by a guy named Boots Deshaw, a retired ex-school teacher and part-time musician I'd met once while doing a story on school violence. He'd started his little B&B side business to help with Louisiana's miserable teacher retirement benefits, but he only rented to music types, and the occasional maverick like me.

No chance Trey would know about it.

Before heading there to check it out, we made an impulse decision to drive back out I-10 to Louis Armstrong International. I wanted to switch to a rental car. Maybe unnecessary, but it couldn't hurt, and it made both of us feel better. We parked in a remote lot, took the shuttle to E-Z Rent 'n Fly and picked out a plain-looking, dark blue Taurus sedan, the kind you'd never think twice about seeing. Then we drove back to the long-term lot and transferred all our stuff out of the Explorer.

Back in town, Elle, still at the wheel, took Carrollton off the freeway, and cut over toward the river, past Audubon Park, and then to Magazine Street. We wound back a couple more streets toward Tchoupitoulas until

I recognized the one I wanted. Boots's next-door neighbors were on their stoop, drinking beer and watching the passersby, especially anyone who didn't belong. It was like the Marigny. New Orleans was a city of neighborhoods, and the key to everything was to be grounded in one, or to know someone who was.

We parked pretty close on the potholed street. I walked up and knocked on the louvered door. No answer. I tried again and after a few very long minutes, Boots opened up. He was about seventy and he still looked good: gray beard, close-cropped fringe of gray hair, jeans and a loose-fitting purple guayabera. It took a moment for him to recognize me. Then he smiled broadly and shook my hand, asked me what I was up to.

I told him I needed a place for a couple of days with a friend. He asked, perhaps only half-joking, if I'd gotten evicted. I said, no, that they were doing some work at my place and I needed a room until Saturday if it was open. I'm not sure he believed me, but he believed in me so it was okay. The duplex in back, bigger than the garage apartment, was vacant. It was midweek and not the high season yet, and he was glad to get the business.

We pulled the car into the narrow driveway and took our stuff in. Boots helped, and if he was any more surprised to see me with a beautiful black woman than with a busted-up face, he didn't say. He did give her an appreciative head-to-toe. Elle chatted with him superficially and then we settled in. It was cozy but not cramped—one small bedroom, a living room with a couple of well-worn sofas, and a clean, stocked kitchen. Every wall was decorated with record albums and photos of Boots and his musician friends from over the years. He played clarinet sometimes at some of the old-school clubs like Donna's.

Elle told him it was perfect. He thanked her and invited us to drop by and talk later if we had a chance, then left us alone.

She went into the bathroom. I finished bringing in a few more things from the car and turned on the window air-conditioner. It was almost November but New Orleans was still a steam bath. I left the shotgun and Colt in the trunk of the Taurus, the Glock still in my duffel. I was so far over the line it didn't even register that I was sorting out my armory.

We sat at the Formica-topped table near the kitchen. It was quiet. I noticed an old Sony radio on a window ledge and found my station. It was hard for either of us to sit still. As if that were an option.

"You want to go get a drink or something?" Elle said, looking at her watch, a mock come-hither look framed with just a glint of hardness and anger. "Do you know a good place around here to take a girl like me?"

I did.

18

It wasn't a good sign that Elfego wasn't at the Rio Blanche, but it wasn't necessarily bad. Could have been his day off. His boss, Quasimodo, subscribed to the negative interpretation.

"You find the sorry-ass bastard and tell him he comes in tonight or he don't come back at all."

"I don't know if I can be much help with that."

"Maybe she can."

"Where do you think he is? Has he been gone long?" she asked.

"Just since lunch. But I'm two people short as it is and the real estate people are in town. We're full all the time. So you tell him."

He brought the two beers we had ordered.

"My brother's a friend of his. We had something to give him."

Quasimodo looked her over. Me, even more, especially the purple hue of my face and nose. If he cared, he didn't let on.

"Your brother? Knows Elfego?"

She shrugged.

"Your brother has a poor choice of friends."

"That's cold, from his boss."

"I ain't his boss. Except when I'm behind the counter. Which I am now and he ain't here. You want anything else? Chips? Po' boy?"

"Just the beers."

He wiped the counter in front of us and walked off to the other end of the bar, where he poured two glasses of red wine and gave them to the only waiter on duty: an older guy, white, tanning salon abuser, gray hair in a ponytail—Venice Beach or Key West look but it wasn't that out of place here, where the nation's leftovers tend to form up like lines of seaweed on the sand. The two talked briefly, looked our way, said something else, and the waiter went off to deliver his goods to a man and two women at a table near the sidewalk.

"What do you think?" I said.

"I think we need to find out where Elfego is."

I raised my eyebrows in a kind of smartass way but then I saw that she was lost in a thought. She looked beatific in the late afternoon light. "You have an idea."

"I'm just trying to remember something Young Henry told me a couple of years ago, about some guy he'd met. He thought it was cool that he had a loft, something around some warehouses."

I looked at my beer bottle and tried to think through the city's neighborhoods. "Maybe it was over by the convention center. But those are expensive for a waiter."

"It was a few years back," she said.

"Maybe he got a place before the rents shot up."

"Or it could be anywhere else. Could be over in the Bywater or Tremé or Ninth Ward for that matter."

"Maybe."

"It'll be dark soon."

"It'll be Saturday soon."

"Three days."

"Three days."

"What do you think?"

"I think we can't sit in this bar forever waiting for him to show up."

"What, then?"

I laughed. "We haven't even tried the phone book." I looked down the length of the bar for Quasimodo and, by and by, caught his eye. When he came over I asked if he had the white pages. He frowned, but pulled a nasty-looking dog-eared copy from under the register.

"He ain't listed." He shoved the book down to me.

I looked anyway.

"Any way you could get us a number?" Elle asked, working her best smile.

"We don't give out numbers. Anyway he wouldn't be there."

"Wouldn't hurt to call."

"Like I said."

I put a twenty on the bar. He looked at it. Turned, picked up some glasses from the washing sink, and went back to the other end. I put the money back in my pocket. Too many questions to a guy who clearly had the capacity to rat out or withhold as he saw fit. And who didn't like Elfego anyway.

"Let's take a walk," I said. "If we can't think of anything we'll come back and try again. And maybe Elfego will show up. Sounds like he runs late pretty often. From what I could tell when I met him, he doesn't seem the type who figures he's obligated to explain himself to a guy like the bartender."

"Or maybe he'll take more money."

"Or that."

We slid off the barstools and walked toward the sidewalk. Quasimodo was busy breaking up some empty liquor bottles in a trash can. We had just stepped outside when the ponytail waiter came up to wipe off an empty table near us. He looked at Elle carefully.

"You really are T-boy's sister. I can see it." He smiled, a slight Floridian drawl. Looking at him again, I was put in mind of an ex-college professor who'd decided on a change of life.

"I am. Did you know Young Henry?"

He laughed. "Yep. It's you. He said you called him that."

"You knew him?"

He glanced toward Quasimodo, who had gone around to tend some of the closer tables to the bar, taking up Elfego's slack.

"What a prick. But Elfego should've showed up. Now we all have to work more. Of course there's more tips so I don't mind so much."

"Were you here the night my brother came in? Before . . ."

The waiter nodded. "I know about that. I'm real sorry. It was hard to believe."

Elle nodded.

"Elfego took it pretty hard." He caught my look. "You didn't think so?"

"He didn't let on much when I came here last week."

"Oh. That was you." He sized me up. "You're her 'friend.' Obviously."

"Maybe I was wrong."

"You were. Elfego's like that. Smartass but I can tell you, it got to him. They were starting to see each other again, him and Terrell."

Elle and I looked at each other. I glanced at Quasimodo, who finally seemed to have noticed that we hadn't actually left.

"We may get some company."

"Yeah," said the waiter. "Anyway, I wanted to let you know. Elfego lives up near Coliseum, a big apartment in one of those old run-down houses. Mercy Street. 121-B, I think. A big white and gray-trimmed house near the corner, with a black fence. He's in the place in back. There's a little Cuban flag drawing or something on his door."

"Do you know his phone number?"

"It's not in the book but information has it. Villareal is his last name. On Mercy Street."

Quasimodo had taken to uninterrupted staring.

"You think he's home?" Elle asked.

"I doubt it. He could be out grocery shopping or up at the mall or hanging out at one of the coffee shops on Magazine." He glanced at the counter inside. "I don't know why Quasimodo's so pissed off. This happens at least once a week. But Elfego's so good and so many customers like him, and so does the owner, who only comes in a couple nights a week, that he can get away with anything." He laughed a little. "Charm, you know? It's part of the business."

"Hey, we got customers," Quasimodo called out. The entire bar looked up.

"Speaking of which," Elle said.

"I know. I better go. Anyway. Call him or go by and if you see him, tell him I told you and he'll be okay with it. We're friends." He looked at us. "Not like with your brother. Just friends. The occasional fuck-buddy." At that he laughed loud, maybe louder than necessary, and broke off with a flourish of his cleaning cloth, smiling bright, back into the bar. Quasimodo frowned, grimaced, and then, his disapproval registered, went back to the business of pouring drinks and ringing up money.

We walked away. After a few paces, Elle turned back and gave a little wave to the waiter, who had never given us his name.

WE DROVE OFF TO find Elfego's apartment, cutting through the Quarter on Decatur and up Magazine Street to the neighborhood near the old Coliseum theater, in the lower part of Uptown close to the Irish Channel. Moss-draped trees filled a small city park, and around it were homes in all states of repair. On Mercy Street, the big three-stories dominated, but most had turned into rental properties, and as such no doubt brought decent incomes for their owners. I should give that some thought, I said to myself, still thinking like I had been doing before finding a body and finding this woman.

Twilight had turned to night but it was easy enough to make out a Spanish-style house with a wrought iron fence and a balcony on the second floor. The white and gray paint was peeling badly. I found a place to park a half-block down. "It's going to get rougher from here," I said before we got out. "Assuming Elfego has the painting or knows anything about it."

She shrugged and opened her door.

We walked up the sidewalk to the house. Under the aura of streetlamps, the neighborhood was Faulknerian, with a touch of Elmore Leonard. Maybe the city was like that.

A light was on in the big front room downstairs but we walked down the driveway. The fence to the back yard had no gate, but a flat stone walkway curved around through the well-kept lawn. A wrought iron patio table and chairs were chained to concrete pads. A flag of Cuba really was painted on a wooden door at the rear of the house.

Elle made straight for it. When she knocked, the door swung open about two inches.

"Get back," I said, catching up to her quickly. "Let me look first."

I pushed the door open a little more and called out Elfego's name. Three times. Nothing.

"Go in," she said, trying to push past me.

I stepped inside, just ahead of her, and felt for a light switch as we hovered at the threshold. I flipped it on.

We both stared.

The place was wrecked. Not randomly, as from a fight. Methodically, as from a search. Drawers upturned, sofa cushions pulled out, ripped open, cabinets emptied. Several oil and watercolor paintings, impossible to recognize, were slashed and the frames broken into bits. The stereo and TV, which an angry lover would have destroyed along with everything else, were intact, just shoved around.

A small kitchen led off to one side and it was the same kind of scene. All the cabinets emptied, cookware and food all over the floor.

"Trey was here."

"Or his sidekicks. I would say so."

"He figured it out, too."

"He knew both of them."

We checked out the rest of the place. In a study off the hall, every book, photo, CD rack or pile of boxes had been tossed around and broken up. More slashed art work. Clothes from an open closet scattered everywhere.

"Don't touch anything. We shouldn't even be here."

"You turned on the lights and pushed the door open."

"Shit. Right. I'll wipe them when we leave. But let's not make any more mistakes."

I suddenly realized she was going into the far bedroom. I couldn't get to her in time. I figured that's where the body would be.

But it was only another mess. The mattress on the queen-sized bed was slashed, a shiny red comforter and silver sheets hanging off a corner. For the first time, I saw bloodstain.

"It's on the sheets, too," she said. "But not that much."

We looked around a little more but that was all.

We made our way back, checking for anything else we might have missed, and also anxious to get out before anyone, especially police, showed up. I pulled out my shirttail to wipe down what I had touched.

We were in the yard in back when I noticed a storage shed at the far end of the yard, next to a huge magnolia tree and a rose trellis. The door was open.

There wasn't much doubt in either of our minds what would be inside. But again, no corpse.

The shed had been tossed pretty well, too. Tools scattered everywhere, a couple of smashed storage boxes. Maybe that's where they thought the painting had been. As my eyes adjusted to the dimness, I saw a stack of stretched canvasses, some spattered rags, brushes, an easel.

I bent down to look at the tubes. They were fossilized, most of the caps off. I held one up for her to see. "So he was a painter himself. Maybe not lately."

She flipped through the canvasses against the wall. All were blank.

I touched her arm. "We shouldn't hang around."

"No."

"We should go."

We walked wordlessly to the car. As we reached the curb, a streetlamp bulb popped nearby and we both looked up as it fizzled to yellow and out.

"We need to be gone," I said.

"Do you think he's dead?"

"No. We can go by the bar again."

"Don't you think we've been there enough?"

"Probably. I don't know. You have a better idea?"

She rubbed the sides of her cheeks like they were itching. Turned around, walked a few paces along the street where there had, in fact, been no murders today. That we knew of. She came back. "You're some kind of reporter, aren't you? Some kind of fake PI? Can't you find people?" Her voice rising.

I unlocked the passenger door, hoping she'd take the cue. "We'll find him. We need to go."

"You have a computer. He must be in public records. Something."

"We can't go to my apartment."

She paced down the sidewalk again, returned, gesturing with her arms like a teacher shaking a kid. "We can figure this out, you know?"

I kept my eye on the street. A block away I could see someone coming with a dog on a leash. It was that time of evening.

"Let's get in the car. We can talk about it. We can go get something to eat."

Her face screwed into disbelief. "Food?"

"I'm hypoglycemic. I can feel the headache starting."

There was a disbelief in her expression, and then a distant blankness. "This is impossible."

"But it's not. Come on, just get in."

She pushed up next to me and kissed me so hard on the lips that her teeth came through onto my lower lip and when she pulled back I felt blood warm in my mouth.

"It's safe back there, with Boots?"

"Yeah."

"Then let's go back there. Let's get something to drink and some takeout food and go back there, Jack, and stay there."

She was pushing herself against me, aggressively. It didn't feel romantic.

"There has to be more. Your brother would've had some other way for you to find the painting, wouldn't he? He'd have a plan, or a contact, something, right? I mean, he wouldn't leave it just up to luck and his sometimes lover?"

It was the wrong thing to say.

"Like I am?"

"What?"

"Your part-time lover?"

"We're not lovers."

She reached down and grabbed me by the crotch. "That's what you want, isn't it?"

I moved back.

She snorted in derision, or exasperation. Then her right knee buckled for a second. I reached out to steady her. I had no idea how she was holding all this together. And she wasn't.

She shook loose and finally got in the car. "Stop for some wine," she said. "You can get a pizza on Magazine. Then home. You know, our home of the day."

THERE WAS NO FAIRY tale build-up or romantic wooing over candlelight or under the waxing moon. There was no time. There had barely been time to get the Bordeaux at the drugstore and the cheese and mushroom pizza at Sicily's.

At "home," in the little room, there was no time for anything but draining half the bottle in a couple of gulps each, not like shots but like some kind of sacrament, some kind of diversion. And then some sitting in silence with the radio on and also the TV on, listening to neither, and then just rising together and slipping off our clothes and falling onto the bed. We made love like people without time. People without injury.

It took time for us to awaken. And for Elle to remember that the cell phone trilling somewhere in the room was in her handbag. It was just past midnight. We had fallen asleep so hard it might have been days rather than just a couple of hours. Having lain still so long, I could barely move. Passion had overridden the pain from Big Red's fists, but now it was definitely back. Elle moved slowly, too, but from grogginess. By the time she got the phone, the voice mail had taken over. She slumped naked at the edge of the bed listening to the message.

"It's Elfego."

The room was dark, other than the bathroom light I must have left on, and a greenish glow around Elle's face from the illuminated screen on the cell.

I worked to come awake, to get into a sitting position. "What?"

"Elfego. I don't know how he has this number. Young Henry, I guess. He said to call him back." She put the phone down and moved close to me. "He sounded pretty high." She ran her fingertips along my side. "Hey."

I winced.

"Sorry."

"It was worth it."

"How do you feel?"

"I'm okay. Stiff from not moving." She smiled faintly. "You?"

"I'm better."

She kissed me lightly as she pushed the call-back button. I could hear a ringing through the receiver. Then a muffled "Hola."

"Elfego?"

She looked at me.

I heard these bits from her end of the conversation:

"You're okay? . . . How bad? . . . It was Trey . . . Jesus . . . Should you go to the emergency room? . . . Okay . . . No, we're in town . . . Really. We just got here. How did you get this number? . . . Okay, no, that's fine. Listen, I need to see you . . . Really . . . Elfego, where are you? You sound drunk . . . Can we meet somewhere? . . . I can't tell you like this . . . Well you say a place. We'll be there . . . Down there? . . . No, okay, okay . . . When . . . Okay . . . Yes. Yes. Just us . . . I'm sorry. Really, really sorry. And I'm glad you're alive . . . Bye."

She looked down at her body, not so much at the form of it but at the fact that it existed and was in this particular place at this particular time. She shook her head repeatedly. "I guess we're going out."

We got dressed—a slow process for me—while she told me what Elfego had said.

THE CHOICE OF BAR was odd, down by the convention center, but also maybe okay, since it was so filled with late-night partiers and tourists, all strangers to each other. A few extra people wouldn't be noticed. The music was classic rock and New Orleans R&B, about the only redeeming quality.

We made Elfego right away. He had found a table back in a corner, as out of the way as possible. Not a guy for understatement, he was wearing a blue and orange tropical shirt and yellow cotton trousers. Also a straw hat and shades. And he wasn't alone. Ponytail waiter from Rio Blanche had pushed a chair up close to him and when we approached, I realized that probably he was there to hold Elfego up—figuratively and literally.

Elle and I crossed the crowds on the peanut shell-littered floor to the two chairs across from our new friends. I was favoring my left side but otherwise loosening up. "How's it going?" I said, sitting with an involuntary groan.

Even behind the sunglasses and straw beach hat, I could see Elfego was pretty beat up. Maybe worse than me. Elle's wounds were on the inside, but no less damaging. What a trio we made. Only Ponytail looked unscathed.

"It's one in the morning and we're in a shitty tourist dive. How do you think it's going?" Elfego said. It was hard to understand him. Inside his badly swollen mouth his tongue was likely cut up. Maybe some broken teeth. He didn't smile enough for me to figure it out.

Elle looked at both men silently. Then, to Ponytail, "So he came to you."

"Por qué no?"

"I didn't mean it that way." She looked at Elfego. "I didn't know you had my number."

"I have lots of numbers, sweet pants."

"You got it from Young Henry."

"Well, duh."

Elle tried to put her hand on Elfego's, but he drew back.

"I didn't come here to chat. Hell, I didn't want to come here at all—"

"—He can barely walk—"

"—I came here because, one, they didn't kill me, and two, I figured if they wanted it that bad I should give it to you, like your brother asked me."

Elle glanced at me.

"You have his painting?"

I tried to stop her but it was out. Elfego cocked his head, looked at his friend. "What painting?"

"Elfego."

"Oh yeah, the one Trey beat the shit out of me looking for? You know, someone might have mentioned that to me. It's hell getting your nose broken having no . . . fucking . . . idea . . . why."

Elfego coughed, so much that his friend gave him a wad of cocktail napkins into which to hack up the blood.

"He needs to go to the hospital. Or a doctor," I said.

"I told him," said Ponytail. "You see how he minds me."

"Is he taking something?"

"Hell yes. I have an extensive pharmacy in my bathroom. Right now it's Percodan."

"Good stuff."

"We may move into something more serious. Of course, he's having some trouble zoning in, as you can maybe tell."

"Fuck you," Elfego said, throwing the bloody napkins to the floor. "They didn't hurt me that bad."

We all exchanged glances of disbelief.

"I have to go back," Elfego said to his friend, negating his own bravado. "Give it to her."

Ponytail—I guess we had all concluded no one needed to know his name—reached into his pocket and then slid his cupped hand to our side of the table. He dropped something and moved his hand back.

She looked at me, and silently conveyed once again an apology for accusing me of taking the necklace from Terrell's body.

"Nobody asked me about it," Elfego shrugged. "So I didn't bring it up."

Elle reached to take the tangled strand of silver.

"Look, I knew he was meeting Trey. He was going to try to get some money from him somehow. He didn't tell me how. I'm not his fucking banker."

"When did he give you this?" she asked.

"At the bar, that night." He looked at me, clicked his tongue mockingly. "See, I don't have to tell you everything, gringo. By the way, what the fuck happened to you?"

"I ran into a door."

He sneered. "Lots of doors out there these days."

"I'd say."

"The door. Name of Trey Barnett?"

"Close friends."

Finally Elfego smiled. I could see blood on his teeth.

"So he gave you this?" Elle continued. "That night, when he was there with Trey."

"He just said to hang onto it until he got back from wherever they were going and if he didn't come back, to make sure you got it. But you know, that little queenie could be soooo dramatic." He coughed again.

"You could have given it to Jack right away. Or called me," she said.

Elfego sneered, as best his mouth would let him. "Maybe I wasn't sure." He let that set just long enough, looked at her directly enough, that it seemed true. "Maybe it was the last thing he ever gave me. Maybe I didn't know who to trust with it, no matter what he said. Or why." He dabbed at the tooth blood, the sneer softened to something else. "I guess now it's different. So . . ."

Ponytail put his arm around his friend. "We have to go."

"Yeah," I said.

Elle let the necklace play through her fingers. "So, did my brother say anything about where he put that painting he wanted me to have?"

"You gonna tell me what the hell it is?"

"I don't know for sure. Did Trey say anything?"

"While his coños were holding me down and kicking me?"

"I'm sorry. I just wondered if you knew. You know, I'm trying to get around this."

"I don't know shit about it other than it gets people killed. Maybe the two of you."

"Maybe," I said.

Elle reached for his hand again. This time he let her cover it and squeeze it. They looked at each other a moment. Only they knew what they shared.

"I'm glad you got away. That was lucky," she said.

"It wasn't lucky. I just hit that shit in the face with the door when we went outside and took off. I know the streets around there better than they did."

"Whatever it was, I mean I'm glad. And I'm sorry about it. We didn't know he'd be heading your way."

"You're not my guardian."

"No," I interjected, maybe a little too strong.

Ponytail exchanged a look with Elfego I couldn't decipher.

"If it wasn't for this little chica here," Elfego said, shifting his attention with clear demarcations from Ponytail to Elle, then me, "I wouldn't have tried so hard to not tell them anything. Not that I knew anything."

Elle squeezed his hand more and said, "Go somewhere for a while. Go to a hospital." To Ponytail: "Take care of him. Too many people drowning in all this misery right now." Her eyes seemed to sharpen even in the barroom light. "Too much of it from the same person."

Elfego looked down at the table and I realized he was having trouble with focus.

Elle toyed with the necklace a moment longer, then clasped it in her fist. "We'd better go, too," she said.

Elfego coughed, and we all stood up. Elle and I walked ahead, with Elfego and Ponytail close behind, so they'd be less visible as we exited. It was a good thing it was late and the patrons were hammered because we must have looked like a hobbling freak show.

I'm not sure where Elfego and Ponytail went but I hoped it was to the hospital. Elfego had taken it hard on our behalf. He didn't seem to like me much and I wasn't sure about him, but I admired his toughness. Same as I did Terrell's, the more I learned of what he had done for his sister.

After a minute or so we stepped out into the street, warm and humid after the icy air conditioning in the bar. We drove back to Boots's to sleep during what was left of the night, and for Elle to tell me what she had seen in that necklace.

I took half a Vicodin before settling slowly into bed. She lay next to me and started to tell me about the necklace, about what was in the locket engraved with the initials "THM." I tried to listen, but the Vicodin worked fast. Her words floated away in my vision of the delight of her body so close to me, of my hand resting on her thigh like it was its natural place in the order of the universe. I tried to come back to focus, to remember that our long quest had brought us to the grail, but it was lights out for the knight.

The electric clock radio said 10:09 when I woke up. Later than I would have guessed. Yet again, it was hard to rally my body. I wanted nothing better than to pop another Vicodin and zone out. But we had less than forty-eight hours. Right now our only lead was draped in a coil of silver chain on the nightstand next to my side of the bed. Recuperation was not an option. I managed to sit up.

Elle was still asleep. I went to the kitchen, found a bag of Community Coffee, and started a brew. I thought a hot shower might help, so I took one, hoping not to wake her. She needed the rest as much as I did. I dug out a pair of clean jeans and a fresh camp shirt from my bag. The coffee was ready by the time I managed to get dressed. I found some brown sugar in a small Mason jar.

I tiptoed into the bedroom for the note in the locket and took it back to the kitchen table. Most of what Elle had been saying last night was still hazy, but I knew the one word on the paper had to do with the secret language she and her brother had used as kids. She said it would take a little while for her to remember how it worked, but it had seemed to relax her thinking about it.

I left the puzzle-word on the table and walked to the rear window to look out into the back yard. Lush and green, surrounded by high bamboo, not unlike the garden at my own place in the Marigny. I had all but forgotten about that part of me. Elle was right: I was living as though each new day brought me a home wherever I was, and that there was no settled place beyond that.

I decided to check my voicemail again. I'd left my cell in the car, but the duct-taped white wall phone in the kitchen was fine. I got a dial tone and only minimal static, and listened through the messages: a callback from Ray Oubre, a check-in from a friend back in Dallas wondering "what the hell you were up to," and something about changing my long distance carrier. Last was another call from Art Becker saying they would be in Atlanta a few days or a week, but that he thought I should try to check in as soon as I could or let me know if I wanted him to go in and look around before they left. In his voice was a tinge of concern, even though he was trying to hide it.

I poured another half-cup for myself and picked out a clean mug from the cabinet over the sink. I had to wake her up. If what she said was right, that the note in the locket would lead us to the painting, it was time to get there.

In the bedroom, I put her coffee on the nightstand and touched her arm. She opened her eyes slowly.

"It's late."

She looked at me as though coming back from somewhere not of this world. "I woke up about four." Her voice molasses-thick. "Bad dream. I couldn't get back to sleep for a while, so I took one of your pills."

I bent down to kiss her. Her lips were there but not much else.

"And now you can't wake up."

"You were right. They take you out."

"It's okay. That's what they're for."

She smiled in what in other circumstances could have been called "serenely."

"What was the dream?"

"Nothing." She looked away. "It was bad."

I sat on the side of the bed, reached out to touch her check lightly. "How bad?"

She sat up, pulling the sheet across her nakedness.

"I don't know, Jack."

"Can you remember any of it?"

"A little."

"Mine usually go away."

"Yeah. Well, it's my line of work to figure out what dreams mean. Not to lose them."

"They get lost."

"Hmmm."

The fingers of her left hand barely grazed mine.

"I was back in my house in Tuscaloosa. They were in there with me."

She drew her hand back and adjusted herself a little in the bed. I watched her closely.

"I just lay there next to you, watching you sleep. And all I could think about was that I felt like I couldn't even take it all in. Like being awake was the dream. Like the dream was at least something with a beginning and an end."

"We're going to make it."

"Yeah?"

"When I was making coffee, it came to me. At least Big Red has faith in us. You know?"

"Or he'd have killed us."

"Or he'd have killed me. Maybe not you."

"You know that's the way it would go."

She didn't say anything for a few moments and I realized she was looking down at my jeans. "Jack. What's the matter with you?" She feigned shock.

I glanced down, too. Impossible, given the way I felt physically.

"Maybe some other time," she said, reaching across to flick away the erection like a hospital nurse. "I need to get dressed."

"You do."

I moved away from the bed and she got up. I had noticed that with Elle the darkness and the light could change places in an instant.

At the bathroom door she stopped, looked at the nightstand. "Where's the—"

"It's in the kitchen."

She gave me a long appraisal. "Why?"

"I tried reading it again. Hell, it's not even a word."

"And?"

"And nothing. I'm just dying to get your translation. So to speak."

She made a dismissive noise, and went into the shower.

"And put some clothes on," I called out.

WHEN SHE WAS READY we walked up to Magazine to a corner coffee shop. We could have driven but my body needed to move. I was going to try to get by without the meds if I could.

It was chilly, which didn't help the ribs or muscles. A mild norther had come in overnight. I really needed to start paying attention to the weather and the world around us. At first I hobbled along, but it got better after the first block. I couldn't do much about the appearance of my nose or the discoloration on my face. A ball cap and shades figured to be a part of my wardrobe for the foreseeable future.

We ordered Mexican coffees and a cranberry muffin for her and a ham and cheese croissant for me and found a table in the far end of the café. I told her about my voicemail. I said I wanted to go by my place after all. My "home," I believe I called it. We decided it would be okay to do so. Maybe a good thing to do.

We took a couple bites of our food and then she took the necklace from her bag, laid it on the table, and smoothed out the note so we could study its one word: "Possmp."

I rolled my eyes and put a huge piece of croissant in my mouth.

She dug in her bag. "Damn. Do you have a pen?"

Veteran journalist that I was, of course I didn't. But I saw a yellow pencil on the table next to ours.

She frowned at the teeth marks and "Geaux Tigers" logo.

"At least those are words that make sense," I said.

"Something to write on, too."

Up again to pick up a flyer for a local band off a stack near a bulletin board. She smoothed the note again, studied the word, then wrote it out at the top of the blank side of the flyer.

She scribbled some numbers under the word. Then she scratched them out. Then she put a new group of numbers in a horizontal line under each letter of the word. Each number corresponded to the letter above it.

"What are you doing?"

"Drink your coffee." She was actually smiling.

She had written: 16, 1, 3, 3, 3, 0.

She looked at it for several moments, then scribbled more numbers to one side. Those, she scratched them out. She repeated that process a few times and finally she put down the sequence she seemed to like, directly under the first one.

She turned the paper so I could read it without bending my head. The lower sequence read: 16, 15, 19, 19, 13 and 16.

She was beaming like a first-grader.

"A combination."

"It was a game we played when we were kids. You start with the first letter and whatever number that represents in the alphabetical sequence. Then each one after that is how many that letter is from the first letter in the word. And it spells something. The first one to guess the word, wins."

I looked at what she'd written, like it made any sense to me.

"We used to try to see how much of it we could do in our heads without missing. Young Henry was quick with numbers and he liked puzzles. He almost always beat me. He could even beat Daddy. But he always made it so much fun nobody cared, and we all expected to lose anyway." She looked away briefly. "And now he's gone."

"It's for a mail box? Or storage box somewhere?"

"Could be."

"But you have two rows there. Which one is it?"

"Which looks more like a mailbox combination to you?"

"The one on the bottom, sort of."

"Me, too. We had a second way to play the game that was easier, for when we just wanted to play as fast as we could, like in the car. You just use the number that corresponds to the position of the letter in the alphabet. You don't have to measure it from the first letter each time. It usually gives you more double digits so it can be little harder to do in a hurry in its own way."

I studied the numbers. Whatever. "So he went the second route."

"Yeah. But he had to do it backwards. See? He made a word out of the numbers on the lock. I guess they didn't really make a real word. It's a preset combination." She looked at it. "Possmp. He was trying for possum, I guess. Or" —she cocked her head— "possible map? Hey, I like that one better."

"Definitely."

"It's our possible map."

"Possibly a possum."

She looked at me.

I looked at the numbers again.

"What? You're checking me?"

I kept looking at the sequences. "Yeah. I see it. Even if Trey got this paper, he wouldn't know what it meant."

"You think Elfego looked at it?"

"Maybe, but he wouldn't know what it meant, either."

"Either way he saved it for you."

"Yeah." She put the pencil down. A couple of Tulane co-eds came by, carrying a tray of coffee and assorted goodies. They sat a few tables over and began talking about a concert at Snug Harbor.

I looked at the paper. "You're sure about this."

"I am."

"Because I'm not sure if I really get it. Not really."

"But I do."

"I believe you. Doesn't matter. The trick is to know what this opens." She put her hand on top of mine.

"I know that, too. Or at least where."

I'm sure unbelief, if not incredulity, telegraphed from my expression.

"He was my brother, you know."

"Yeah, but—"

"I know his habits."

I smiled, took a long drink of my coffee.

"You know where Broad is, right?"

"Sure."

"Let's go."

"Where on Broad?"

"I'll show you."

We got up from the table. Outside, on the sidewalk, she stopped me.

"You don't believe me. Admit it."

"That's not true."

"Liar."

She kissed me, just enough not to hurt. We walked back to get the car. She kissed me again, pinched me on the butt. Actions that could be described as playful. But it wasn't about me. And it wasn't about anything in the present. If I had to guess, I would say it was summer in Rosedale, decades ago, when time had yet to manifest.

21

Broad Street is a busy crosstown thoroughfare where you can find anything from a beauty shop to a liquor store. For our immediate purposes, it also was home to Mid Town Pack 'n' Mail, where you could dispatch via UPS or Fed Ex and where people like Elle, who needed a local delivery address for her business correspondence, might keep a rented mail drop. And where a brother who emulated his older sister in all practical matters could do the same, should the need arise.

We had taken both possible sets of numbers but she was right, the combination was the second: 16-15-19. It went with the box number: 191316. The sequence of numbers was broken perfectly in half. I guessed he did the combination first and box second because that sequence came closest to a word. Maybe Terrell really was clever, though obviously not in all matters.

The box was in the middle row on the left wall inside the alcove next to the packing and wrapping counter and copying machines. The teenaged attendant in a blue-and-white-striped company shirt was helping an older woman weigh a package, and nodded at us when we walked by, that kind of chirpy sales clerk thing that had infected the retail world. But if you wanted a job, you did what you had to do, and I was happy to see the kid at work.

The little store was bright, almost sterile, odd for a neighborhood that was about as rumpled as you could get. It almost didn't figure except that the world, even this ancient one at the delta of the great river, was becoming transient and people who bore their abodes on their backs, more or less, needed places to get checks and letters and government notices. It was probably a damn good business to get into. And it was the kind of place to be anonymous, unless the cops or the feds were looking for you in a hard way, and then there wasn't much you could do to hide, anyway.

No way a painting could have been in that little mail drop, but I assumed—I know that's always wrong—its contents might lead to another, larger storage box in the same store. But why expect anything to be easy? All that was in the mail slot was a letter, two pages, handwritten either in a hurry or while under the influence of something. It was folded up in thirds, not even put in an envelope, which I also figured to mean it was done in haste.

When she unfolded the letter, a small brass key fell to the floor. I picked it up. There was no marking other than the name of the company, Yale, that made the lock the key would fit. I showed it to Elle and she gave it back to me. I put it in my pocket. Elle closed the mailbox door and spun the combination dial. She gave the letter a cursory glance and then refolded it and said we needed to leave.

We went back to the Taurus.

"Just drive somewhere. Anywhere."

I found a street lined with two-story houses that looked as decrepit as they did vacant, the sides of the street lined with old cars and a lime green van on concrete blocks with one wheel missing. I parked.

She was already reading the letter. She shook her head, pursed her lips, then leaned her head against the seat rest and took a deep breath. "Young Henry, Young Henry."

"Does it say?"

"It says."

I reached for it but she held it firm.

"Read it, then."

"It's to me." She took another deep breath, and started:

Ellie: I guess if you get this I'm not going to be around to read it because you wouldn't need to have it. It also means Elfegito did the right thing. I knew he would, even though he tries to put up a front, he's not so bad in a jam, and I am in a motherfucker of one, maybe. I'm going to meet Trey later on. He's going to want that Spanish painting I was telling you about, and thinks I'm going to give it to him, or maybe sell it to him, whatever. But I'm not going to. I hope Lenora has talked to you already and if not you need to call her right away. She can tell you the shit. I can't. I hope you don't even need to read this. But if you do, get the painting and take it to this address in Houston: Beldon Gallery, 11120 Shepherd. It's near Rice University I think. Ask for Jackie Beldon. This is the number: 434-5555. Tell her what you have. She'll know about it already. It's worth a lot. Don't take less than a mill and a half.

Minimum. It's worth way more than that to Trey but without him you just have to take what you can fence it for. Just do it quick, okay, Ellie? Don't wait. Take the money and get the hell away.

The other thing, Lenora can tell you about. I'm so sorry. The asshole. But it could be big for you, you little tush-baby, all that money from Junior. But you need to stay away from Trey till you get it, or you never will. If you get this you know what he did to me. Shit, I'm scared big sister but I'm also so pissed off. I really want to fuck him over and this is a good way. Without this damn art he's in big trouble with the mob, 'cause he owes them a fucking bundle. They'll kill him, straight up.

Look, I gotta go. No way Trey could get to this letter but if he does and if that's who's reading it, go to hell, rich boy bitch, you'll never find anything.

But figuring it's you, big sister, you can think where it is. We went there one time when I visited. 21. You should remember. Shit, this is the last place I'll ever be if you're reading this. I'm a history teacher. I can appreciate it. But it doesn't mean I like it. If you really are reading this, then at least that means it's going to be okay and you are and then it was all worth it. Put my ashes in the river, like we always said.

I love you, Ellie, lord how much I do, but you know that.

Kick ass, may the Lord watch over you forever,

Love, T. Henry.

p.s. to myself: If I get to this on my own, God help me I'm going to wise up.

Her eyes were moist when she was done and for that matter so were mine. She folded the letter and touched it to her face.

"You go with God. Blessed are the angels that fly with you." She kissed the letter and held it in her hands, looking out the window. I could see her lower lip quiver.

"That was a fine brother," I said.

"Amen. Amen. Amen."

"Are you okay?"

"I'm fine." A quick glance my way, and her lips tightened in vain, and then she began a quiet sobbing. "Just drive," she said. "Anywhere. Just drive and find some music."

I dialed up O-Z, which was playing traditional second-line jazz, and drove toward City Park, and then looped around through whatever street came up, and on back to Magazine, where I pulled into the lot at Audubon Park. We got out and walked around the loop, not saying much.

At a bench, we sat down.

"So you know where it is?" I hadn't wanted to press her although I have to say I was pretty sure I knew, at least generically. Maybe I was good at puzzles, too.

Joggers and walkers passed us on the oval asphalt track and nodded in greeting. We were such a nice couple, if you didn't look too close.

"21 is U. It's where I put some things when I first got my apartment here."

"You mean U-Haul?"

"You're getting the hang of it."

I rolled my eyes. "We've got the key. We just need a lock."

"Isn't that a blues song?"

"Something like that."

"Jack, I do know where this lock is."

I took her hand. "You think this will be it?"

She pulled her hand away. "Don't be like that."

I was wrong to have said that. But I was right, too. But mostly wrong.

Somewhere so far inside I could but feel the first sickening pulse of the electricity of its resurrection, a crack opened. It manifested, as usual, as a laugh line. My life had come down to a children's math puzzle. But the laughter could no more be expressed than the demons writing the divine comedy. I knew what I wanted to do. I knew why I was in New Orleans. I knew what I needed to do. I knew where I was going. I was going as far south as you can get.

She started walking again. The leaves on the trees had not yet turned, given the latitude, but it was in the air that they would.

The U-Haul was on Tulane, not all that far from the mail drop, which made sense. Terrell probably had been in a hurry. I must have driven by the street dozens of times and never noticed, although it was easy enough to spot if you were looking.

We passed through the gate, surrounded by a high wire fence, and parked in front of the office. The last trick in Terrell's book had been to force the person coming for the painting to show some ID, and for that reason he had listed both his name and his sister's on the three-month rental agreement. The clerk was on duty alone and at wit's end with a middle-aged guy wanting a trailer hitch on his SUV, despite a posted notice from corporate headquarters that hitches couldn't be installed on that model.

Elle showed him her driver's license and he gave her the number and the code to get into the "climate-controlled" storage building next door. He asked her if she needed the spare key but she said no. Nice touch, I thought. Leaving an extra. If it all got this far, no point getting hung up on a key that might have been dropped by a sister, presumably, by that point, grief-stricken and frightened. No idea she'd be with a guy who had morphed into a freelance mercenary in a war of no defined length or boundary.

We left the office as the customer was berating the clerk, who gave us one of those sorry-about-the-asshole looks and a complicit smile as we got out of the way. Elle walked over to the storage building while I parked the Taurus close to the entry. She punched in the code and we went inside.

A staircase took us to the second level and down a concrete hallway past corrugated, retractable red doors festooned with locks of all kinds. The fluorescent light made everything surreal. Halfway down was the 8x20 unit we sought: 217. I couldn't figure any significance to the number, nor could Elle, and there wasn't any. It was just the unit available at the time Terrell Henry Meridian, coked out or freaked out, maybe both, played the gamble that he thought would save his sister's life. Ended up costing his.

The key fit. I unclasped the lock and pulled the noisy, roll-up door up and open. The unadorned overhead bulb illuminated a slender, cold space: tin walls and a concrete floor, filled with what at first appeared to be nothing but a square cardboard box at the far end, open at the top and apparently empty.

I followed her inside, weary with the hide-and-seek. Before my petulance had a chance to blossom, we saw it. Another box, thin and rectangular, about chest high, just right for holding a painting, was tucked against the corner next to the door. Not really hidden, just pushed aside enough that you might not see it right away, focusing instead on the decoy. So that you'd have to go in all the way to find it. I don't know why. Maybe some kind of half-conceived escape plot. I had learned that there was really no end to the justifiable paranoia in this entire enterprise.

"It's here."

"It's here."

"Pull down the door."

She did.

The second shipping carton was sealed at both ends. While I was tearing off the tape, Elle went to the first box we had seen and kicked it. Empty.

I carefully slid the interior part of the carton from the outer shell. I could feel the weight of a heavy frame and the smell of something very old inside, but it was wrapped in a couple layers of dark plastic, also sealed in tape. It was short work to take that off and then we finally were looking at it. The object of so much desire, the suffering for which enables the First Noble Truth.

I carefully moved it away from the carton and propped it against a wall. We both stepped back, like visitors to a fine arts museum.

"My God," she said.

"Jesus."

It was the Virgin Mary, all right, but it conveyed a power I had never seen in anything that called itself art. She was captured inside a thick wooden frame, intricately carved and adorned with gold leaf. She was standing on a narrow trail on a rocky hillside filled with giant cacti and thick bushes of bright red roses. She wore a green cloak with a red-and-black-striped serape draped across one shoulder. The hood of the cloak was fixed over her head.

Her face was oval, deep copper skin ringed by dark black curls. She was Aztec. She was European. The perfection of her beauty was impossible: flawless, graceful, sensual. Hovering above and behind her were flights of tropical birds of every color imaginable, and among them scores of winged cherubs. In the background, a golden sun rose from the rim of high desert mountains. Rays of light pierced a sky of purest azure.

I had seen Guadalupes and Virgins. I had seen beauty to break your heart. But nothing like this.

"No wonder," I finally said.

"It's perfect."

"How could anyone ever steal something like this?"

"How could Trey get to be somebody who would?"

We couldn't stop staring.

"It's worth a lot more than we thought."

She reached forward to touch the surface, slightly. Then she said something that broke the spell.

"Young Henry said it had been in Mexico City. On loan from some Mexican oil guy."

"What?" I looked at her hard.

She looked at me sharply. "I wasn't hiding anything."

"I didn't mean . . ."

"Yes, you did."

I settled down on one haunch. "Okay, I did."

She looked me over, and then let it go.

"Anyway, he supposedly loaned it out again as a kind of penance to a cathedral and it got stolen. Drug lords. I gather that's how Trey got wind of it. Look, I don't know. Seeing this now. It's powerful, you know. Things are popping into my head."

I stepped forward to touch the surface, too. The oil was hardened, and almost certainly needed a cleaning. Nothing popped into my head that wasn't already there. But I knew what she meant. It was like being in a presence.

"Can you see the signature?"

I let my finger glide just above the brush strokes, working down to the lower right corner. "There it is. Echave."

I moved back and she air-traced her finger over the name. We studied the painting more. That is to say, allowed ourselves to be captured by it.

"It's psychedelic."

"No. It's like being possessed by the spirit. It's what people experience when they are taken. I've seen it a hundred times in churches. Jack, it's why I'm remembering."

With that, Elle moved the frame a little to the left, carefully, to reduce the glare from the overhead bulb. She cradled the edges, as though she were holding the most breakable of bones, and tilted the frame toward her. "Look," she said, indicating the thick, yellowed canvas in back. A protective backing of padded brown paper was badly torn.

"What is it?"

Gently, she pulled back one of the torn strips of paper. Then she propped the frame against the wall.

"I don't know." She shifted her weight to stand akimbo, lost in a thought.

"What?"

"What Young Henry said. Maybe there was something to it. I wish I'd talked to him more." Her glance told me she hadn't truly let go of my earlier comment. "But with the coke. . ."

She shook her head. "This is the really goofy part. He said it was an art dealer, that one in Houston probably, said there's been a rumor for years that this really might be a paint-over of another oil underneath. Wouldn't that be wild?"

I looked at it more closely.

"Okay, here's the story. So there's the Aztec peasant—"

"—Juan Diego—"

"—up on the hill in Mexico City, seeing the Virgin, and all the legend that came out of that, like we talked about. The usual kind of thing you see in these Guadalupes all the time."

"But?" I dropped to one knee, trying to follow the color lines in the work.

"But what if there was somebody else on that hill?"

I glanced up at her. She was like a docent with a pet theory. If that docent were inside a U-Haul storage shed. Running from killers. But none of that was real to Elle in the presence of the Virgin.

"A Spanish trader, nobody remembers who, brings home to Madrid a painting by another Aztec peasant who also claimed to have seen Mary. Not Juan Diego. This Aztec knows how to paint. A priest had given him some brushes and oils. Somehow the trader gets the Aztec's painting. He smuggles it back to Spain to give to his wife. But before he gets home, she dies. The trader ends up giving it to his friend, the painter Echave, in return for his doing a portrait to remember the late wife."

I stood. "And that's this?"

"It's just something my brother told me. Like I said, maybe it was coke. Echave was either crazy jealous of the peasant's work or ultra-devout and thought it was a sacrilege. Whatever, he painted over it with his own version of the Virgin."

"On the back, you think maybe there's an original underneath."

"It seemed far-fetched at the time. I didn't even remember, until . . . but now, standing here, in front of it . . . I mean, Jack, can't you feel it?"

Suddenly a loud "bam" rattled the building. We both jumped.

"What the hell?" I looked quickly at the door. Still closed. She took a step toward the painting.

In the next second a rush of cool air came in through a vent in the ceiling. Climate control had kicked on.

"Jesus."

She was trembling. I took her in my arms and held her. She nestled her head against my chest. Whatever energy was rippling through the storage unit was coursing through us, too. Good and bad.

"So, you felt it?"

We unclasped, walked back to the painting.

"I used to pray to her all the time. Now, I don't know what that ever meant."

I started picking up the wrapping bags and padding and parts of the shipping carton. "I think we need to go."

"Yeah."

She helped me. She took in a final, long draught of the roses, the birds, the sun rays, the mother of God. Then we covered the painting with the bags and re-tied them.

"I need to go outside," she said.

"Go. I've got it."

I continued with the packaging as she pushed up the roller door and walked down the hall to the stairwell. Her footsteps on the naked concrete echoed like a death-row inmate's last stroll. I resealed the box with the tape. I turned out the light, pulled the door back down, and locked up.

She was leaning against the car, her head back, eyes shut against the clouds drifting in from the southeast. The cool morning had turned warm-ish, languid. Maybe a storm in the Gulf, maybe a hurricane at the tail end of the season, maybe the gathering of the gods to bring on the end of the world with fire and thunder and flood and pestilence. Gods tired of humans trampling in their domain, to ends that never seemed to turn out for the best.

23

It had gotten to be late afternoon and along with the dull throbbing in my body was also a kind of nausea. I felt dizzy, driv-ing back into town. I told Elle I needed something to eat. I pulled into the next convenience store, the kind that sold more lottery tickets and beer than anything else.

Before I could unbuckle, Elle was out the door and into the store. She came back with a white plastic sack and dug into it for a carton of orange juice. I emptied it in about two swallows. Then I ripped open a pouch of cashews and swallowed a lot of them, and followed that with several gulps of milk from another carton. I let my head lean back against the seat back and closed my eyes.

"Better?"

"Getting there."

"We're not in a hurry."

I didn't say anything, just let my mind drift off, maybe into that swarm of birds and angels strafing a Technicolor field atop an Aztec mountain.

I must have gone to sleep, just for a few minutes. I woke up to my door coming open and Elle caressing my cheek.

"Can you move over into the other seat? We should probably leave. The clerk inside is starting to look at us too much. Not to mention those two creeps over by the pay phone."

I shook my head like a dog and still felt groggy but in no mood to argue. I pushed the seat back down so I could maneuver and fairly awkwardly got myself into the passenger seat. She took the wheel.

"Sorry."

"No problem."

She backed out and we zoomed past downtown on the interstate and then dropped off to pick up Carrollton and more or less back toward Magazine Street. My nausea was gone but now the pain of the beating was back.

"Can you eat something else? Maybe you should."

"Yeah. Something. Meat. Protein."

"You sound like a caveman."

"It's my new look."

She pursed her lips.

"I'm okay now."

"I can see that."

"Really. I just let the sugar drop too low. Hasn't happened in a while."

"I thought you got some extra sugar last night."

I never seemed to know when she was going there. I tried to say something appropriate but just smiled.

"Maybe you could take another Vicodin."

"I need to be awake. We need to get this taken care of."

"We still have a whole day and a half." She laughed. "Thirty-six hours to avoid the mob."

"A French movie."

"How about there?"

The Camellia Grill usually was crowded but we didn't see anyone queued up outside, and there was a parking place only a half block down.

This time of day the late lunch and early dinner crowds both were absent. We got a quiet corner on the far side of the counter. The waiter was friendly and professional in the way they were in the city and in no time I had a big cheeseburger in front of me, a toasted cheese for my partner. I ate half of mine before coming up for air.

I hated this hypoglycemic thing, but I could see how I'd strung myself out so far it was bound to happen. I rested my elbows on the counter, around my plate, staring across the pit in the center of the U-shaped counter to an old man on the other side sipping a milkshake. I was living in a theme park of violence and flight. One could struggle with meaning in such a situation. A semi-diabetic lapse wasn't the worst that could happen.

Someone tapped on my shoulder.

"Earth to Jack . . ."

I looked over at her, back from wherever.

"Oh, hey."

"Any messages?"

"The usual. Boy meets girl."

"Some girl."

"Some boy."

She was working on her food pretty good for a change, no daintiness at all, even dipping into the fries. I wanted some but I knew I couldn't. Carbs turn to glucose.

She leaned over, not that anyone around us was listening, or could, with the din of the orders being taken the cooks calling out to each other.

"What do you want to do?"

I drank about half my iced tea, wiped my mouth with a napkin. "I want to get it off our hands."

"Big Red?"

"Well, yeah."

I could see she was thinking.

"We have to."

"I know. I was just wondering if there were another way."

I took a bite of my dwindling burger.

She ate a fry.

"You have to admit."

"I know."

"The even weirder thing is that it might be covering up something even more amazing."

I popped the last bite into my mouth. "No time for all that."

"Just enough time to send it to a one-room show in a drug lord's house?"

She was going to be hard about it. Fine. But it was impossible.

She looked at me directly, then her gaze shifted just slightly, and then she reached for her tea. "You saw it. You know we found something we didn't expect."

"What I expect is that if we don't give this up, we're dead meat. It's fairly simple."

A young couple, one white, one black, like us but in reverse, came in, sat nearby. The black guy nodded at me. Then he looked a little harder. I could see he wondered how I got the face. I nodded back, shrugged, made a sign with my hand like a door slamming on my nose. He chuckled, turned back to his girlfriend. I waited until they started talking.

"Look at me," I said.

"I have been."

"They don't ever give up. The mob. Ever."

"I was just thinking."

"What I think is that you never know how these things go. We don't know where she'll end up. Could be the Louvre for all I know. She's been a lot of places."

"Our Lady of Storage."

"The Virgin of U-Haul."

We were bemused by our cleverness for about the right amount of time. Then not.

"It will make it hard for Trey this way, right? Giving it to that Red guy."

"Very hard."

"If they have the painting, he doesn't have the money. They won't need him."

"Plus they don't like him. You know, it's really not so different from what your brother was trying to do."

She nodded, made a low growling noise. Her eyes were glowing.

"You okay now to go?"

I turned on my stool, took her hand, leaned close to her. "I love you, Elle."

"Y'all want dessert?"

Elle turned from looking into my eyes, smiled, and melted the waiter, the way she can do. "Just the check'll be fine."

"You got it, darlin'."

Her mouth was in a little smirk. "You sure can pick the romantic moments."

"Look who's talking."

The waiter came back with our ticket. "Hope to see you again," he said, looking a lot more at her than at me.

I left the tab and an extra five so we wouldn't have to deal with the cashier and we went outside, down the tree-draped sidewalk to the car. We were almost there when she stopped, pulled me to her and kissed me. Like I was saying.

It didn't much matter that traffic was rattling down the pot-holed boulevard or people were walking by us, or that the river was churning a few hundred yards off, beyond the levee, or that someone in our immediate circle of acquaintances probably wasn't going to see the other side of the weekend. What mattered was what she whispered in my ear:

"Of course I love you."

The smart bet was to call Big Red right away but instead we went back to our room. The idea was that I would lie down and rest for an hour or two and then we'd make the call and meet wherever he said. I didn't even know if he'd be in New Orleans, although my guess was that he had an idea that's where this would all wind up.

We drew the blinds and turned up the air-conditioner. I pulled off my shoes and no sooner had put my head on the pillow than she was on the bed, next to me, sitting on her knees, taking off her dress. She touched my ribs lightly and asked me if I could handle it. I lied and said I could. After, I drifted to sleep.

I awoke as she pushed hard on my shoulder. She was sitting on the side of the bed. She had dressed again, and held her phone in her other hand. Her hair was damp and comb-lined from the shower.

"He called."

I raised myself on one elbow, rubbed my face. I was naked under a light quilt. I guess she had put it there.

"Who?"

She was across the bed again, one knee curled under her. She looked at the phone in her hand, as though it were some alien presence. "Trey."

I sat up all the way, for some reason pulled the quilt over my lap.

"I guess everyone has my cell number."

"He knows where we are?"

"No. But it doesn't matter."

Her face was flushed from sex, but inside of that, pale and taut. I think I knew what she was going to say before she said it. Maybe I was catching the second sight.

"He has my aunt."

24

What had seemed a lucky find at the U-Haul yesterday was looking a lot less that way when we woke up Friday morning. We were to meet Trey at 9 P.M., although we wouldn't know the location until 8, when he was to call with directions. So now we had a day to fill, as last night after Trey's message also had to be filled, although exhaustion and Vicodin bridged that gap pretty effectively. Elle woke me up once, a nightmare she didn't want to go into, and then fell asleep with her head on my chest. But today we had plenty to do. Things were going to be moving fast and I had to contemplate an abrupt, violent and permanent exit from the city. Diddy-mao, GI, for sure. I wanted to get to my apartment now more than ever. It was possible there'd be something there that would help us, or help Lenora. It seemed at least worth a drive-by. And we couldn't just sit still.

Elle said Trey told her he'd picked Lenora up in Jackson after she'd left Rosedale and we'd gone to New Orleans. He said he knew I'd met Big Red, and that I had been given an assignment. That's what he wanted to talk about. He thought it would be better to give him the painting as soon as we had it. Especially it would be better for Lenora. Apparently he wasn't afraid of her anymore. But he didn't dwell on it. If we didn't bring the painting to him, he said, he'd have to give Lenora, and us, more thought.

He also said something that I could tell was twisting Elle up. She told me his first words when he called were, "Hey, little darlin', it's your brother."

We packed up. It was unlikely we'd be coming back before, or for that matter after meeting Trey. I left an envelope with a hundred-dollar bill and a few twenties to cover our stay, and then some. Boots wasn't home and I didn't want to just leave as though we'd skipped. If we did make it back, we could decide if we wanted to keep the place any longer; if not, well, he could handle it however he wanted. It wasn't like we'd really been there, unless he said so. It was a strange feeling. The monks say leave no footprint behind, wipe the sand clean. Until now, I had always thought that sounded enticing.

We had a late breakfast just off Napoleon and started threading across town. There was just no fast way to get from Uptown to the Marigny no matter how you went, but I gambled on Magazine then through the warehouse district and on across Canal to Decatur. We did pretty well until we got close to the old Jax brewery, reimagined as a mall, where a mule-drawn buggy full of tourists blocked the only clear lane.

We both stared blankly at the human tableau: shorts and T-shirts, Midwestern khaki conventioneers, suits who couldn't leave the cell phones even for a half-minute, the steady infiltration of black-clad Goths and losers from every part of America who got here because that's where the river dropped them off. In *Dog Soldiers*, Robert Stone said Vietnam had been the place where American kids went to find out about themselves. "Bummer for the gooks," he wrote.

Ditto for the Big Easy.

The traffic cleared a little and I cut up on the back side of the French Market past the Café du Monde and finally into the Marigny. Too late, I realized I was about to drive down the block where I had found Terrell.

"It's okay," she said.

I passed along slowly where he had been. I stopped on the far side of the street. We both looked at the curb.

Whatever blood had been there was long since gone. An empty plastic drink cup lay in the gutter.

I eased forward.

When we got a block away from my street, I slowed to a crawl again. A taxi had been behind us and squeezed by, somehow. I tried to get a quick recon.

The street was mostly empty. I could see the trash had been picked up, although as usual the trucks had left behind a small trail.

I parked near the end of the block and we walked to the gate. I opened the padlock and then we went single-file down the shaded, narrow path that led to the garden and then my apartment at the rear. Despite everything else going on, Elle was extremely interested in seeing just where, and how, her new boyfriend lived. Or maybe it was just a way to pretend for a short time that something about what had happened with us was in any way normal.

I knocked on the Beckers' rear screen door while Elle walked through the garden, admiring the multicolored flowers in their well-tended beds.

I waited over a minute and no one answered so I figured they must still be in Atlanta. I walked back to my unit.

Whatever hesitancy I'd had in my gut about actually coming back here got what the shrinks call validation as soon as I opened the door.

"Oh, my god," she said, fanning the air in front of her face, retreating midway into the garden.

My eyes were watering and I had to spit to try to get out whatever had come into my lungs and mouth.

I looked back at the Beckers' door. A bad thought came into my head. I think she got it at the same time.

"You don't think—" she called out, still scowling from the smell.

"I'm going in."

I took a couple of breaths, pulled the front of my shirt from my jeans to reach over my nose and entered.

Not only was the odor putrid, the place was way too warm, like the gas heaters actually had been left on.

The wreckage was total, but before I could take inventory, I had to be able to breathe. I hurried to the kitchen door at the back, which I rarely used, since it led to nowhere but the wooden fence near the alley. But I didn't have to push the door at all; it had been jimmied and swung open immediately.

I let that thought go for the time, and opened the window over the sink. The smell was hitting me hard again, so I turned on the cold water and splashed my face.

I was pulling a dish cloth from one of the half-open drawers to use as a bandana when I noticed the stove. The burners on top weren't lit, but heat was coming from somewhere.

The oven door was partly open. I pulled it all the way down.

Whatever had been inside was mostly a big mass of fur and well-done entrails, but I was pretty sure it was a cat. Maybe two.

I turned off the gas and shut the door.

I still needed to see if there were any deceased Beckers lying around. I wet my face again through the makeshift bandana and went to the bathroom, then the bedroom. Ransacked, but no human corpses. Yet the smell of death seemed to intensify, and there were flies near my upended futon.

I waded in through dresser drawers and clothes pulled from my closet. I tugged the futon to one side.

I had to get out.

In the garden, I tore off the bandana, and couldn't even talk to Elle, who had moved over into the shade under my landlords' prize orange tree.

"Are you okay?"

"Stay over there. I probably reek of it."

She did.

"I think I found it."

"What?"

"They trashed it good."

"What?"

"I have to go back in. I'll bring it out."

I took a few fresh breaths and re-tied the bandana on my way through the door. I went to the kitchen closet and pulled out several trash bags. I tore one apart and used it for gloves. Then I opened the oven door again.

Definitely cats. Gutted. I pulled out the entire metal rack on which they had been piled and dumped it all into one of the garbage bags. Intestinal cord and blood were seared into the bottom of the oven. I pulled a wooden spoon from a clay pot next to the stove and scraped out as much as I could, lumped it into the bag. Then I put that bag inside another, and tied it all up.

I closed the oven door again and headed back to the bedroom with another garbage bag. This time it was a raccoon, also gutted, inside a clear plastic bag with a hole cut in it so that the swollen entrails would fester and pop, amplifying the stench.

I double-bagged it, too—carefully, so that the body wouldn't fall apart on me like that woman's corpse in Dallas when I was covering the cops. My eyes were watering so much I could barely see. A breeze had started to drift in from the southeast through the open windows and doors but it was still plenty humid.

I carried both black plastic sacks outside.

Elle took a few steps back. I went directly out to the street and dropped the bags on the curb. Pickup wouldn't come until Monday but there wasn't much more I could do. Except hope stray dogs wouldn't tear the bags open.

I pulled off my bandana and left it on top of the heap, rubbed my face and went back to Elle, explained between breaths and short coughing fits what I had found. A kind of sick expression covered her face, and then one that looked angry.

We sat down on the green wrought-iron bench near the flower beds.

"I have to go back in and open some more windows and turn on a couple of fans."

"Jesus, Jack, who does something like that?" She rolled her eyes as soon as the words were out of her mouth. "Still, you don't think they hurt your landlords, do you? I mean, should you check?"

I looked back at their place again. "They're out of town. That's what Art's message said. It looks that way. The doors are all locked."

I went over and pushed against their back door. It didn't seem jimmied. I looked through the curtain on one of the back windows and all seemed intact. Nor could I smell anything bad coming out from around the seam of a window pane. I turned to her and shrugged. "Looks okay."

"Can you call them anyway?"

"I will."

I took a few breaths. "So, I can't really show you my fashionable bachelor pad."

"Can I help?"

"Just stay here. No point both of us smelling like hell."

I went back inside, while I had the momentum. I looked around much as I could stand. The TV and stereo were busted up but still there. Ditto my laptop, CDs and so on. I didn't get the impression anything had been stolen. Books and the files on my desk were strewn about. Everything in the place was a write-off.

I opened every window I could and turned on the fans. I left the air conditioner off, since it might just make things worse even if it still worked. I was going to have to think of a good story for the Beckers.

I was on my way out when Elle came through the door. "Just a quick drive-through," she said, dodging me when I tried to stop her. I went on out. Had to.

Two minutes later, if that, she'd had enough. She hobbled to the edge of the garden, bent over, and threw up.

"I'm usually cleaner," I said when she sat next to me. I must have smelled pretty bad because even through her own vomit-breath, she got up right away and moved off.

"Can we go back to Boots's? We need the shower."

"I shouldn't have come."

"You had to." She sniffed at her clothes, made a face. Then her head shot up. "Damn. I wonder what my house in Tuscaloosa smells like by now."

I tried smelling my shirt but it was beyond acrid. "That was before it really got going, you know?"

"Before you shot the help."

"Yeah. Before that."

I stood up. I hated to go back in but I needed to wedge the kitchen door shut. Not that I was really worried about burglars. But no need to leave it wide open, either. I locked the front door behind me when I was finished.

As we were leaving, I checked the street door to Art's place and it hadn't been broken into, either. I used his new garden hose, neatly coiled on a yellow hanger near the gate, to wash off my face and hands. Elle did the same. It helped.

Going back across town, I took Claiborne north of the Quarter. Traffic moved pretty fast, although it also seemed to take forever. We kept the windows down and the A/C on full blast.

Props to Trey for a hell of a statement.

In a way I was glad. The unreality of what we were doing had become an atmosphere around us, blocking out time, history, everything but some imperative to move forward into whatever it was that we were supposed to do. Find a painting. Deliver it. We were living as if nothing else existed. Or ever would.

I didn't tell her, but each whiff of death and decay that lifted off my clothes and hair as the wind whipped through the open windows was like a summons. The crack that had opened up grew wider, deeper. Demons spoke like angels. A discourse of revenge.

We got to Boots's, who still wasn't home. I got a suitcase with some of our clothes from the Taurus's trunk and carried it inside. We disrobed and put our clothes in a trash bag. We took turns in the shower. It was too unappealing to wash off the filth together, but not enough to keep us from lying in bed afterward for an hour, listening to the radio, barely talking, and then doing what naked people trying not to think about things might do in a similar circumstance. Late afternoon shadows had started to set in when Elle rose, put on black slacks and a classically embroidered, Chinese-style tunic, her black slippers. I had one last pair of clean jeans, and a gray and blue camp shirt.

It was my turn to make a phone call.

25

"Say what? Hell, I'm over here in Biloxi. How can I get there by nine?"

We were crossing town again, but now the congestion was bad and getting even worse. I didn't like doing the cell phone in that kind of traffic, but Big Red seemed to want the details again, so I had no choice but to talk it through. I had thought he would just want to know I was ready to deliver a day earlier than the deadline and be happy about it. I was wrong.

"I don't know what else to say. Like I said, Trey called us. Now I'm calling you."

"This very minute, he called." Red's gravelly voice in the receiver was so loud that Elle was able to follow both sides of the conversation if I held the phone just a little off my ear.

"Okay, last night."

I heard a mutter of curse words. In my mind, thinking of it phrased exactly that way as I listened, I thought, "murder of crows." It made me want to laugh. I didn't know why. I should have. I never did.

"I thought we might be able to take care of it. Then I knew we couldn't."

"So you can't put him off a day?"

"I tried. The number he left on our cell doesn't answer. So I can't reach him again."

"He'll call you. He likes to mindfuck."

"He does." I looked quickly at Elle. She rolled her eyes.

"I told you I was going fishing."

"You said on the weekend. This is only Friday."

"Plans change."

"Tell me about it."

"What I'm telling you is I need to figure out what we're gonna do about all this." Pause. "You definitely have the painting."

"Definitely. Shit." I hit a huge pothole on Tchoupitoulas and nearly dropped the phone.

"What?"

"Nothing. Traffic."

Pause. "You're taking it to exchange for, what was it, some damn aunt?"

"I'm leaving it where it is."

"Which is?"

"I'll take you there. I'll tell you everything I know about it."

Pause. "So what are you planning to do?"

"I'm going over there at nine tonight. What else can I do? It's her aunt."

"And you figure he'll let her go just because you show up."

"No. I figure there will be a problem. That's why I'm calling you."

Elle shook her head. I'm not sure whether at me or at Red.

"Is that a smartass thing, again?"

"I'm not giving him the painting and I am getting Lenora out of there. But there's just me and my friend. A little short on muscle."

"She with you now?"

"Of course." Elle waved silently, impatiently.

"Hang on," he said. Through the phone, I heard what sounded like the slapping of waves against a boat or dock. "Go ahead."

"Thing is, about the muscle. I don't know who Trey has partnered up with."

Exasperated breathing. Thudding noises. "Wait a second while I get this shit stowed. Fuck."

I thought about telling him about what Trey did to my apartment, but didn't.

"Jesus, I stink of fish. I gotta go to the casino and clean up."

"So you're coming?"

"If he's trying to cut me out . . . that wouldn't work out copacetic. For him."

"No." I could see it in Elle's face, too. "By the way, that painting. It's really something. You a religious man?"

"What?"

"No. I mean it's got something about it."

"So you're an art critic and also a writer."

Elle put her fingers up to her lips, as if to tell me to just leave it.

"I just mean somebody's going to want pay a lot to get it back."

"Not your problem."

"Okay."

"So I'll be there. I figured it would all come back to the city. Just not so soon."

"I sort of figured you thought that."

"It started there. It ends there."

"Let's say things go bad."

"Yeah?"

"You have to get the painting from Trey."

"I 'have to'?"

"I mean that's what I would hope. If something goes bad."

"Son, it's already pretty bad, wouldn't you say?"

I put on the brakes hard coming to Canal. It was green my way but a dozen conventioneers wearing name tags and walking like they'd already gotten shit-faced were crossing the street, oblivious. God bless 'em, I guess.

"But if it all works out, you get the painting, we're clear?"

"We've been over that."

"Okay."

"Son?"

"Yeah."

"What exactly do you have in mind?"

"I have in mind blowing his fucking head off."

Much laughter. Not from Elle. "Hell, I might have a beer with you yet."

"We'll have to wait until my jaw is better."

Pause. "Right." Pause. "Isn't there something you want to tell me?"

I got across Canal and turned up to pick up St. Peter and on to Decatur again. I looked at Elle to see if she knew what he meant. "No. I mean all I know is we're to be there at nine."

"What I'm saying."

"What?"

"Where, Shakespeare, where? You wanna give me some kind of LZ coordinates?"

I CAN'T SAY I had much of an appetite but we had to do something other than drive around drive around until we heard back from Trey. Dooky Chase for some of Leah Chase's fried chicken would've been perfect, but nothing was perfect and we didn't have the time. Anyway, I had to keep on my ball cap on and shades, so we needed a bar, but not one were I was a regular. And definitely not Rio Blanche.

We settled on a little Thai place at the edge of the Quarter. The main attraction was that it was dark. I ordered chicken pad thai and a beer. Elle asked for the vegetarian version. We picked at the food. I forced myself to get a little protein down although I kept thinking of cats in ovens. We lingered as long as we could, had sweet filtered coffee for dessert. It gave us exactly the buzz we needed.

Afterwards, we walked up to Frenchmen toward the neighborhood park where I'd left the Taurus. The early evening crowd was starting to fill the clubs. The tropical depression that had been pushing in was beginning to dump itself onto the city in a light but steady rain that likely would continue at least a couple of days.

"Worse case scenario, we give up the painting for Lenora," she said, when we got to the car.

"Worst case."

"Best case?"

"Best case we get her and give up nothing."

She pulled me to her, kissed me, pushed me away.

"That first day, you wanted me, right over there on Elysian Fields."

"The first minute."

She pulled me back tight against her, kissed me again. Then the ribs spoke up.

"Sorry." She released the pressure.

"It's okay. In an hour we'll be done with him."

She stared at me with that look from another universe.

"You know what I want."

"I know."

"You don't want the same thing? You just said you'd blow his fucking head off. Unquote."

"If it comes to that."

"At least I admit it."

I opened her door and went around to my side of the car.

WE HEADED UP ELYSIAN Fields toward the moneyed neighborhood fronting Lake Pontchartrain. She'd gotten the call a little before eight. I passed the LZ on to Big Red right away. He wasn't any happier than when I'd told him we had to wait on Trey to give us the location. At least this time he didn't hang up after calling me "the dumbest motherfucker in motherfucking history."

I wasn't familiar with the address Trey had given her, but I knew it had to be a big place. Just before Robert E. Lee and the UNO campus, I turned left. Then a couple of blocks and then left again and after a few more streets a right and there it was: a big, sand-colored ranch-style on a corner lot, with a shingled roof that even in the dark called out for repair. A garage, similar architecture, toward the back. The lot was filled with moss-draped oaks, and also a poorly trimmed line of shrubs along the front. It wasn't on the water, although it was easy enough to smell and hear the lake.

I noticed a yard sign in front for a local constable race. The neighboring houses were of similar design, either that or a two-story, faux-plantation style. Nouveau riche, professional bourgeoisie, and oldish money crammed together as if they fit. The house was dark. It didn't seem right.

I parked across the street along a stretch of lawn from a two-story brick imitation colonial. We both looked through the rain-spotted windows for signs that anyone was there. Only one light was on, in the rear, the kind that draws more burglars than it deters, but I figured in this neighborhood anybody with any sense had an alarm system.

A couple of cars came by, big SUVs no doubt from the neighborhood. Elle looked at her watch. It was 9:05.

"You sure this is it?"

"11067. I'm sure."

"What do you think?"

"I think nobody's home."

"Yeah."

"The fuck is he doing?"

She looked at the house. "I wonder if he even has Lenora."

A bad thought came to me. I put the car in drive and moved away, toward the lake.

"What are you doing?"

"Is anything behind us?"

She looked around. "No."

"I don't see anything either."

I followed Lakeshore upriver toward Canal. The waves were getting whipped up, but looking out at water made me feel calmer. But I wanted to get back on a big street.

"You think it was a set-up."

I made a quick check of the mirror. No one was tailing us. "I'm thinking."

She moved restlessly in her seat. "Where do we go?"

"I'm just driving."

"Maybe we should go by the house again? Just to be sure?"

I slowed for a homeless guy with a shopping cart shuffling across the street.

"I don't think we give them another chance."

"It was definitely the right place?"

"It was the right place. I'm positive. You took the address."

"I'm just asking."

I kept driving. I cracked my window for fresh air from the rain. Elle did the same. The pre-storm breeze felt good. Then she pulled her cell phone from her bag. She pressed call-back. "It still just keeps ringing."

"It's a throwaway."

She clicked off.

"You have a number from Oxford?"

"I can try information."

The listing she got was for an office, Barnett Properties. She rang, got a machine, clicked off.

I was more or less headed up Uptown, and decided just to keep meandering that way. Looking all the while for black Volvos with Mississippi tags. Or blue Suburbans.

We had just gotten to Canal when her phone rang.

I could only hear her side of it:

"What the fuck, Trey? . . . Why? . . . You're joking . . . Okay, Okay . . .

Shut up. Don't ever say that again . . . As soon as we can. Twenty minutes. Maybe less . . . Yes. Of course we do. What about Lenora? . . . She'd better be . . . Say the address again . . ."

She turned to me. "Julia Street, just down from Magazine. It doesn't have a number on the front. Delta Gallery. How original." Then she looked away, focused on the voice in her ear. "Whatever, Trey. Okay." She clicked off.

I took a left. "He changed the location. Classic."

She slammed the phone back into her bag. "Prick. Called me his big sister again."

Driving, I used my own cell to try calling Big Red about the location switch but I got a busy signal. I followed Canal to the edge of the Quarter and hooked a right on Magazine. I tried Big Red again. Still busy. No way I was going to leave a message. I couldn't believe he didn't have call waiting.

The closer we got to Julia Street, the main drag of the Arts District, the more cars. And pedestrians, despite the light rain. They weren't touristy-looking, in the sense that they weren't dressed that way. Most of them were coming in and out of crowded doors here and there. We looked at each other, getting it at the same time.

"Jesus, it's a gallery night."

26

We found a place to park on a side street, waiting longer than need be for an older couple and their friends to open the doors to their burnt gold Mercedes, drop their drink cups in the gutter, blah blah blah—all so they wouldn't have to appear to be hurried into giving up their prime space to another car. It just gave me another thing to be pissed off about and I was glad.

Elle walked up the sidewalk, pausing next to a meter as a group of Uptown swells walked by, talking about an upcoming LSU football game. I locked the car and went back to the trunk. I rummaged through my duffel until I found the Colt. More stopping power than the Glock and it was going to be close quarters. Looking around to check for more passersby, I tucked it in the back of my jeans, under my shirt. The metal was cold against my skin. I caught up to her. Neither of us had an umbrella.

We passed isolated packs of the arts crowd as we got closer to Trey's gallery, which was about two blocks upriver of Julia, toward the convention center. She gave me her cell and I made another call for Red. This time it rang and then a beep came on, no greeting message. It made me wonder who might be listening. I still didn't want to leave a message but just in case it would do any good I just said it was Shakespeare and we'd moved to an art gallery, near Julia. I figured he'd know which one. I said to call me right away.

It wasn't one of the really big nights, like White Linen in August, when the entire district is filled with locals who want to see and be seen. Most actually do come in some sort of white outfits. They cruise the galleries and museums and line up for the etouffée and wine served under the white tents on the blocked-off streets. You had to love this city. It was rent by a horrendous caste system and locked into poverty, about to disappear any given year under a direct hit from the Caribbean. But it was open, not closed to itself, tolerant of all manner of eccentricity, and dedicated to at least the pursuit of happiness regardless of the odds. Which of course was another of its liabilities. It could have people like Trey Barnett right under its skin posturing in white linen and opening an art business. While on one hand it was good that it didn't matter what went on inside anyone's storefront, on the other hand it did. On the other hand what was going on right now mattered a lot.

We walked on.

"If she's hurt—"

"She'll be okay."

"You don't know that."

"No. But it wouldn't be good business to do her harm."

She gave me a sidelong glance.

"You know what I mean."

We stopped at the corner. I still couldn't see a sign for Trey's gallery. It was on an off-street, also home to ordinary business offices and a bar, its neon light fuzzy in the rain. Another block farther was a small pedestrian boulevard catering mostly to the convention center and casinos.

"So we go in, we get Lenora, we give up the painting," she said. "That's it."

"What choice is there?"

Her eyes flashed.

I took her arm. "What?"

She shook me off immediately.

"And your mob buddy?"

I wiped rain drops from my face. "Red?"

"What's he gonna do?"

"He didn't say."

"You know what I mean."

I could feel my head tightening. "Leave all that to Red."

"If he even shows."

"He will."

I pulled out my own cell and punched in Red's number. My eyes locked on hers. I got a busy signal. She flinched in the stare-off.

"I don't know," I said, clicking off, looking down the sidewalk. "You want to wait?"

"No."

"Me neither."

We crossed the street.

"So. We get her. We leave. Then what?" she asked.

"I haven't worked that part out."

"Me neither."

"We should just stick to the plan." I tried for a reassuring tone. "We have to."

"I know."

"The priority is to get out with Lenora. Just keep saying that."

"Jesus, Jack."

I stopped again. I didn't have to take her arm. She turned her body right into mine.

"We'll get through this," I said. "We have something he wants more than your aunt."

"I know that." She flipped her head to throw off a sheen of rainwater.

"Red has a very big interest in this. He's not going to leave it hanging."

"I wish I had that faith."

"Me, too."

I thought I saw her expression settle, what we used to call a battle face.

"Are you ready?"

"I was born ready."

"It will be like back in Mississippi."

She touched my face. I don't know why. "It's all been like Mississippi, Jack, hasn't it?"

TWO DOORS FROM TREY'S gallery we saw the lights from the windows and the oversized glass door. I was trying to think if I'd seen the place before. Like most of the buildings in this one-time skid row district, it had been refurbished. The bricks were either new or steam-blasted, and the deep blue trim around the door and front window repainted with care. The only sign, Delta Gallery, was stenciled in black deco letters near the edge of the window. Très artsy.

On the door was a more temporary white sign with carefully hand-inscribed block letters: "Sneak preview tonight: 7–9 only." When we got closer we could see a small table inside covered with plastic cups, a couple of liter-sized bottles of wine, and a plate of picked-over cheese and crackers. The exhibit room behind it was empty, except for the white walls on which rows of small watercolors in stainless steel frames, all about nineteen or twenty inches diagonal, the size of a TV screen, were precisely arranged.

"Unbelievable. He invited us to an opening." Her mouth crinkled in contempt.

I tried to size up as much of the set-up as I could. But within fifteen seconds a door at the far end of the viewing room opened.

As if on cue, he emerged and walked toward us, a big smile on his tan face. Like Elle, Trey was dressed all in black—in his case an expensive silk shirt and matching slacks, slick Italian shoes. He opened the door to greet us with the same flourish of his strut across the gallery floor: directly, grandly, even, as though we had come to buy his entire inventory. Which maybe we had.

"Welcome to the Delta," he said. No doubt he'd named the gallery that way so he could say just that to the prospective patrons. "Come on in."

Elle looked at him hard. I nodded in greeting, I don't even know why. Elle walked directly to the center of the empty room. I followed, making a quick check of the surroundings and the possible exits. Only two. One at the back and the other through which we had just come.

I heard the lock on the front door click. I turned to see Trey pull the sign from the window, and walk to a panel on the corner wall to enter a digital code. An elaborately rigged set of blinds moved in from each side of the display window and then folded shut, a separate system for the door. The outside world was sealed away.

"We had a decent turnout, even with the weather. But you know, kind of serendipitous in a way, raising money for storm victims and all that."

He came up to Elle, who had turned to watch her flesh and blood— and murderer of her brother. He glided down the walls, looking at the art, perfectly highlighted by the track lighting on the ceiling. The layout alone must have cost him a bundle. Each piece was titled the same: "Red Gator," with subtitle written in elegant cursive just below.

The one nearest me was "Red Gator: Oxford '65." In it, a large alligator with a surreal glint in its jet-black eyes, done up photorealist, was sprawled at the front gate of the Ole Miss campus, which was tiny and ugly and out-of-scale. The gator had inhaled an angry-looking Governor George Wallace all the way to the waist. He was holding a sign that said, "States' Rights!"

Just to its right, "Red Gator: Sand Dooms," showed the title creature on a Gulf Coast beach on a blanket, facing the water. On one side was a black man in a green swimsuit and on the other a blond woman in a white bikini. All three were holding hands, or claws.

I didn't want to look at the art, that not being the purpose of the visit, but, as I may have mentioned, I have a propensity to dissociate in times of life-threatening stress. Ergo, I had to admit the show wasn't bad.

"You like them?"

"Not bad. Glad you had time for painting. You know, between gutting innocent animals and baking them in my apartment."

"You have such bad taste, what did it hurt?"

I took a half-step and he moved back, more like a boxer than someone afraid. I could have pulled out the Colt but we hadn't seen Lenora.

He shrugged, that baiting kind of smile guys give to each other just before they try to take each other's head off. I returned the expression.

I saw Elle looking toward the back of the room at the rear exit, a closed double door. Trey could tell what we were thinking. But for him, the game was just beginning.

"Elle? What about you? You like this work?"

"Where's my aunt?"

Trey mockingly smashed his fist against his heart. "The worst criticism of all. To be ignored." He waited a beat. "And by family."

I moved next to Elle, keeping everything in my peripheral vision.

He came closer, looking at her, smiling. "So, you really didn't notice?"

"What?"

"The artist."

"I don't care whose stuff you're pimping."

"But darlin', darlin', you do. You really do."

She turned her back to him, moving to the double door. "Where's my aunt?"

He followed her until she stopped. She turned to look at him and he spread his arms as though making a sweep of the room for a visiting audience of nobles.

It was all between them. He had lost interest in me, other than a perceptive regard for whether I would try to kill him.

"Why, darlin', can't you see? These are all mine. It's my debut into the art world as one of its own. An artist, not just a businessman." He walked up to a row of the works. "I call it the Red Gator series. See? Gators. Red. It's going to be a big hit, big sister. Blue dogs gonna kiss my Mississippi ass."

He was beaming with pride. I wondered if it would be reviewed in any of the arts papers. I was actually thinking of journalist questions. I needed to start thinking of questions from my other previous life, the one where you got into situations where people shot at each other.

Elle glanced at one of the watercolors. I don't know what she was thinking but it could have been that they were political in a way not to have been expected from a guy like Trey. But then that was the South in America, wasn't it? Hardly anything made sense straight on.

"Why do you think I changed the meeting place to bring you down here? A lot more interesting than an old dope house up by the lake, wouldn't you agree?"

Cold-blooded and bound for hell that he was, he really did want Elle's approval. The vulnerability in his expression only lasted a second, but it was there. I could feel something zing between the two of them to which I could never be a party. Not just the kinship. Maybe not even the childhood days before everything went bad. Something else. It was like being present in a room with a huge and violent storm that you could feel but not see, not even explain.

Then Trey's eyes went hard again, and when I glanced at Elle, I could see nothing in her face that resembled kindness, let alone aesthetic appreciation.

"It figures you'd be into reptiles." She stepped up to the closest watercolor, "Red Gator: Delta Blues," showing the alligator in a chain gang. She cocked her head, pursed her lips as if considering the aesthetics, then spat directly onto it. She backed off, looked at it again. "It just needed that detail."

Trey crossed his arms on his chest, gave me a quick once-over, and looked at her a long time. Then he smacked his mouth open and shut, like a swamp creature.

Elle stepped off hard toward the double door. When she got to it she stopped. She stared at it as though it would open of its own volition. She was like Moses at the Red Sea, waiting for the consciousness of God to catch up.

"Open this now."

"Why, sister, that's just the delivery and prep area."

"I know what it is."

"Why so anxious? Everything's going to work out just fine." He walked slowly toward her. So did I.

Elle twisted the door handle but it was locked.

Trey stopped a few feet to her right side, clicked his tongue. I was close enough to touch her, or to take him out with a hard kick, like the one Red had given me. It got very quiet, then Trey pivoted around on one heel of his Italian shoes and ambled back to the wine and snack table.

"Wait," I said to her under my breath.

We both watched Trey pour himself a plastic cup of the house white. He raised the cup in a toasting gesture, drank it in a single swallow. He made a slight face, set it down. "This stuff isn't bad but not really my personal favorite."

Then he came back to us. As he did, I heard voices from behind the closed door. So did Elle. I adjusted my stance again anticipating the need to hit something. It occurred to me I'd actually been doing that from the moment we had spotted the gallery.

"As requested," Trey said, and took a key from his pocket. He looked at it and then at Elle. I thought he was going to stroke her hair but seemed more to regard her with a fascination from over the decades. "When we go in, you need to think about what you want out of this and how you're going to help. And by the way, I don't see any large container with an obscure Spanish oil painting in your possession." He clicked his tongue again. "But then I probably wouldn't have brought it, either."

He put the key in the lock, twisted it, and then paused. "But on the other hand I did bring what I promised."

He pushed the doors open to a long, rectangular storage room crammed on each side with double-decker shelves full of frames and boxes and the various tools of the trade. A couple of cluttered work benches were pushed together at the back, next to another door, probably leading to the alley. A tiny closet with toilet and sink were just inside the entryway, to the left.

I stepped in ahead of Elle and Trey. Two guys were at the back, by the tables. One, with a goatee, was leaning on a wooden cane, pants bagged out like they might be concealing bandages. That would be Reggie. The other was a skinny, youngish kid with unkempt straw-colored hair and a purple and green "Biloxi Rocks" T-shirt.

Then there was Lenora. Elle spotted her at the same time. I heard a small, suppressed gasp as she spun toward Trey and shot him a look beyond mortal rage. In the next second she was running to her aunt.

I'd seen a lot of things I wish I hadn't in the course of my careers. What people could do to each other had long ago settled into that crack in my head, or soul, that started reopening yesterday. This would lodge in there pretty well.

They had suspended Lenora from a support beam at the far left corner of the room. Her hands were bound up above her head, a gag made of gray tape lashed across her mouth. She was completely naked. She might as well have been crucified.

Elle looked around in a panic for something to cover Lenora's almost limp body, cursing at Trey as though each epithet were a hollow-point bullet.

I spotted a folded white drop cloth about the size of a bed sheet on one of the shelves, grabbed it, and took it to her. Nobody stopped us. More like they found it amusing.

"Lenora, Auntie Lenora, are you all right?"

Lenora seemed to bring her mind back from someplace far away. Tears streamed down her cheeks. I had the feeling it was for the first time since Trey had kidnapped her.

Elle pulled off the tape. Lenora gasped, taking in fresh breath. Then Elle draped the drop cloth around the small, trembling body as best she could. "Cut her down right now you sick piece of shit."

"We'll have a little talk first, I think."

Elle started toward Trey until the kid grabbed her. I moved toward him but Reggie limped forward much faster than I would have thought, intercepting me. He raised a Beretta to my head. "Give me a fucking excuse."

I stopped. After a moment, Elle stopped fighting against the kid.

Trey looked at us like trapped animals. Which we were. Which can lead to multiple outcomes. "Nobody's going to hurt you if you stay calm. Like I said."

Elle pushed again against the kid's hold. "Take her down. Let us go."

Trey laughed. "Sounds like the old days playing down by the river."

We stayed in position for a moment, some evil piece of choreography. Then came a faint but resolute voice: "I'm okay, child. I'm okay."

Elle stopped struggling, but in the same moment she noticed, for the first time, that the top joints of the middle two fingers on Lenora's left hand were missing, caked over with dried blood. I guess the overall shock impact of Lenora's condition had blocked the details. Elle's face seemed to dissolve in horror.

"I see it," I said. "But the bleeding's stopped. There's nothing to do right now—"

"No shit." The words were still in Reggie's mouth when I felt a blinding slash across the back of my head. I stumbled forward a couple of steps, but regained my balance. All I could see were flashes and pinprick sparkles. "That's a start," he elaborated. "Looks like you've already had a little pay-back, though."

I turned to look at him, best I could. His face was twisted in hatred and gloating. A few scabs from stray No. 5 pellets. I could see his cane leaning against the wall.

"But not nearly as much as you're gonna be getting." He bitch-slapped me across my nose with the back of his hand.

More sparkles. It was getting hard to just stand straight. I thought about going for the pistol but it would be suicide. Mostly I hoped they didn't see its outline under my shirt. They hadn't even frisked me. Maybe I should have told Trey he needed to improve the quality of his help.

"I promised Reggie a free one," Trey said, coming up to me. He took my face in his hand, not gently. I could see him trying to look into my eyes. Then he let me go and moved back.

"Let's just keep this confined to them," he said to Elle.

She had broken free of the kid, or maybe he just let her go. She tried to steady me. "Why?" she yelled at him.

"I'm okay," I told her, straightening up into the pain.

He grinned at her, ignoring me. "Got you here, didn't it?" He gestured toward Lenora. "She was always kind of a bitch to me anyway, wouldn't you agree? Put the fear of god—or at least those gods of hers—in me every time I was around her. Hell of a nice body for an old broad, though. Guess it runs in the family."

"I'm okay," Lenora said again. "It's okay. . ."

I nodded for Elle to attend her aunt. She did, pulling up a table for Lenora to sag against and take the weight off her upstretched arms.

Trey smiled. A small, twisted-up kind. It was eating him alive at the same time it gave him pleasure.

"Mary washes the feet of Jesus," he said, in the tone of a pompous art lecturer.

"Go to hell."

"He will, child." That was Lenora.

Trey dropped to one knee, perusing them as though studying a mildly interesting nature trail. "You're both so terrifying. Considering."

Elle was trying to get a good look at the fingers. I knew she was trying to be professional, from her medical training. "All this," she said to Trey as she tried to comfort Lenora. "All this. You really thought we were hiding that damn painting?"

"Well, yes, come to think of it."

"You still do?"

"I've become more enlightened. Still, I knew you wouldn't let Big Red down." He stood, sniffed and wiped his nose, walked away a few paces, seemingly lost in a thought. It was like time meant nothing anymore, here, in this place.

My mind began to clear again. I rubbed the knot on the back of my skull. There was a little scalp blood but mostly just another bruise. I was going to look like an eggplant again. As if it would matter. "You plan on taking it, then?" I asked him.

"I think that's why we're all here, no?"

"He said you weren't to get it. That I was to give it to him. Period."

"Thanks for reminding me. By the way, not to get to business in a rush, but you do have my Echave, don't you? I mean, this would all be so boring otherwise."

"Why did you have to do that to her?" Elle said, as if repeating the question would bring a better answer.

"It was kind of a waste. She didn't have a clue where that little whore of a nephew of hers had put it, in the end."

"But you thought we would know?" I asked.

"I knew he had told something to Elle that she would figure out. Given some incentive. I mean, she's my blood, right?"

Elle ignored it, rearranged the cloth a little more, about the only thing she could do. In the process, she leaned in and Lenora whispered something in her ear. Elle's face drained. Then it went deep crimson, and finally she pulled back as if electrocuted. She tried to hide her expression but it lit her up like molten lava.

"Do share," Trey said, coming up close to her again. "So everyone will know what a couple of fingers were worth."

27

From a physical standpoint, she was only a woman in her sixties, and she had been alone, stripped of everything, no thought of rescue or hope. Maimed by a man whose lifelong fear of her apparently had been transcended. Yet even in her torment and despair she had fought back in the only way she could. The same way I imagined Terrell had, in those last hours, those last few minutes, that final second as Trey smashed in the back of his head. Whatever she had given up, it had been a feint, a strategic ploy. Trey never got from her, any more than he had from Terrell, what he really wanted.

At least that's how I came to think about the ensuing half hour in the gallery, after Lenora had whispered to Elle the secret that, once released, made everything fit together at the same time it was exploding all our lives apart.

Recoiling from Lenora's revelation, Elle tried to steady herself against the wall. She scratched out in the air in Trey's direction with one hand but it was like a nerve twitch from a corpse. In the next moment, her legs buckled and she sank to the floor, slumping against the wall like a rag doll spat out by a Rottweiller.

I took a step toward her, but I was off-balance and Reggie had managed to get close again and pin my left arm behind me. Now his Beretta was pressed into my cheek.

"What the hell, big sister, you didn't even know Rose was alive."

I had never seen news delivered with such enthusiasm and sadistic glee, and I had once made my living among practitioners of the art.

"Go to hell . . ." Her voice broke off, something that couldn't rise from the bottom of a dank well.

"The fuck do you care anymore? It's not like you were much of a mom."

"I'm sorry," Lenora moaned. "I'm so sorry."

"It's okay," Elle managed. Then, flatly, evenly, "It's nothing."

Trey laughed. "Nothing?"

"It has . . . nothing . . . to do with this." Stronger with each word.

I started thinking about the best way to slap the gun away from Reggie and grab the Colt. Except that would leave Elle and Lenora vulnerable.

"I think it has a lot to do with it. But hell, don't let me be the judge. Share. You know. Your darlin' daughter. Tell us all about her. Tell all of us about Rose. Tell your boyfriend here."

Elle looked up toward me.

"Don't," I said.

"Shut up." Reggie tapped the muzzle against my nose. I tried not to show the sharp zing of pain.

"Leave him alone." Elle raised herself to her feet slowly, finding support from the wall. She leaned there more than a minute. Nobody said anything.

"I'm so sorry," Lenora said again, and began singing softly, some kind of hymn.

"Rose is my daughter," Elle finally said, each word a discrete agony. Her eyes tried to convey added meaning. Same as when she'd had to tell me Trey was her brother. All I could do was hope my eyes spoke in kind.

Trey relaxed against one of the wall shelves. Hard to say what had happened to his face. It was arrogant, and smug, but more than that.

The kid, Ernie, was sitting on one of the tables, watching everything with a cheap grifter smirk I was more than eager to erase.

"I haven't seen her since she was born." Elle cleared her throat, choking down any hint of suffering.

"It was fifteen years ago. I was in college. We all were." She paused. Her jaw muscles twitched. Lenora continued singing, the words in a melody too slurred to understand. She had checked out.

"It was the holidays," Elle said, looking at me, more erect now, hands pressed against the wall, maybe digging into it with her fingers. "We had all come back home and decided to get together, talk about getting away to college, that kind of thing. First couple of days it was okay, but you know, we had changed a little. Trey, especially."

He smiled, crossed his arms.

"He was drinking a lot and had started in on coke, although back then it didn't seem like what it got to be." She stopped for a moment and looked at Lenora, as though she had just remembered she was in the room. She knelt to pick up the drop cloth that had fallen off her aunt's naked shoulders and draped it around her again. Lenora smiled and continued to sing.

"You don't have to say anything," I said, before Reggie slapped the muzzle against my ear.

"Stop it," she said to Reggie, with that same authority she'd used on the redneck on the river trail back in Rosedale. Then, to me: "I'm going to. Tell it. I'm going to now."

Trey clapped, watching her. "Bravo, big sister. Sweetheart. Whatever. Get it all out. This is soooo arts district."

"Shut up."

He zipped his finger across his mouth. In that instant, I knew what I would do to him. I didn't know how I would get there, but I knew. Reggie wouldn't make it, either.

"So one night Trey wanted to drive over to Clarksdale to hear some music and we all went, the three of us. We heard some of the local guys in a little place downtown. It wasn't built up like it is now for the tourists. It was pretty rough."

She stood next to Lenora, stroked her cheek, smiled at her and turned to face the rest of us full on.

"It got to be late and we'd all had too much to drink. Young Henry said he'd met someone and was going with him and would get a ride home and for us not to worry about it. It seemed okay, and then Trey and I went outside, down toward the river and railroad tracks back of town. Trey's mood went funky the more we walked on. I think he was pissed at my brother."

He made a face of mock indignation.

It fueled her. I could see the power of her wrath course back into her body.

"So we were behind this warehouse building and the moon was almost full, and it was getting cold. I said we needed to get back but neither one of us were in much shape to drive so we decided to get a room at a little motel up on 61. Remember it, Trey? The Dixie Inn?"

He feigned a yawn, looked at his watch. "You're telling the story. Tell it how you want."

She took a step toward him. Ernie jumped up, ready to do whatever he was commanded.

"Make my day," Reggie hissed in my ear, pulling my left arm up a little higher.

Elle checked her impulse and stayed put. I could see in her eyes that she wouldn't for much longer. I wouldn't, either.

"So we had gotten double beds, one for each of us, and we went in and it seemed like it was just the end to the night. I'd just come out of the bathroom and was ready to crawl in my bed when he got other ideas."

I could feel Reggie's ugly breath against my ear. "Don't cry," he said. "You'll get over it real soon."

Elle glared at Reggie to shut him up again, then back at Trey. It worked. Even Lenora had stopped her singing and seemed to be conscious again of everything around her.

"So basically he ripped off my clothes and smacked me around a couple of times and he raped me." She was looking at nobody but Trey. "The worst. The worst . . . he said he loved me."

I don't know what was passing between their eyes. It sucked the energy out of everything else in the room.

"And then I passed out and I think he did, too. We woke up in the morning and he acted like nothing had happened. I guess I did, too. I just wanted to get home and I had nothing to say. No one to tell it to. We'd gone away, got drunk stayed in a motel. Who'd believe me? A black girl's word against the rich white boy? We left before lunch."

Trey sniffed, wiped his nose again. I realized he'd been doing coke before we got there.

"But the real news came about a month later. I thought about an abortion, but I couldn't."

Her eyes went down a long moment. She looked at me and I knew it was just to know that I was there. Then back to him. His face was blank, as if he wasn't sure how it was affecting him, hearing it.

"I dropped out of school for a semester. I moved in with Lenora in Jackson. Even my mom and dad didn't know where I was. I sent them letters from other places and told them I was working a semester with some friends. I had the baby a month early. We named her Rose."

At that her voice started to break. "The nurses took her and the adoption people came and that was the last I ever saw of her." A long pause. "I was so worried there might be something wrong."

She took another step toward Trey. "But she's fine. I guess that especially means something to you. Now."

Then she was on him. But he caught her right arm as it swung toward him in an roundhouse arc. Then he seized her left. He twisted both until her face showed the pain.

Reggie wrenched up my arm and put the muzzle against my throat. "Like I said. A fucking excuse." In doing so, he almost lost his balance with the bum leg. I almost went for him, but checked myself to see what Trey would do. Something was still missing.

His face glowered, inches from hers. "You want to blame someone, talk to your aunt over there. She knew about us all the time. Why you think she took you in like that, with the baby? You think she wasn't ready to deal with things if some little incest monster came out of your pussy?"

"Shut up." Her body struggled but he was stronger than he looked.

"Ask her."

Elle got one arm free but he grabbed it again.

Lenora tried to straighten up. If there were any way another ounce of misery could show on her face, it made an appearance.

"Don't, auntie. You don't have to do anything he says."

"I just wanted to take care of you. Your momma and daddy couldn't know. They couldn't go through all that." Then she slumped until the pain in her arms forced her to stand again.

"Hell, they didn't have to, did they," Trey said. "Mine, neither. Dead people don't feel a damn thing. You think my daddy's plane crashed by accident? Hell, he knew what had come up from all this."

"What?"

"His lawyer found out. Told him the whole deal about our little Rose. He was really quite ill about it." He paused. "Beat the hell out of me. Actually he didn't but some friends of his did, all the way out in Stanford. Hell of a deal. We never seemed to get real close after that."

"You're lying. Junior would never do that."

Trey let Elle's arms go. In the next moment he backhanded her so hard across her face she reeled almost to the shelves.

With that, Ernie was across the floor and behind me—quick little shit—holding my other arm, pinning me between him and Reggie. I didn't move. If I struggled and they found the Colt, we had no chance. But the math was still bad. Even discounting Lenora, Trey would be one on one with Elle. One of the hardest things to teach a soldier is to stand your ground even when you're getting pummeled, and wait for the right moment. Because the wrong moment favors the enemy. It gets you killed.

"Just a little taste of what your beloved Junior could do," Trey snarled. "Trust me, sister, you never got to see the pugilist side of your dear old daddy. Me and mom did."

Elle regained her balance, legs apart, glaring, her hand on the red splotch on her cheek.

"Anyway, Jack, my old friend, she seems to have lost the thread of this little saga. Ernie, watch her."

He obeyed and went to stand next to Elle in what I'm sure he felt was a pose of menace. Reggie decided to get a better angle on the gun and pushed the muzzle into my upper spine. I didn't know how much longer before he might realize I was armed.

"Sorry, got to watch you kids." Trey moved to the center of the room. I computed my vectors of attack. "Anyway, I'll cut to the chase and say that our little Rose went off to live with who knows who, who knows where.

But this little voudou queen of an aunt knew. Sure did. She had her hand in everything, one way or another, didn't you sweet?" He approached Lenora. Even in pain, her eyes had gone as hard as Elle's.

"You've gone down a bad way, Trey Barnett," Lenora said.

"Nice talk. Considering you're hanging naked inside my gallery."

Elle shifted her position and Ernie stood directly in front, as if to block her.

"So like I was saying, I was talking to dear Lenora here earlier tonight, in the back of a delivery van, touching up her manicure and so on."

Elle glared at him. "Shut up. Just shut up."

"Hey, baby sister, you told us your little tale. Thought you'd want to hear mine."

"I don't." But her glance to me said that she did.

He sniffed.

"He can't stop talking," I said. "White line fever."

I knew the blow was coming and didn't care. It came. But I managed to stand straight this time. What wasn't killing us was making both of us stronger.

"I mean," Trey said, winking at me, shark-grinning at her, "I want you to listen real close because at the end there'll be a quiz. It'll be like, 'What do I have to do to keep from flying up to heaven to see my faggot brother?'"

"Screw you."

"Done that."

She held.

"Turns out that to make the will work—for you, so you could rob me of my rightful inheritance—they would need an original birth certificate. Because otherwise who the hell would believe we're related?"

"We're not."

"Pay attention, now, son." It was Reggie, that bad breath again.

"I know, culturally and all that we're not, but of course by the iron laws of genetics it's a lock. Now, I did a little looking through a lawyer friend of my own. Thing is, that birth certificate isn't in the hospital records, or with the county, or anywhere at all that I know of."

He went back to Lenora, the coke trailing off, making him jittery. "But she does. Like I said, she had a hand in everything in that family."

Elle went to stand next to her aunt. Trey didn't stop her.

"I was helping Pearl," Lenora said.

"Well, be that as it may, you were messing me all up." He walked close to Elle. His words came out a coke-y combo of steely staccato and syrupy drawl. "And here's the kinkiest thing about it. Your brother, when he wasn't fucking everyone else and stealing paintings from me, he was going to find that birth certificate and get it to me for a cool hundred thou in cash. That was the deal. You know: we meet, he gives me the painting, all is forgiven on that, and then for a little extra change I get the birth certificate and you know, life goes on. Hell, you never even would've known."

"Nice plan," I interrupted. "So you killed him instead."

Trey waved one hand up to forestall Reggie's expected bitch slap, as if it wasn't worth the trouble. He came over to me, looked me over, shook his head, clicked his teeth.

"That's the fact, Jack. I shut him up. Right here, actually." His soul-dead blue eyes shifted away toward a pile of 4x4 wooden staves for making custom shipping boxes. "I mean, he took a swing at me, what was I gonna do?"

It was clear why she had stood her ground for this, letting him blather. She knew him. She knew he would eventually tell her what had happened. White line fever or not. She knew he would deliver unto her his confession. But she was going to make it into something else. She advanced on him and paused, a lioness waiting to spring.

"Had to, you know? I mean, you know, it bothered me. Old friend and all that. And anyway, little T-boy, well, he sort of double double-crossed me, didn't he? Didn't bring the painting or the freakin' birth certificate. Even bragged he was fucking with me the whole time."

She was an arm's distance from him. Their eyes were locked together. "You never could get the best of him."

"Well, maybe this very last time I did."

"You just killed him is all," Lenora called out, the drop cloth slipping off again.

"Fuck you. Some hoodoo lady you turned out to be."

"Fuck you," Elle said. "Why didn't you just ask me about it, any of it? I would've told you. You didn't need to do any of this."

He looked at her for a long time. "Bullshit."

"No bullshit, Trey. I never would have wanted anything to do with you, even for money."

He breathed out hard. Looked at her some more. "Well, too bad about that now," he finally said. "But turns out your aunt wouldn't tell me where the birth certificate is, either. So I said, what the hell, then I'd just have to whack Ellie. And here's the really good part."

He went to one of the work benches. Ernie came up to keep Elle in check. Trey opened a drawer, pulled out a small metal case and from it a small plastic baggie. He poured out a line of coke on the top of the bench, bent down and snorted it.

"Whee-yuh!" He put the stuff back in the drawer. "Whee-yuh doggies! You know? So anyway, when auntie here tells me where Rose was—that she's alive—she actually said that she was telling me because I ought to know. Because—this is the part I especially like—I wouldn't kill you. Since I wouldn't kill the mother of my own daughter. Can you believe? For thirty million and change?"

He twirled around, like a tango dancer, finishing with one arm in the air and the other across his chest. Held the pose.

Then he took a deep breath, threw his hands open in a dismissive gesture. He looked at his prisoner hanging on the ropes.

"But shit, Lenora, that just means now I probably have to take care of Rose, too."

Elle tried to get past Ernie, but he did a move I didn't think he had and slipped around to seize her from behind, pinning her arms again.

"I don't even know who's in there anymore," Elle said, ignoring Ernie's hold. "What happened to the boy I grew up with, the three of us playing together down in the Delta?"

"He grew up. Like you said."

"Everyone grows up."

He looked at her, opened his mouth as though to speak.

"Do it," she said to me.

Trey's head turned in my direction, quizzical.

Whatever he was about to say to her, he never got the chance.

Whatever my intention—to somehow grab my Colt and shoot Reggie and Ernie without harming Elle and hope that would buy me a few seconds to deal with Trey—I never got that chance, either. Good thing.

Trey's cell phone rang at the same time that a loud banging, like a hammering with a big air jack, came from the door at the front of the gallery.

I caught Elle's eye. The message was still to fire at will. But I didn't.

Trey looked at his caller ID, glanced at his two pals, and at me. His smile had more teeth than it really needed as he spoke into the receiver.

"Hello, Red."

"Trey, you bastard. We've been out here knocking for five minutes. What the fuck?"

The booming, pissed-off voice seemed to propel Ernie from the viewing gallery back into the storage room like a Cat 3 hurricane. Hard on his heels were my old pal, Big Red, and a wingman. The extra muscle was nearly as much a tank as Red, maybe a little thinner, easily over six feet. To Red's Hawaiian shirt outfit, he wore tan slacks and a dark purple shirt, shiny black Italian loafers. His hair was slicked back to Red's wild-in-the-city look, and with his mustache he looked vaguely like Magnum, P.I., New Jersey version.

Trey walked up to Red with an outstretched hand. "Welcome to the Delta."

Ernie made immediately for the back of the room. Reggie lowered his weapon and took a step back, but stayed within muzzle-slap distance of me. And vice versa.

Red and his backup ignored Trey, stopping in the middle of the room, pretty much as Elle and I had done, to take in the scene. As a frieze of modern life in the Big Easy, our little tableau had its place.

"God almighty," Red exhaled. The other guy shook his head, frowning.

"This is where we prep the material," Trey said, the hail-fellow-well-met arrogance in his voice hiding who knew what. "As you can see, we've been getting some new works delivered."

"The fuck is that?" Big Red snapped, staring at Lenora. "The fuck are you doing?"

"By the way, what the fuck are *you* doing here?" Trey answered. It must have been the coke talking because it was an insane thing to say.

Made even more obvious by the way Red glared at him.

"For god's sake cut that old lady down. Now. And put that piece away, Reggie. The fuck kind of cowboy are you?"

Reggie immediately lost his interest in me and turned toward Ernie. "You heard the man. Let her down."

Ernie started to comply but stopped, looking to Trey for the final okay.

"You got a problem with that?" Red snapped.

"What the hell, she probably needs to sit for a spell," Trey said, and nodded to Ernie, who had made the unforgivable error of mistaking exactly from whom he was supposed to take his orders.

"So as I was saying, welcome to the Delta," Trey continued. He walked forward and extended his hand to Big Red and friend. Neither responded. Trey shrugged.

"My name's Trey Barnett," he said to the friend, again extending his hand, again declined. "And you would be?"

"He would be Antonio. You can call him Tony the Barber. Most of his business acquaintances seem to favor that," Red said.

Tony the Barber nodded, a faint smile on his lips. He looked steadily at Trey, but I could see he was also aware of every move that Ernie and Reggie were making.

Elle and I both looked at each other with something between relief and fatalism.

Ernie pulled out a shiny lockback knife and cut the ropes that held up Lenora. Reggie went through the motions of helping her sit down to rest against the wall. When they were done, Elle covered her aunt once more with the drop cloth.

Red came up to me. "You get yourself in some shit, don't you, Shakespeare?"

"It's a gift."

He studied me, not in the manner of a rescuer. His voice sunk to a growl I had heard before. "So what the fuck is going on? You got something for me, bringing me all the way here?"

My impression was that he was really talking to Trey, whose body posture had lost all its theatricality.

"Like I said, this one over here called, said to come by here first."

"I know that already."

"He changed plans from the first meeting place. I tried to call you. A lot."

"Did you? I must of been busy." Big Red took a step closer to Trey, eyeing him like a piece of day-old fish.

"I left a message on your voicemail, too."

"Well, I'll have to check it sometime—hey, don't bunch up over there," he said to Reggie and Ernie, who had gathered in front of the work bench at the back of the room. They moved apart a few paces.

"Don't worry about the phone, though," he said, talking to me but watching them. "Turns out Tony was out there by the lake, saw you drive by. Followed you back down here."

I looked at Elle. She kissed her aunt on the forehead and rose to her feet again.

"Kind of a shitty thing to do, wouldn't you say, rich boy?" Red said.

I thought he was talking about Lenora. But he was more focused.

"What, you've never changed a meet at the last minute?" For the first time there was anxiety in Trey's voice, as though he were calculating that he hadn't calculated everything.

"So . . . the fucking painting?" Red, back to me.

"We have it. We just didn't bring it. You know." I stared at Trey, who ignored me.

"I definitely know," Red said.

Tony the Barber moved a little nearer to the back of the room, almost next to Ernie and Reggie.

"It's my painting. I was going to deliver it to you. It's my right."

"You were already told I was getting it from this schmuck." To me: "No offense. You got no business in this." Back to Trey: "You should of known that."

"I know I need to make sure I get credit for getting it for you."

"You calling me something?"

Trey shrugged. It was like he was trying to get control of the situation again. "I'm just saying that if I personally deliver it to my client, my client knows where it came from. It's just standard business." I still couldn't tell if he had balls or was just high.

Red looked at Lenora, at me, at Elle. "This is standard?"

"They have my painting. The one her fucking brother stole to get this all screwed up in the first place. All I have to do is go pick it up. Then you can have it."

"This is crap." It was Tony. First thing he'd said all night. His voice was low, smoky, like a DJ's.

"Yeah." Big Red turned, went to the side of the room, looked at a watercolor propped on one of the shelves that wasn't in the show. It was of a gator eating what looked like a Bible. "Interesting. Twisted, though. This your name in the corner?"

"Take it. It's a gift. 'Red Gator Taking Sacrament.'"

Red looked at Tony. A second later they both laughed. Then Red came back close to Trey. "So you have the million-dollar art, or what?"

"I was about to get it when you dropped by." Trey looked at me.

"What I thought," said Red. "I'm doing business with the wrong man."

"We only came for her," I said, pointing to Lenora.

Red looked at her again, sitting against the wall, then back to Trey. "About that. You want to tell me how you came to tie up and cut the fingers off an old black broad by way of getting me a painting you're not even supposed to have?"

"For all I knew, they'd be in Mexico and I'd still owe the Francosis a lot of money."

Red and Tony exchanged another look.

"If you think I went too far, fine." Trey grinned, tentatively. No one else joined him. "Whatever. It seemed the best way to get myself a little insurance." His voice dropped an octave and he looked directly at Red. "You know, I just want out from under this with the family. I was taking care of it."

"I can see that shit." Red looked at Tony again. "But back to the question. Where's the friggin' painting?"

"I'll show you," I put in.

"Fuck him," said Trey. "He's nothing."

"He's the only one's done what I asked him so far. Except for coming here instead of straight to me." He shot me a hard look.

"But seeing this"—he shifted his view toward Lenora and shook his head—"seeing this puts everything in a whole new light. I'm with Shakespeare on that. You're a sick fuck, Barnett. Business? You think this is good for business? Now what you gonna do with all these people? Say, 'see ya, have a nice day, sorry about the fingers?'"

"It's my mess. I can clean it up."

Elle, who had been taking it all in, walked up to Red. He stood a head taller but it didn't bother her. "The thing is, that's my aunt," she said, her voice even and icy. "You know Trey already killed my brother. He wants to kill me, too. I'll get your painting for you. He can kiss it and the inheritance goodbye."

Red to Tony again.

"Inheritance?"

"It's nothing," said Trey, stepping up as though he was going to push her away. "Something from my family. The painting's where the money is."

"That's a lie," she said.

"A big fat one," I added.

Trey took a step toward me but stopped.

"Trey and I grew up together, is the thing," Elle continued, only about an arm's length from Red's chest. "Want to hear?"

"Make it fast."

"Turns out we grew up out of the same daddy. We all sort of just found out. Trey's view is that with no siblings, or even half-siblings, there's nothing to split up from the estate. You want to know what Aunt Lenora is doing over there? Not to get the painting here." She shot Trey a hard, hard ray of hate. "To get me here. Deal with him however you want." A pause.

"Whatever you think is, you know, fair. In your world."

Red listened with a half-smile, looking across at Tony. Ernie and Reggie hadn't moved the whole time, other than to shift feet and wonder what was going to go down.

"She's smart and good-looking," Red said to me. "Hope it's been worth it."

"She's a great fuck, too," Trey said, his face working itself into some kind of mask of sadism. "She forgot to tell you we were more than brother and sister. Hell, we're mom and dad." He let it hang there. "At least for the time being."

"Shut up," she yelled, the first time she'd really done that.

"So go get the painting for the man, wherever your fucking brother stowed it, and let them be on their way so we can go on with our party. And then maybe I can go visit our little daughter. You know, talk to her about our family."

Elle's lips snarled back to show her teeth and gums. She looked wildly about, like she was trapped.

And it happened.

She rushed to Trey, lioness to her jackal nemesis at long last, so quickly it almost seemed everything else in time went into slow motion, slamming him toward the tables at the back of the room.

Recoiling from the attack, he tripped over an electrical cord used for the track lighting, lost his balance and fell, hard, toppling a table as the back of his skull hit the concrete with a loud crack.

For a millisecond, she stopped, as though some immense gears needed but one more click to engage.

Then she leapt upon him, straddling his torso and pounding him with her fists. He covered his face, cursing her, blinking his eyes into focus from the force of his fall.

Red and Tony let it happen.

When I started to step in, Red put his arm in front of me and shook his head.

No one really saw the move, but the next time Elle raised her arm to strike, she was clutching a long, plastic-handled screwdriver in her right hand. On the downswing, a dull sound of metal crunching through ribs filled the room. A splurt of bright red blood flew up.

Trey convulsed, reached for the screwdriver, but couldn't pull her hands away from it nor pull it out.

She leaned forward and with all her body weight drove the chisel-nosed blade deeper into his body. The spurting stopped. Trey coughed, put his hands around the screwdriver handle, and then lay quietly, his shirt drenched in his own blood, his face gone pale and expressionless.

I looked at Red as we both made an instant evaluation of what had happened. On the floor next to Trey lay an overturned carpenter's box, its contents spilled out: a hammer, measuring tape, some nails, carpet cutter, and several screwdrivers. Minus one.

"Damn," Red said.

"You bitch!" That was Ernie, who made his last mistake of the evening, rushing forward, trying to pull a pistol from the pocket of his trousers. He almost got it out when the straight razor sliced his neck just above the Adam's apple.

He stopped, like he wasn't quite sure why a spray of blood was splattering the back wall. Then he toppled forward, gurgling, eyes wide open, barely breaking his fall with his hands but hitting hard on his face, which thumped and then turned sideways, weirdly, because his head was only about two-thirds attached.

Tony the Barber stood next to him, knees flexed, as if ready for anything else. Which wasn't coming. Blood from Ernie's wound spread out in a thick puddle. His eyes stared out across the floor, not like he was looking for anything, just open. Tony looked down, emotionless as the cutter in a poultry processing plant. When he was sure it was over, he bent down and wiped the blade on Ernie's jeans.

Reggie froze, staring at Red, his mouth slightly open, an occasional glance down at Ernie, and at his own blood-speckled clothes.

I pushed aside Red's arm to get to Elle, still straddling Trey's body.

I knelt beside her. Trey was breathing slightly. I could see a faint gurgling around the opening where the screwdriver had impaled him. Her hands still gripped the handle. His hands loosely encircled hers.

I pulled at Trey's fingers to get them away before the death grip locked them forever. Then I worked at her fingers. Those, I couldn't loosen. She raised her head for the first time. Her eyes were wide, nostrils flared, jaw tight and pulsing, mouth twisted in a way I'd never seen, or ever wanted to.

Then she stared back down at her half-brother. "How's that feel?"

He tried to say something but it was just a hoarse gurgle.

"Let it go, Elle. Let it go." I kept saying things like that, prying at her fingers, hoping to overcome the adrenaline strength.

Then I was aware of Red, towering over us.

"Can't we get her off?"

Before I could answer, he bent down and slapped her on the cheek. She glared at him but also let go of the screwdriver handle. Then he pulled her up and away.

I stayed down, next to Trey's body. His eyes were going glassy and out of focus.

I think he was looking at me. I stared back, maybe with the same expression Tony had expended on Ernie. All my time on the meditation pad, working at the Eightfold Path, changing my life and letting go of past perfect and imperfect—all for naught.

I pushed down on the screwdriver handle and twisted it sharply to the left, so the tip would slice to the right, inside, into his heart. He gasped. Then—and it may have only been my imagination— seemed to smile.

But he wasn't looking at me. He was looking up at her.

"He was going to kill all of us," she was saying, almost swallowed up inside Red's forearms.

Trey had one last word. I think that's what it was. It sounded like "Mama," but not the way some people revert to infantile longings when dying. I don't know if Elle heard it. It might just have been my imagination. Then he was gone.

Tony the Barber had put his razor back in his blood-spattered trousers and moved over close to Reggie.

Lenora, meanwhile, had gotten to her feet. She let the cloth slip off her shoulders but this time wore her nakedness like a suit of regal power, advancing step by step toward me and Trey. She went right past us to the wall shelves and reached for the little framed Red Gator that Big Red had been looking at.

She pulled the painting from the frame, then, almost slipping on the slender pool of blood spreading from the wound on Trey's chest, came to kneel on the other side of Trey's body.

With the index finger of her right hand, she touched one of the ragged joints on her left, and used the blood from it to mark an "X" on Trey's damp, clammy forehead. Then she dipped her finger into some of Trey's blood and made another "X" below the first mark and said something, some African words, I couldn't make out. Like back in Rosedale.

She crumpled the Red Gator canvas and crammed most of it into Trey's mouth, still partly open.

"Evil grows where evil goes." Then she got up.

I did, too. For the first time, I saw her back. In the center was a dark, ugly raw scorch mark in the shape of an iron. Around it, what looked like cigarette burns.

No one much knew what to say.

Red let Elle go and she went to Lenora, held her. I went for the drop cloth. We were wet and sticky with his blood, all of us.

"Damn," said Tony the Barber. "Damn. You figure it was going this way?"

"Call somebody," Big Red told him. "We need to clean up and get the fuck outta here."

29

Big Red took a look at Trey's body, kicked the legs just to be sure there was no response, then walked over to where Lenora had been strung up. "Jesus," he said, shaking his head again. "What a fuckin' freak."

Tony the Barber was on his cell phone, talking in a low voice, looking unhappily at his clothes.

Elle helped Lenora to the far corner of the room, glaring like she was guarding the entrance to her lair.

Red looked Reggie over, hard. Then went back to the upended work bench, pulled it upright, and sat against it. He dropped his head for a moment, deep in thought. No one moved. Finally he exhaled heavily and looked up.

I was quietly wiping my hands on my jeans. Red nodded toward a box of disposable utility rags on the floor near the toolbox. I picked one up, wiped myself some more. I tossed a couple to Elle.

"I know you're strapped, if you wondered."

"I didn't know what I was walking into."

"But you do now."

"You want it?"

"I do, I'll let you know. Just keep it in your pants, as they say."

"Hey, over here." It was Tony and I threw him a couple of rags.

"Everybody better?" Red said to the room, but mostly to me. "We need to take care of business now. You got business for me?"

I dropped my rag to the floor. "I made the deadline."

"So you gonna get it? Now?" I was reminded of his short fuse.

"It's a short drive from here. Over on Tulane."

"You can drive?"

"I think so."

"What about them?"

"We're going with you," Elle said. "I need to find something for her to wear."

"I'm okay. Just use this thing," Lenora cut in.

"There's got to be something else." Elle looked around the cluttered room, as though it weren't thick with blood and bodies.

"She okay? Really?" Red asked.

"Compared to what?" Elle adjusted the drop cloth, now streaked and smeared.

"Hell, Shakespeare, that's a tough crowd you run with. All writers like that?"

"I'm not sure."

"A guy'll be here in half an hour," Tony called out from the back of the room.

Big Red looked at the watch on his thick, heavily freckled wrist.

"You stay. I'm going to get our package. With them."

Tony looked at him, thinking it over. "Yeah, okay."

"You're finished, you meet me back down on the coast. Call me when you leave."

"What about our boy Reggie here?"

Big Red stood, walked back over to Reggie, who had managed to retrieve his cane. The look on his face was several degrees shy of happy. Other than a spray of Ernie's blood across his trousers, he didn't seem to have been harmed. A thought he was obviously processing.

"So, Reggie. How's it gonna be? I know you got detailed to this shithead, and shot up for it, but, you know, now you're in the shit yourself."

"It was just a job, Red. I never liked the bastard."

Red patted him on the shoulder.

"What I wanted to hear. And as far as that little creep Ernie, all this"—he gestured around the scene of death and gore—"you feel the need to talk about it to anyone back in Memphis?"

Reggie's eyes darted everywhere. "I'm just doing a job. You're the boss. You know I know the play."

"Copacetic." He looked at Tony. "So he stays with you and helps with the crew. Whatever you need."

Tony nodded. "Jeez, fuckin' ruined these pants. That sink over there work?"

"It works," Reggie said quickly, then looked at Red.

Tony rolled his eyes and walked up to the toilet closet at the front of the room.

"Any problem with what I just told you?" Red asked.

"Hell no. But Red, I mean it. I was just told to ride with him."

Red put up his arm to wave off more analysis. He patted him again, a little rougher. "Good boy."

Reggie tried for fake confidence as he walked back to lean against the shelving, his cane between his legs, taking most of his weight now. On the way, he gave me a look.

I let it go. He no longer existed.

We heard water running at the sink, then a muttered "fuck" from Tony.

Red turned to Elle. "So, you wanna tell me how you think this is going to play out from here? How you smoke this little shit right in his own place of business and walk away from it?"

Elle was helping Lenora into a metal folding chair that had fallen behind one of the tables. Her aunt seemed beyond feeling her wounds. The medical guess would be that she was finally dropping into shock, but her face wasn't pale and she was breathing fine. It was more like she had other things on her mind and would get to the issue of the defilement of her body soon enough.

"I'm talking to you, honey."

"I heard you." Elle dabbed at Lenora's face with one of the rags, and continued to fuss with the drop cloth, frustrated that it was far from enough. She turned to look at Red with that wilting stare. Even he looked away after a few seconds.

Elle patted Lenora on her shoulder, and walked up to the big guy.

"You were saying?"

"I'm saying we've got two dead bodies here and that wasn't part of any plan."

"Three."

"What?"

"Three bodies. My brother is already gone."

Red looked at me, as if I might have a comment. I didn't.

"Right." He shook his head. "Look, I can't get into that. I'm here to pick up some goods. Period. Shakespeare here says it's really something. Maybe so. It was enough to get a lot of people killed. So far."

"So far."

"You not afraid of much are you?"

"What's to be afraid of?"

"Look," I broke in. "It was a bad thing between them. You didn't like him anyway."

"I had no reason to waste him."

"Other than that he was going to rip you off."

"Tell me something I don't know. But business is business."

"Like you said, we all need to get going," Elle said. "I need to get my aunt to a doctor. You have to meet your own people. Somebody needs to take care of all this. What don't we agree on?"

Red laughed, looked across at Tony. "In court they call it witnesses." I think maybe he expected a reaction he didn't get.

"To what?"

Their eyes were locked.

"Y'all walk out of here, we clean up your mess? You think that's really all there is to it?"

"From what I know, this solves a problem for you, too."

I could see a vein standing out in her neck, which still bore splotches of Trey's blood.

"In a way. In a way, not."

"Why?"

"I have to explain?"

I stayed silent. It wasn't me he wanted to hear right now.

"We can improve your business situation, is what I'm saying," she said, breaking their stare-fest.

"Such as?" The hint of a smile through his beard.

Elle's eyes flashed my way.

"Let's say I could tell you who has been looking for that painting, other than Trey, and wants to buy it back. You don't go through any middlemen. Make the sale yourself, give the money to your boss to cover his investment. Maybe keep a cut for your trouble."

"That's not my orders. Not my style."

"Then give it to your boss and he can sell it to the name I give you. And he owes you one for turning him onto some big money. Or something."

Red looked at Tony, still dabbing at his clothes with wet paper towels. Tony shrugged, as though hearing a reasonable idea, and walked to the back of the room.

"I'm not a witness," Elle said, walking over to the shelves, leaning against them, cooler than Bacall in a Bogey movie. "I'm the fucking killer. You know?" She held up her hands as exhibit A. "I have no reason to tell anyone on the outside anything. None of the rest of us do, either."

"That's a given."

"Then?"

Red looked at the mess around him. At Reggie. At Tony.

"I got no interest in adding to this. On the other hand I got no motive not to."

I followed Elle's lead. "Look, think about it. Trey was never going to give the painting to you. He was going to sell it himself and just pay you whatever he owed your boss, and pocket the rest. Then probably kill us. Or at least try to"—I shot Reggie a murderous glance. "He stood to make eight or nine mill profit."

Red looked at Tony. "That's the value?"

"It's what my brother said. Up to ten million. He knew."

Red looked down at Trey's body. "What a pop dick. I don't know how we ever got in business with him."

"I think he got in business with us," Tony said, watching Reggie.

"Yeah, you could say." Red looked at me. "But back to my point. Don't all of us necessarily need to leave this little soiree."

"What else you want?" she said, her tone not alarmed, but insouciant.

"Whaddya got?" He laughed, looked over at Tony. "I always wanted to say that."

"James Dean."

"Yeah." Then he stopped laughing. "So, what do you got?"

Elle looked at Lenora, who was following the conversation with something like approval. She looked down at the blood all over her. She looked at me. Then to Red.

"Look, I'm going to come into some money. November eleventh. Veterans Day. That's my birthday." Her eyes back to mine for an instant. "I'll be thirty-five. Let's say by New Year's Eve you have one hundred thousand in an account you set up. As gratitude."

Red's sunburned brow furrowed. He glared at Reggie, who did everything possible to pretend he wasn't listening. Tony was pursing his lips and nodding his head, slowly.

"Two hundred thousand."

Red and Tony shared a quick glance. "You can guarantee that?"

"It's guaranteed." Still leaning against the shelves, she waited for his answer like an impatient, temporarily insane school principal.

He shook his head. "All this is weird Mississippi shit, ain't it?"

"If you say so."

He looked down at Trey's body again for a moment, then, with a slow shake of his head, at his watch. He was back in charge. "We're here too long. Let's take a ride. Tony, call me. I'm going with the kids."

Tony nodded.

"That back door okay?" Red asked Reggie.

"Goes to the alley for deliveries. Streets run off either way from it."

Elle and I took a couple minutes to use the washbasin to clean ourselves as best we could. I could hear Red and Tony talking lowly but it could have been about anything.

We left. The cover of night would help, but it couldn't avoid being a tough hike for a mixed-race crowd, one of whom was dressed in a bloody white sheet and half-carried by two wild-eyed people with suspiciously stained clothes. On the other hand this was New Orleans.

30

Red led, ducking his head into the weather. The rain had some wind in it. We got to the Taurus wet but without incident. I clicked open the lock for Red to get in front and helped Elle and Lenora into the back. While they settled, I opened the trunk, ostensibly to make room for the painting and to get Vicodin from my duffel for Lenora. I had so much adrenaline running through me I didn't need it. But mostly I wanted to stow the Colt.

"Smart move," Red said when I got back in and buckled up.

I put the key into the ignition.

"With that psycho, it was okay. But now, yeah, I don't want to see you with hardware anymore."

I looked at him, nodded without comment, and cranked the engine. I squeezed out of the parking space and onto the street. It didn't bear much speculation, but I had to wonder: Could I have taken all three of them, before Red arrived? If he hadn't shown? I had counted on it then and I wasn't going to second-guess now.

I cut across town toward Tulane, looking in the mirror at Elle off and on most of the way. Lenora, face gray and drawn, was leaning against Elle. Lenora had taken two of the pills with some bottled water.

"We should go to a hospital," I said.

"I'm okay," Lenora said, ever more weakly. She began to slump down and Elle helped her to stretch out on the seat.

"That's your call for later," Red said. "Now we got business."

"Let's just get this done. She's stable and she'll be sleeping in a minute," Elle said, cradling Lenora's head in her lap.

In about ten minutes we were pulling into the U-Haul lot. I parked at the front door of the main storage building, like before, and turned to Red.

"You coming?"

"Every step."

I looked in the back. I thought I saw a change of expression in Elle's face, some sense the first wave of anger that had propelled her was dissipating. But it might have just been exhaustion. Where she had been, you didn't come back that quick.

"They stay. Lock up and bring the keys."

"Go on. We're fine," she said.

The rain eased off, or maybe it had been localized down in the Quarter; rain did that in the city sometimes. At the entry door, I stopped, feeling a little stupid, and went back to the car to ask Elle for the code.

I punched in the numbers and Red and I went upstairs to the unit. I opened the door and turned on the light and showed him the packing box. He wanted to grab it and leave but I told him he ought to see the goods and that I'd feel better if he did. So he'd know I wasn't shining him on. He shrugged, as if I'd have to be a total idiot to try a switch after all this, and glanced at his watch again. Told me to hurry.

I pulled the inner box out and unwrapped the painting and stood it near the side of the room, as Elle and I had done earlier.

He moved a few steps back to get a good look. Maybe I sensed what he would see and maybe I didn't.

"Son of a bitch."

"It's something, isn't it?"

"Not that I'm a big art fairy but I been to a few museums. Hell, it's like a movie or something."

I could see his eyes tracing every corner of it, taking in every frequency of color and light.

"You Catholic?"

"No."

"I am."

He looked a few minutes longer, then exhaled, shook his head as though reentering the planet. "Okay, let's go. I've seen it."

"Okay." I started the repackaging.

"Trey Barnett. How's he get stuff like that?" He seemed really to wonder.

"He was an art dealer, I guess. They're in their own world."

"I figured it was from all the other stuff he was dealing."

I kept working. "Can I ask you a question?"

He shrugged.

"Let's say your boss gets this. You think he'll get it back to the owner? Maybe put it in a museum? You know, take care of it?"

"That's the question?"

I slid the inner box into the outer, resealed the tape.

"Just asking."

He looked at me in a way that very nearly reminded me of conscientious.

"I got one for you."

"Yeah?"

"What she said about what this is worth. That's straight up?"

"Her brother told her. He knew about art. Taught it in school, I think."

"He did all this to keep Barnett from taking down his sister?"

"That's the way I see it."

I propped it against the wall.

"Back there, she just lost it?"

"You know, on top of killing her brother, he raped her."

"Raped her?"

"When they were in college."

"Shit Leroy," He reached for the box. "Give me a hand. I don't want to drop this damn thing." We started out. "And you just walked in on the whole thing."

"I found her brother's body. It all went from there."

We stopped in the hall while I flicked off the light, locked the unit.

"Where now?"

"Back to my truck. You'll drop me off. I need to get back to the coast."

We hurried outside to get the painting in the trunk before the rain started up again. I had thrown an old plaid road blanket from the Explorer into the trunk of the Taurus when we had transferred our stuff and grabbed it for Lenora after getting the painting storage box secure. Driving away, I felt strangely like celebrating, although it was far from over. Coltrane was on the radio. "A Love Supreme." Barely audible, Lenora whispered the words and huddled against Elle for warmth.

THE FORD F-250 PICKUP was parked along a back street in the warehouse district near the convention center, where Red had met Tony. Red said it was as close as he could find at the time. I pulled into a space nearby, partly blocking an unloading driveway but we wouldn't be there long.

Elle pulled the note from her brother from her bag and read off to Red the name and address for the Beldon Gallery in Houston. He wrote the information on a pad he kept in his front pocket, looked at it a couple of times to be sure it was right and repeated the phone number. It had come to him how much it was worth. I think it also was coming more and more to him the scope of what Trey had nearly pulled off.

"The decent thing to do, if that means anything to you, would be to get this Guadalupe to a big art museum," Elle said, leaning up close to Red. "If it goes to your boss, it'll be lost to the world, you know?" She seemed ready to say something else but didn't.

Red turned to look at her, then me. "You knew what you were getting yourself into?"

I managed a half-smile.

"I know what you mean, darlin'," he told her. "It really is something. Like I said to Shakespeare here, damndest thing I've ever seen outside of a church." He cleared his throat. "Thing is, it's not my call."

She stared out the side window.

"But I'll bring it up. You know, if it could play out that way, business-wise."

It was a close as he could get to acknowledging his debt to her. That he even had a human side was something that amazed me, especially considering the state of my body, which was starting to reassert its right to remind me it had become a punching bag. In a weird way I had started to like him. Stockholm syndrome, maybe, but there was something about him I respected, and apparently vice versa. Not that it would stop him from killing me whenever he wanted. Business-wise.

The rain had started up again on the drive over, though not hard and wind-driven like before. The painting was protected in its wrapping inside the cardboard box. I helped him carry it to his truck and stow it carefully in the extend-a-cab compartment. Red closed the door. I looked at the box through the window. It was a long way from belonging to me, but I felt a little protective.

"Art class is over. Let it go."

"I know." A car came by slowly, filled with young women, probably looking for a parking space to head out clubbing.

"So I'll be hearing from your friend in a few months."

"You will. Same number?"

"If it changes I'll find you."

I almost shook hands but that was going too far.

"How's your ribs?"

"They hurt."

"Coulda been worse."

"Yeah."

"Where you going?"

"Now?"

"Now. Later."

"Now, I think we need to get Lenora to a doctor."

"That was bullshit, what he did."

"Yeah."

"So all that back at the gallery. It'll be gone?" I needed to ask.

I think he understood. "Probably already is. Or will be soon. Some people, that's what they do for us in some places. New Orleans is one of those places."

"What about Reggie?"

"What about him?"

"You trust him?"

"No."

I wiped rain off my forehead, tried to see into his eyes. He wasn't going to say it any more directly.

"So this is it, then."

"You haven't answered."

"What?"

"What after this? After the hospital? You and the chick. Elle. She's all right."

"She is."

"You gonna stay with her?"

I looked down at the pavement. A couple more cars passed by.

"The thing is, if we do, or whatever we do, do I have to worry about"—I paused— "you know, anything?"

Red leaned against the truck, looked up, the rain splattering his face like something almost holy.

"Again. What are you going to do?"

I looked at him. "You mean other than Elle?"

"Like for a living."

"I told you. I'm a writer. Pretty much."

He smiled and shook his head.

I had to laugh myself. "Okay. So I'm not so sure anymore."

"'To be and not to be' shit?"

Caught me a little by surprise.

"Saw the movie."

"Hunh."

"Myself, I got 'to be' doing something, I'm not working. My ex told me reading would be good for me. I even joined a book club up in Memphis."

"Yeah?" I kept looking at him. For what, I didn't know.

"But it didn't work out." His eyes glanced away as if he were remembering something and considering whether to share. "Still, I take stuff when I'm fishing. I like that guy, Robicheaux, the coonass."

"Yeah. He's good."

"I saw that movie, too."

"Yeah, that was good."

"Yeah."

We stood there a moment, probably each trying to figure what was going on in the head of the other. At least I was.

"Well," he sniffed, then spat, "since you don't seem to have a fucking plan, my point was, you ever need some odd work now and then, you let me know. You're not much with your hands but you got some balls. And smarts. You started a fire-fight back there, I'd of walked in on a lot of bodies. Hell, even your woman has balls."

I knelt down, picked up a pebble, flicked it out into the street. "I'm not in your league."

I looked up. His expression was somewhere between wistful and a scowl. "You was, though, once upon a time, weren't you? You think you hide it but you don't."

"I outgrew all that."

"Yeah. Me, too."

We sort of laughed.

"It's not like we go to college and get a degree in muscle. You follow orders, it all works out."

A flicker of lightning came from upriver. I stood up.

"Hell, now it's really coming down."

"Yeah." Then a thunderclap off in the distance.

We looked at each other, run out of things to say. He really was a big guy.

"See ya."

"See ya."

I went back to the rental car and he got into his truck. I waited for him to pull out, and watched until he got up to the corner. Then I started my own engine.

"So we're done?" she asked from the back seat.

"We're done."

I could hear her breathe out. "You got anything left?"

"Not much."

"Me, neither."

"What about Lenora?"

"Pills knocked her right out."

"Where do we go? Charity?"

"We can't do that. When you were getting the painting, she asked if we could take her back to Jackson. Tonight. She has friends there, the kind who don't ask questions, and a doctor like we had in Rosedale."

"It's what, three hours, about?" I looked across the seat at her.

"It's pain, mostly. You know, she didn't bleed that much. Did you see her fingertips? They're cauterized. Same iron he put on her back."

I felt my head drop and closed my eyes. Like Elle, I wasn't interested in absorbing it all right now.

"So can you drive that far tonight? It's late."

I pulled forward into the rain-pelted street. "I'm okay. We'll get some coffee. You?"

"I'm wide awake."

A big Japanese sedan appeared behind me and started to take my space, then, seeing the one Red had left, made a beeline for it.

I picked up a street taking us to I-10 and eventually to I-55 out past Kenner and the airport. I turned on the heater for a half hour until it and our bodies dried out the dampness in our clothes. Then it was too hot and I turned it off, let in fresh air. I could hear Lenora's ragged breathing. I picked up a station playing classical.

We drove on into the deep, wet forests and glistening empty highways of the Southern night, nothing out there more real than everything in here.

"I guess those Red Gators will go up in value," Elle said, after a while.

31

The rain must have been coming in from the north because it stayed with us most of the way, off and on, hard. After an hour or so, just enough for the wipers to come on at intervals. Radio stations faded in and out, but kept me awake. We talked enough to remind ourselves we were alive and well, but otherwise it was a good night for quiet. I kept replaying the scene at the gallery and it never got any less gruesome or more explainable.

Lenora snored softly, jerked a couple of times but never really woke up. I stopped twice at convenience store gas stations for coffee, and some cashews to keep up my blood sugar. One of the clerks gave a long look to my soiled clothes but for all she knew those could be wine stains, and a disheveled late-night traveler in rural Mississippi wasn't really an extraterrestrial event.

It was nearly three when we hit the outskirts of Jackson, too late to call anyone to stay. We didn't want to go to Lenora's place right away, so I found a chain motel not far from downtown and booked two adjoining rooms. I told the clerk we'd gotten a late start from Mobile and apologized for my appearance and for waking her up. As if she cared one way or the other as long as I had a credit card.

I carried Lenora inside and put her on one of the queen beds. Elle followed with a couple of bags. Elle took her aunt's pulse and watched her to be sure she was resting well. I went into the second room to shower and change and put my gallery clothes in a motel laundry sack. Elle did the same in Lenora's room, and borrowed one of my T-shirts for a nightgown.

We sat on the bed next to Lenora, watching her, but we both started nodding off. Elle said it would be better to stay close to her for the night and so we both just lay back on the thick motel pillows. She pushed up next to me and we held each other as though some part of the earth were falling from under us. For a few hours, a few hours of an oblivion I had never so welcomed, we slept.

In the morning we went down into the old Farish Street neighborhood and found the clinic where Lenora knew a doctor named Benares who attended her wounds without unnecessary questions. He said she could get cosmetic surgery later for her fingers, and maybe the scar on her back if she wanted. We had been living off the radar for so long that it didn't even seem odd to discuss such matters.

We stayed at the motel the next two days, Lenora and Elle in one room, me in the other. All of us slept a lot, watched HBO. I picked up our meals and brought them back. I called the rental car company to extend my contract. I checked my machine, nothing new except someone still wanting to be my new long distance provider. I called for Art Becker, which I'd forgotten to do despite my promise to Elle. They still weren't back from their trip. I did a wash so we'd have clean clothes. I threw away the bloody ones.

We made two trips back to see Dr. Benares to change the bandages and check the progress of the burn. He told her she was very lucky and that he would drop by to see her once she was back home to follow up.

I was feeling better, too. The switch to Advil was working well enough, although at night I took the prescription stuff.

I missed Elle, lying in the room by myself, drifting in and out of sleep. Once, when we were next to each other on the bed, Lenora asleep, we thought about sneaking over into my room, but it was just a thought. I brought up Rose, but Elle changed the subject so quickly I knew it would have to wait.

ON THE THIRD DAY Lenora said she was ready to go home. Late that morning we stopped by a place near Millsaps College for coffee. It had a patio and Lenora wanted to sit outside. She said she hadn't seen the sun in too long. She told us a little about life in Jackson and we worked out how we would get the birth certificate.

Lenora's was a nice bungalow near the campus, two brick columns on a big open porch in front, a weathered oak tree for shade. I remarked on it, that she must have some rich clients. She said she also knew her way around the Dow Jones.

Elle asked to stay with her aunt one more day to be sure she was settled in on her own and not just pretending to be better. I made a crack that no one thought was amusing about it running in the family. For dinner, I went to a nearby deli for takeout sandwiches and salads. We ate perfunctorily, like people on a trip who'd spent too much time together. Like balloons losing air.

Later in the evening, sitting on the wicker chairs in the back porch, it all came out. It had hurt beyond words when they used the knife to cut first one finger, then another, and put the hot iron to the tips. She was already numb from the pain when they stripped her naked and put the steam iron on her back—Black and Decker, a weird detail she couldn't shake—and that was when she told them about Rose.

She said it was just like Trey had said, that she thought telling him might keep him from killing Elle. That he wouldn't kill the mother of his child if he knew the child was still alive. That otherwise, no matter what she confessed, he would have killed Elle anyway. Then she passed out, and when she woke up she was in the gallery, not the back of that van. And then we had showed up. And the mob.

She told Elle that there had been nothing else for it after that, that Trey was a dead man no matter what. That in a way, dying at Elle's hand was the kindest way he could have gone, that it was probably the most loving thing that had ever happened to him.

Then she said that it was important for us to be cleaned, and blessed.

IN THE BACK YARD, sheltered by the shrubs and high wooden fences, we stood inside a ring of several candles on the ground. Lenora had rubbed oranges over our heads and bodies to cleanse us and now we waited for her to come back from a shed near the back of the house. It was late and the good Christian neighbors slept under the Mississippi moon, blissfully unaware of secret voudou gardens and pagan ceremonies.

Lenora came back carrying two pigeons bound up with string. She pulled off their heads and used their blood to dab an encircled cross on both our foreheads. It looked a little like a vévre. Then she passed the bodies of the birds over each of us, head to toe, and threw them to the side.

She chanted a prayer to the African gods and dotted our foreheads with the sacrificial blood. She told us to pray in whatever manner we chose. We should ask to be cleansed and healed of our sins and also of our deeds and our thoughts; for no matter how justified, we had taken lives and harmed others.

The moon rose in a half circle through the misty clouds. Looking closely at Elle, Lenora said she wanted to do another reading. She took out her broken coconut husks, threw them several times, speaking to the husks, or maybe just to herself. Finally she gathered them, looked at both of us.

"The spirits say you will move past this. They won't tell me more."

"What about Rose?"

Lenora threw the coconut pieces again, a few more times. Finally she shook her head. "Rose can't reach you now. The spirits won't let her."

Elle touched the blood marking on her forehead.

"Too much dark in you right now."

She tasted the blood on her finger. "But they will."

"They will if you let them."

"Throw again."

"I don't need to."

"You did before."

"I wasn't sure what I was hearing. Now I am. You got a heavy load, baby. It's not the time for you to make that connection now."

Elle shook her head and walked away a few steps. I left it between them.

Back inside we followed Lenora's instructions. Elle bathed in the tub in Lenora's room and I used the hall bathroom shower. Each of us had a half-gallon plastic jug, filled with a thin, milky liquid that smelled of smoke. I poured it over myself and rinsed off. Elle soaked in it in the tub.

We slept separately. We were supposed to rise in the morning with a prayer on our lips before making any other sound. I didn't have one. Couldn't form the words. I don't know about Elle.

We left about noon for New Orleans and the birth certificate, the final piece of the puzzle. Driving south, it was as if something were missing. No one was following us, to kill us, to steal from us, to violate us from the past.

32

The St. Martin de Porres Spiritual Church of Jesus was in the Ninth Ward, downriver of the Quarter. The red brick building and its several annexes took up a half-block on a mostly residential street close to a busy intersection currently flanked by a fried chicken stand, a loan shark check-cashing office and a liquor store.

The drive had taken longer than expected, but we'd stopped for lunch. Still, the appointment was for five-thirty so we'd judged the time pretty closely. It was just after the hour when we pulled up on the gravel shoulder outside the sanctuary's main entrance.

A playground had been added behind a high wire fence. In front of it a long breezeway connected the sanctuary to a small, free-standing structure of aluminum siding and concrete blocks. I figured it for the rectory office. A weather-worn marquee sign along the front of the complex listed the hours for services, weeknight prayer, and Bible study. The week's motto: "Jesus Wants You for His Army of One."

Lenora had set it up with the minister, the Reverend Learned Bathing. She had known him from when they'd been at college in Tennessee. Bathing had been born in Mississippi, part Choctaw, named after the famous federal jurist, Learned Hand. His father, a cop, moved the family to the Big Easy for better pay, and wound up getting shot and killed a year before retirement. By another cop.

Reverend Bathing had also known Pearl, Elle's mother, from visits she and Lenora had made to New Orleans over the years after he was ordained. Although trained for a more mainstream denomination, he had found his calling in one of those powerful spiritual tributaries that flourished in the city: a little Catholic, a little Protestant, a little African voudou. Lenora and Pearl thought he was a brilliant preacher, even though Pearl was generally more straight-laced.

Lenora had filled us in with all this so we'd know a little about the man who had babysat the document that would make Elle a rich woman, if one wanted to look at it that way. To him, it was only a very old, probably forgotten favor to a long-ago romance.

Lenora said that you didn't just drop in on the Reverend Bathing anymore. He had become a figure of influence and reputation. That was good for the church but not so good for the personal visits and confessions and even salvations for which he had been known since his earliest days in the pulpit. I guessed he had learned to juggle his appointment book. For special guests, he could open up his schedule.

Two pre-teen girls strolled by, talking loudly, laughing, and looking behind at several boys about the same age. The street in front of the chicken joint was filling up with after-work traffic. We weren't all that far from my apartment in the Marigny. But in New Orleans, everything is a part of everything else, one neighborhood blends into another. If you ever forget the linkage, reminders will materialize.

"You ready?"

"It's still a few minutes early."

She sat up in the seat, stretched her legs and arms out as much as she could.

"Man, we've spent some time in this car. Can't wait to turn it back in."

"I'm pretty sick of it. I might just walk around for a week."

"Yeah."

She was looking into her bag for something, then closed it, sat with it on her lap. I fiddled with the steering wheel.

"Reminds me I haven't been to church in a long time. Other than back in Oxford," she said, making conversation.

"Other than that, I don't know when."

"That was a nice church for Young Henry."

"They did a good job."

"Yeah."

"And then he had to show up." Her mouth quivered but then she firmed it up.

I took one of her hands in mine. She squeezed my fingers.

"He did," I said.

"Yeah."

"But he's not going to anymore."

I could see her eyes moisten.

"Maybe this is too soon," I said.

She pulled her hand away and shook her head. She adjusted her blouse. "We've talked this to death." That made her laugh a little. "You know."

"We'll talk about it as much as it needs."

She tilted the rearview to see herself in it. "I still look better than you. Let's go."

"You're sure?"

"Yeah. I'm sure. I'm more than sure."

She got out. I did the same and locked up, reconned the street.

WE WALKED THE CRACKED sidewalk leading to the breezeway. I made a short detour to get a look at the sanctuary through the window in the chapel door. A small balcony ringed the back, with a chorus pit and a dais for the preacher up front. At least twenty rows of varnished wooden pews on either side of the aisle.

"Bigger than I thought."

Elle took my arm and turned me gently back. "You're checking things out. You don't need to."

I opened the office door. Just as I did, a woman and her young daughter, both sniffling and teary-eyed, hurried past. The girl looked up. She was maybe ten or so and I didn't know what had gone wrong in her life, but there was a bruise along her cheek.

The modest reception room was cramped with an old, cluttered wooden desk, a couple of metal folding chairs, and a file cabinet in the corner decorated with years' worth of stickers and children's drawings stuck on with magnets or tape.

We were alone, but could hear a man in the other room talking on the phone, making arrangements for a banquet. In a minute or two we heard the receiver click down then the Reverend Bathing came out to greet us.

He was of average size, gray mustache and close-cropped hair, and although he had to be in his sixties, he looked ten years younger. He wore the uniform of preachers: dark blue suit pants, white shirt, blue tie. He looked tired after what may have been a long day.

He took Elle's hand, introduced himself, remarked how he was glad to finally meet Lenora's niece. Then he turned to me, though with more formality. He held out his arm in the direction of his inner office, and showed us to a pair of wooden captain's chairs with worn red padding on the arms. He walked around to the other side of a cypress-knee coffee table to settle onto a navy blue sofa. His own desk, almost as cluttered as the receptionist's, was backed against a window looking out to the playground.

He asked about the drive down and the weather and then said he was sorry about Terrell. Elle told him about the services in Oxford, putting the ashes in the river. He thought that was the right thing. But time was precious and he got directly to the point. It was a thoroughly professional move, so polished in the segue you had to admire it even while thinking of yourself as just one more number in a long line of customers.

"I have to admit it took me a little looking to remember exactly where I put that old letter—"

I could see Elle's eyebrows arch slightly.

"—but never fear, I'm not that dottering just yet." He laughed and we did, too. "Actually we have a bank we use for things like this." He sat back, made an open-palm gesture. "You'd be surprised how often our congregation needs things put away, saved, kept for a better day, and so on."

He stopped speaking and looked past us. I turned to see a man of about forty, in work overalls, standing at the doorway. "Oh, didn't know you were still here, Reverend."

Bathing rose. "Hey, Marcus. Just running a little late tonight. Can you work over in the church for a little while and come back?"

The man looked at both of us, nodded. "No problem."

The reverend sat back down. "Marcus works here part-time, janitor kinds of things. He also teaches over at Addams but, you know, times are hard and he needs two jobs these days."

"Well I don't want to keep you long, Reverend," Elle said.

He put up one hand to say it was okay, "We're fine. We're fine. Now where was I? Oh, right, the box."

"You were saying about the congregation."

"That's right. That's right. We have lots of need for people wanting things saved for them. Sometimes it's money. They don't trust the banks— even though that's where it winds up, basically. Or maybe it's some kind of religious or family thing. A lot of my folks, you know, they have to live in places that get robbed. Anyway it kind of grew up that we could take care of that sort of thing. And you know"—he smiled—"it's not so bad for business. We get a lot of lifelong members that way."

His gaze wandered over to his desk, maybe at the papers, maybe at the clock. "But like I was saying, I was trying to remember exactly where I'd filed the letter she gave me back when. But it wasn't so hard. Excuse me a second."

He went to the desk and picked up a brown folder, the kind with a flap and tie string. He came back and put it on the table in front of Elle.

"I want to tell you about this before I give it to you, just a little."

We looked at the folder.

"You know what this is? What's in that letter?" she asked.

He smiled. "That I do. I just never knew exactly what would come of it. Something good, I always hoped."

She glanced at me quickly. "I hope so, too."

"Pearl, your mother, she was a good woman. So was Abe. I think maybe so was . . . that other man."

"It's okay. I know about all that now."

They took the measure of each other, let that settle in.

"Junior Barnett."

"My father."

"Abe was your father."

"I don't mean it that way."

"I'm just saying it."

"Okay."

Both their eyes fell on the folder.

He put his arms on his knees to lean in closer. "When that happened, after you were born, I think your mama was scared. You can imagine. Junior got the birth certificate away from the official records—I'm just telling you all this so you'll know—but he wanted it kept somewhere safe. Even then, I think, he wanted to protect you. Lenora said he was so sad about everything, that he could never even let on about you to anyone."

"I understand."

"Lenora came to me, because I was far away from all that and because I guess she knew she could trust me. We were good friends back in college, you see. I was a little older."

"She sort of hinted at that. I know she thinks a lot of you."

He smiled. "That's good to know. People say she does black magic and voudou and all that sort of thing and I know she does but I don't think she does bad work. She keeps the African ways. I admire that. A lot of people do, even the ones who say they don't, and then show up on her door." He smiled, thinking about something or someone.

"But like I was saying. Where was I? Oh, about that certificate. Lenora brought it down here, told me what had happened, that your mama loved your daddy and was sorry for what happened, that Junior was a good man in his own bad marriage. I prayed with her and for your mama and daddy. Lord knows I see the weakness of the flesh day in and day out. You saw that young girl and her mama when you came in? The father's back in jail for assault. It goes on and on . . ." He drifted off in thought again. "So I took this letter, she told me what it was, and we looked at it to be sure it was the real thing, and we had it sealed up by a notary public and it's been here all that time. I guess you must be getting to thirty by now—"

"—Thirty-five—"

"That's right. That would be about right. Anyway, I was sorry to see him go like that. I guess his wife died, too. Like your parents both, so sudden and young like that. So many gone like that I once knew." He shook his head, pressed his lips together. "Still, I hope they're all at peace now with the Lord."

"I hope so."

"This young man here, your aunt tells me he is helping you. But it's more than that, isn't it?"

Our looking at each other proved his point.

"I trust Jack."

He looked at me longer than I liked. "You had some kind of trouble?

"Fender-bender. I got a little banged up."

He nodded. "Well, you got to watch that traffic."

"Absolutely."

"Yes, sir," he said, slowly, looking at Elle, then letting it go. He reached for the folder and passed it to her. "This is yours now."

She unfastened it at once. I'm not sure what either of us expected to find inside. It was a thick white envelope with a blood-red wax seal.

"They say you have to wait to break that seal at the lawyers. I think they're in Jackson."

"They are."

She held the envelope up to the light from the window. "Reverend, you're sure it's all in here?"

"I'm sure. I'm very sure. You can open it if you want, I guess. I'm not much of a lawyer. That's just what they said way back then."

She examined it some more, passed it to me.

"He's right. You should open this in front of your lawyer."

"Sure enough what I'd do," he said.

I passed the envelope back to her. She put it back in the folder, tied it up. "I wasn't doubting your word."

"I don't take it that way."

She tipped her chin up in agreement.

"So I guess we'll be going, then."

He rose, and so did we.

ELLE WALKED TO THE door and I took her elbow, almost formally. But we'd only taken a few steps when she stopped and looked back. The reverend had paused next to his desk. He flipped at the pages of a frayed book, maybe a Bible commentary, and seemed to be running something through his head.

"Just a minute, if you don't mind. I was praying over this and I want to tell you something. Something you should know. I think. Now that all this is open." He let the pages go. He seemed to have trouble framing whatever it was he wanted to say.

She glanced sidelong at me. "What is it, Reverend?"

We went back toward him.

"Have a seat, please."

She looked at me again. We sat. The chairs were still warm.

He returned to his place on the sofa. He looked at her steadily, as if trying one last time to make up his mind.

"All along, your daddy, he knew."

Her head tilted at a defensive angle. It took a long time for a word to come from her mouth: "What?"

He looked across the room, at me, then back at her. In a way, the conversation was already over. Just the blanks needed filling in.

"Lenora told me, said I could do with it as I wanted. Like I said, I asked the Lord for guidance." He breathed out hard, his face still bearing that inner glow, but shaded now, for what he was saying brandished a thousand hidden thorns if rendered the wrong way. "I think you should know."

Elle attended to the folder perched on her lap, making very sure the string was knotted tightly. All very orderly. "That's what I should know?"

"It's okay, child. It's okay." He got up and pulled over another captain's chair from the corner of the room near a lamp, set it next to Elle.

"You're saying he knew about Junior? And Mama?"

I looked at him hard, but his return gaze was calming.

He took her hands away from the folder and held them in his.

"Not right away. It came up when you started school and they needed your birth certificate for something. There wasn't one and they had to do the research to get a new one. Turns out the doctor said something to him, not knowing, and he took it back to Pearl. She told him the story."

Elle was rocking, slightly. The file dropped to the floor. I reached down and picked it up.

"I guess for a year or more, Lenora told me, they didn't get along well. You might not ever have known. But Abe got over it, had to admit he had been the one almost broke the marriage up, that let Junior and Pearl even get close. I see that all the time here. But they stayed together and he always took you as his own."

"He . . . .never . . . said . . . .anything."

"Never would. I met him once when I was up visiting Oxford for a church conference at the university. He was a good, honest man. Talked about his kids, his wife, his job, about being a good deacon."

"But he worked for Junior."

"That's the miracle, if you want to look at it that way. Each of them knew the truth, but never spoke of it. How could they? You see that all the time down here, too, don't you? But they needed to work together and they did that and I think they even liked each other. Junior, he always treated your family right?"

"Yeah . . ."

She was drifting off. In less than two weeks, her whole life's history had been turned inside out. It wasn't a lie, not a bright shining lie. It was a fiction.

"I know this is hurtful for you, child, but mostly I see it as a good thing about your daddy and mama. Overcoming all that. That's why the Lord wanted me to tell you. It's something you should know, now, a grown-up woman, all those people passed on anyway, nobody of them to hurt anymore."

She looked at him but didn't speak.

He kept both her hands tightly in his. He closed his eyes. "Pray with me."

She closed her eyes. I closed mine, too, but only for a second.

"Jesus, love this child of Yours. Keep her always to Your side. Protect her now and let Your love fill her soul. She has suffered, Lord, but is a good woman. Jesus, love her, O Lord, bind her to Your side. Hear her now, Jesus."

They prayed silently. After a minute or so they opened their eyes.

"Amen," he said. "Amen."

She was looking at him steadily, not crying. He had not let go of her hands.

"But they were okay then, when they died. Mama and Daddy."

"They got over all that years ago. Last time I spoke to Pearl, after your daddy was gone and before she found out she was sick, she was so happy. She just talked about you, about your brother."

He let go of her hands and glanced at the clock on his desk. "I hate to say this, but I have to be at a meeting in fifteen minutes over in the Tremé. Folks trying to figure out the mayor's race. Kind of thing I have to show up at."

Elle stood up, clutching the folder. "I know we kept you."

He rose and I did, too. "It was no problem. I hope it was a help."

We shook hands. Then he hugged Elle, like a father would a daughter, and walked us to the outer door.

"I'm always here, Good Lord willing. You can come back any time and we can talk more. You go visit your priest, too. You keep close to God either way."

33

Something other than hewing to the spiritual path was going through my mind as we pulled away and crossed the Ninth Ward. I didn't want to go back to my place or even deal with it, and instead drove along the lakeside edge of the Quarter on Ramparts, also dense and complex—maybe the whole city was—aimlessly heading Uptown. The chaos that had enveloped our lives was but a part of a history whose entanglements seemed to have neither beginning nor end.

I played dodge-car down Poydras to Magazine and then a slow two-lane drift toward Audubon Park, past the antique shops and bars and cafes, laundries, coffee shops, throngs of people gathering at watering holes, street corners filled with people waiting for the next bus, cop cars, miscreants waiting for their moment.

Just past Jackson, I slowed and pulled into a space by the curb. I told her I was tired of driving to nowhere and she said she was, too. Neither of us wanted to go back to Boots's, it wasn't Elle's week for the timeshare, and my apartment was uninhabitable. I suggested we go back downtown and stay the night at a boutique hotel I knew a couple blocks from Canal. Let tomorrow take care of itself. She was for it.

I let a valet take the car and carry up our bags, including the duffel with the sidearms, watching that he left the shotgun case. We got a sixth-floor room with a decent view, giant bed, and bathroom with a tiled shower and spa-sized tub. We went down to the bar, found a quiet corner and split a bottle of California cabernet. We nibbled at cheese and crackers as the early autumn sun faded outside and business types began to filter in to lay siege to the evening.

That was no good, so we took the elevator to our room to sort through our things. We didn't want a restaurant so I called room service. I turned on the wall-mounted Panasonic TV, found nothing, and then tuned in jazz on the stainless steel Sony radio on an adjacent shelf. Billie Holliday. We ate our sandwiches and drank our bottled water without hurry at a bleached pine table by the window. We watched the city below. It was cloudy, but you could see the lights toward the river, Gretna on the other side. We watched the night settle.

"It's good to be back," she said.

The city looked back in at us, filled us with its longing. She pushed back her chair, came to me. She kissed me, the taste of tuna and beef and grapes mingling on our tongues. She smiled and said she wanted a bath. I thought that sounded fine. When I heard the water running, I flipped on the TV to scan the news, but it remained of no interest. I turned it off and turned the sound back up on the radio. In the tub, she sang along to "Strange Fruit."

She came out drying her hair and wrapped in an oversized white towel. I told her she smelled good and she said the music sounded good and I went in for a shower. We could have done all that together, but it didn't need remarking.

When I came out, she was still in her towel and I was in mine and then we weren't. We fell on the bed. My ribs and nose still hurt but she didn't care.

There wasn't much foreplay. She lay back and told me she wanted me in her, fast. It was not athletic, nor rough, nor even lustful. I would describe it as what the Buddhists call mindful. Aware of everything: every feeling, every thought, every ounce of ourselves contained in the other. Another word would be love. We made love. Another word would be "coda."

In the morning, we lay next to each other on the tangled and sweat-stained sheets. Dawn through the edges of the drawn curtains threw a narrow beam across her thighs.

"You snored a little."

"Sorry." I touched my nose.

"Still sore?"

"Somebody roughed me up during the night."

She turned on her side, ran her arm up my torso, kissed the corners of my lips. I loved her breath, her touch, her face, everything. In her eyes was everything I wanted. But I knew it wasn't going to be.

"A whole day coming up with no one chasing us," she said.

I turned on my side to face her.

"In my job, we would say it hasn't sunk in," she went on.

"That the technical term with shrinks?"

Her eyes were so perfect they were almost unbearable. She wasn't smiling.

"I mean, it's just . . . trying make sense of it."

I let my head drop to the pillow.

"It was all so so fast," she said. "I don't mean us. Or this. I mean every-thing else."

She rolled onto her back, looking not at the ceiling but through it, through the building, through the cap of the solar system.

"It's like something is scratching inside my brain and I can't make it stop."

I rolled on my back, too. "It'll go away. Pretty much."

She knew I was lying.

"I just have to say it."

"So say it."

She kept examining the ceiling. The brush pattern was very interesting. Asian, perhaps. "Okay . . . look . . . I have to be by myself for a while. I can't be with anyone. Especially you."

I knew it was coming—had to—but that didn't make the knowing easier. I looked for some words. "It was what we had to do. It was a lot to do."

"I understand that. Logically. Just not in here." She touched her chest with her hand, patted it. For a long time. "Not in here."

I looked for some more words. "We can get to Birmingham by mid-afternoon. We can get your car." I mean, wasn't being a man with a plan what I was all about?

She took my hand. Held it while I didn't talk anymore. "Yeah."

Then I did. "We could stop by your place in Tuscaloosa on the way."

Her grip tightened.

"Or I could just fly from here," she said.

"Or, yeah, that."

"It might be easier that way, you know?"

"I guess."

"Jack. Don't."

What a pair. I let go her hand and sat up. I tucked my head against my knees.

"Not after all this. Don't go that way now, baby," she said. It's not fair."

I felt a sound come from my chest but it was not a word.

"What?"

"I said, all right."

She sat up, too, swiveled around and scooted up to me. She caressed my shoulder.

"I'm not running away from you."

I pulled my head up from my knees. "No."

"I mean it."

"I know."

"Kiss me."

I did.

"And you know, I have to find out about Rose."

34

It took a month to move it all forward, but the time went fast. I went back to my apartment but couldn't stay because of the stench. After throwing out most of my old stuff, I ended up going back to Boots's apartment for a week while I had my place fumigated and painted.

The Beckers returned from their vacation and I told Art there'd been some trouble over a woman but that I couldn't talk about it just yet. I said I'd naturally pay for any damages. That seemed to cover it for both of us in a city where sometimes a polite stretching of the truth was both expected and appreciated. Other than to ask me how I was feeling, we never spoke of it again.

When I did move back in, the only odor was a fake mountain pine scent. I ordered a new gas stove and it arrived, and then everything else new, futon to window screens. I got a new laptop off the Internet, and found a zafu through a health food store bulletin board. I found it impossible to meditate, but it was nice to know the cushion was there. It's a sad commentary on your own state of enlightenment when you can't find the time to try to achieve it, but my mind was locked into a set of gears that would be turning for quite a while, and in fact had been turning most of my life. I stocked up on food but took almost all my meals out. Where there were people, noises, distractions—evidence of a world of separate existence.

In the next week, I dabbled with some travel pieces for which I had lost all interest. I sent a follow-up to a magazine on the story about that Nigerian carpenter. I called Ray Oubre and told him we'd have to talk soon. He asked me if I wanted to do a late-night tail on a wandering spouse in the Garden District. I needed the money, but said I was busy the next couple of weeks. He wanted to get a drink. I put him off. He wasn't mad but he wasn't stupid. I knew he'd want to know what was going on, and maybe he would be the right person to tell. Sometime.

I talked to Elle only twice.

She had picked up her car in Birmingham, put the hefty parking fee on her credit card—our cards had gotten workouts of late—and driven back to Tuscaloosa. She said she had been afraid at first to walk inside her house but as soon as she pulled up in the driveway she realized that after what she'd been through, nothing much would scare her.

The house had been tossed all right, but nobody had left any rotting creatures. Cleaning it up gave her something to keep herself busy well into that first evening home, after which she fell asleep on her couch and didn't wake up until the phone rang the next morning. It was her answering service, wanting her to clear two weeks' calls.

It took a few days to set her absence straight with the university. She explained that she had needed extra time to take care of her brother's affairs. They were very supportive.

She said everyone at the clinic was, too. She said she didn't look forward to turning in her notice, and was very concerned about some of her clients, the young women and single moms, including the contract patients in New Orleans. She was trying to find them replacement counseling. I told her not to worry, that she had other things on her mind.

She said she thought she was "functioning normally within the psychological circumstances" and that I probably was, too. She said we needed time to come to terms with our actions, our thoughts. She said it was like soldiers coming home. The ones after World War II returned on ships and had time to reintegrate themselves. In Vietnam and since, it was by air. One day your job is to kill people and the next morning you're supposed to pretend that was just a passing phase. She said I probably already knew that. I did.

She said she knew she was talking like a shrink. She was right. But the talking was good. She said that we had become our own triage therapists. It was meant as a joke.

At night I missed her; also days, walking through the Quarter. After a couple of weeks, I took on some work for Ray. We had that drink and I gave him the Cliffs Notes on what had happened, under his oath of confidentiality. He knew some wise guys and that Big Red was an enforcer for the Francois. He thought I would be okay. He thought it might even be good for business, having survived. I believe he was actually impressed. He thought I should just do P.I. work for him from now on, maybe even get a license. I said I'd give it some thought.

Most nights I hung out at Berto's, sometimes at the Urban Bayou, but it wasn't the same. Other than coming home shit-faced a couple of times, I didn't even feel like going out. At heart, I wasn't a George Jones drown-your-sorrows kind of guy.

What kind of guy was I?

I missed her.

TRUTH IS, IT TOOK something out of me. "It" being her and them and everything that had connected us, from Terrell's corpse to the screwdriver in

Trey's chest. I didn't want to admit it. No one ever does. First time someone tried to kill me, on a rice paddy dike outside Incheon, something got taken out then, too. But it was different. You don't care about an infiltrator trying to blow you up, because it's his job. He can take away some sense of permanence and immortality and put fear of unexpected death it its place, but it's a righteous fear and you can handle it. You can shoot him in the throat, too, and handle that. I got it, but, once again, the getting it wasn't enough. Maybe that's what I didn't want to admit. That not every riddle has an answer. Can be fixed. That the mystery can come from a bee sting, a bullet, a kiss. That it remains mysterious. That life is.

She began to call more often, a few times a week. I couldn't tell if she was keeping me up-to-date or just talking because she missed me, too. It didn't matter.

A week after her birthday, she went to the lawyers in Jackson. The attorney for the estate, a old Mississippi liberal type, Cornelius Weathers, said he had been surprised, having wondered if she would ever turn up. The wax-sealed birth certificate was acceptable, and he went over the details of the estate, in effect the "second will" left by Junior Barnett. The holdings had been kept in a hollow trust, its funds administered by a brokerage company hired by the firm, with some commissions deducted and duly recorded. Weathers had been a boyhood friend of Junior's and felt it his duty to keep everything strictly in order.

Elle would indeed receive half the assets, after which the other half could be released to Trey. Which raised the question of his whereabouts. By then, he had been declared missing. The *Times-Picayune* had run a positive review of his Red Dog collection, noting that the Delta Gallery's part-time staffer, Weldon Greenbriar, had been unable to locate the artist and thought he might have gone to Europe unexpectedly, as he sometimes did. All the paintings had sold and were expected to increase in value, just as Elle had said. I thought about visiting the gallery. I never did.

Elle said Mr. Weathers didn't care much for Trey, but felt that his responsibility was to fulfill the terms of the will, so the firm had stayed in touch with the NOPD after the missing persons report became public. Nor did anything more come of the shelved investigation of Terrell's murder. Officially.

Just before Thanksgiving, she called to tell me that $5.9 million had been transferred to a new investment account set up for her in a Jackson bank. The estate's worth of $12 million (after legal fees and tax reserve) was less than the $30 million Trey had estimated, but Weathers said various global market recessions, the lingering effects of the oil bust, and some "risky investments" had cut into the portfolio. She said she hadn't pressed for details.

Still, not bad. And if no one heard from Trey in a year, and he were declared legally dead, she would receive the balance. Until then, his share would remain in a separate account from the original trust.

She had dinner with her aunt the night of the official opening of her account at a French restaurant in North Jackson. She said they talked about how everything around her would change—yet again. She said Lenora had healed fine and would get the plastic surgery on her fingers soon. Lenora had given her another cleansing bath and she had been to mass a couple of times. She said she missed me.

They drove to Rosedale in December and put Artula's house on the market and set up for her to move to Jackson for better treatment for her and for the baby, Vanessa. Elle got her lawyers to create an account for Artula that would roll over to the children when the time came. Elle promised to become their guardian. Artula thought she had about two more years.

Elle bought a new house near downtown Tuscaloosa, worked when she could. Her patients in New Orleans were referred to another counselor. New Orleans was the place she most wanted to go and the one place that, for now, she couldn't.

The second week in December, a couple days after my birthday, I went to my bank to withdraw some cash and deposit checks from Ray and from *Southern Focus*. The drive-through clerk seemed exceptionally friendly and made a comment that this had been a good day for me so far. The pneumatic tube sent me my deposit receipt. Instead of $5,453, which I had expected, it was $205,453.

I called Elle right away. When I objected, she said that if she was going to have to give that much to Big Red, she could do the same for me.

I tried to celebrate that night but couldn't get past the first Jack Daniels at the Napoleon House, and had to walk around through the crisp cold night, unable to stop or sit. She had handed me everything I needed to start up whatever I wanted.

She had given me my freedom.

SHORTLY BEFORE CHRISTMAS, SHE called to ask if I'd heard from Big Red. I hadn't. An exact date for the payoff had never been set, but she said she thought he was probably getting anxious and she wanted to get him his money and be done with it, before New Year's Eve. I said Red was the kind of guy who would let me know if the payment were overdue. She asked if I could come get the cash and deliver it to him in person right away.

I drove up to Tuscaloosa that same day and got in about seven. It was dark and cold in Alabama but her house was warm and clean and she greeted me with a kiss and a hug. She was beautiful as ever. Eyes, still, to die for.

She explained her plan to pick up the money at the bank in the morning. We went to dinner at an Italian place near campus, but the conversation was muted and the wine went down badly. It wasn't until we got back to her house that we talked about the past. Or tried. I couldn't get to the heart of anything because she wouldn't let me.

I stayed the night, sharing the bed but nothing more. Eventually it was dawn. I turned on a space heater and read the paper while she got ready for work. Lots of troubled patients over the holidays needed her help.

A little before nine we went to her bank, where a particularly unctuous assistant manager escorted her to her safety deposit box. She came back holding a briefcase-size suede pouch, zippered shut. She gave it to me and we walked outside. I didn't count it. At our cars, we kissed goodbye. I drove back to the city.

35

It was cold in New Orleans, too, but I couldn't sit still. I stashed the leather pouch under the futon and walked all the way from the Marigny to the Napoleon House. I drank too many Jack Daniels pretending to be in a holiday mood with some tourists from San Antonio clumped around the bar.

So naturally I had to walk over to the Rio Blanche. I didn't go in but I thought I saw Elefgo, or at least someone with his wardrobe. I was glad to think he was okay but it wouldn't have done any good to go in and say so.

The alcohol warmth was dissipating, and I headed home briskly as possible. I turned on my new stereo, jumped around to some be-bop, poured myself another couple fingers of Jack, and looked in the pouch. It was impressive: a hundred banded packs of Benjamins, twenty in each. I closed it up, stowed it back under the futon, and passed out watching *Seinfeld* reruns.

I called Red the next day. The number transferred to a beeper, and I punched in my own number. A half-hour later he called back, wouldn't say where he was, but that he could meet me the following day at 2 P.M. That would be Christmas Eve but he said that was the earliest he could make it. We settled on the Moon Walk overlooking the river.

I almost enjoyed the fresh winter chill as I walked to the rendezvous, my bare head into the wind, carrying all that cash through Jackson Square like it was a bag full of beignets.

I found him leaning against a rail looking at a barge pushing upriver past one of the casino boats.

"I always like coming up here," he said. He was wearing a Saints cap. A tropical shirt stuck out from the bottom of his leather jacket.

I handed him the pouch. He opened it, flipped through the money packets inside like some kind of high-speed counting machine.

"Looks good."

"It is."

"How's she doing? You?"

"You know. Getting along."

"And?"

"And I'm okay." I looked at the water rushing toward the marshes and the Gulf. "I think my ribs have healed. Mostly."

"Like I said, business."

"Yeah. It comforts me."

He looked sideways at me. "Don't mean I like smartass any better."

I watched the barge. Like I cared anymore.

He zipped up the pouch. "You think any about what we talked about?"

"It crossed my mind. But, really, I wouldn't have a clue." The river seemed exceptionally gray and ugly in the flat winter light.

"Who does? You know, like we said. I never thought I'd wind up with the family. It just happened I knew how to do a couple of things, and then a couple others, and there I was."

I turned to study him. "And where is that?"

He didn't like the question.

"I'm not criticizing. I'm asking. It's something on my mind about myself."

"Huh."

"I mean, where you are. You want to be there, I mean where you are, or would you rather be somewhere else?"

A pause. "It's like I said before. I'd rather be fishing." He turned his body sideways against the rail, facing me. "You know, it crossed my mind to sell that painting straight out to that woman in Houston, take the money and run. It'd last me a couple of lifetimes."

"And?"

"And then I'd have to worry every day of this lifetime when they'd show up. They always do."

"But it crossed your mind."

"Yeah, it did. Don't never say that to nobody."

I shrugged. "Thing is, you thought about a change."

"I think about it all the time."

We fell silent, looking at the water. It was going to rain.

"The painting. What happened with it? I'd like to tell her."

"I took it to my boss, gave him the name of the bimbo collector in Houston."

"He saw the painting?"

"Hell, yeah."

"He liked it," I said, already knowing the answer.

"Yeah." He stared at the river. "Said it would change his life."

"Huh."

"Huh."

"He's gonna keep it." I knew that answer, too.

Red threw up a hand, clasped it back on the rail. "Fuck do I know."

"That would be too bad."

"Look, Shakespeare, you never know about these things. Guys might like hanging on to something at first. But then later on they like having the cash more."

I glanced at him. "So maybe—"

"Fuck do I know."

He looked into the pouch again.

"So it's done," I said.

"It's done."

I let that settle a moment.

"Can I ask you something?"

"Shoot."

"Anybody else, I mean, you know Tony or Reggie or Delmore or anyone else, ever going to show up, you know, looking for me? Or for her?"

He gave me a sizing up look.

"We went over that."

"I know. But now, still the same?"

"First, Reggie, he won't be a problem. Tony, he plays in a whole different area most of the time and he does what he's told, plus he gets a taste of this you just gave me. Anyone else, no. And nobody's sorry about how it all played out back there that night, either." The slightest of smiles. "I might of told them I whacked the rich-boy prick myself. You don't mind I get the credit."

I looked him in the eye, something I rarely had done.

"That make you feel better?" He held my gaze.

"I just wondered."

He turned away, spat out over the railing. "Look, I gotta go. You wanna talk later, you get in touch."

He put the pouch down, reached in his jacket pocket for a piece of paper, then into his jeans, and finally found a business card for a boat shop in Biloxi. He turned it on the back and wrote down a number. "This is a service. It's good for a year unless I change it. I do, I'll find a way to let you know."

I put the card in my pocket.

"See ya," he said. "Stay out of trouble."

He walked away, down the steps toward the market.

"See ya," I said, mostly to myself. Then I turned the other way and cut across the big parking lot on Decatur and into the hard, shadowed streets of the Vieux Carrê, the Old Quarter, the American landfall for the fallen.

I HEARD FROM HER on New Year's Eve, about six. She called to say she was feeling better, had decided to go into therapy with a doctor she trusted. She was thinking about setting up a foundation for at-risk young women. She missed me.

She had finally gone to Atlanta to learn about Rose, drawing in some favors and hiring lawyers. What she found was that the girl, now a teenager, had run away. The guess was some kind of domestic abuse in her adoptive family. No one had heard from her in almost a year.

I had been thinking of many options. I had been thinking of staying here and opening a café or bar with the money she had sent me. I had been thinking of going into a business deal with Ray Oubre. I had been thinking of running off to a monastery in Japan or Korea for a year. I had been thinking of the Big Bend, where you only knew other people if it was by mutual agreement and you could drive a pickup to Mexico over a low spot in the river.

But now I was thinking: I wonder if Big Red could help me find a missing person that he didn't need to kill.

///////

SOUTH, AMERICA

About the Author

Rod Davis is the recipient of the inaugural Fiction Award of the PEN Southwest Book Awards in 2005 for *Corina's Way*, described by Kirkus Reviews as "a spicy bouillabaisse, New Orleans-set, in the tradition of Flannery O'Connor or John Kennedy Toole: a welcome romp, told with traditional Southern charm." A member of the Texas Institute of Letters, Davis is also author of *American Voudou: Journey into a Hidden World*, selected as one of the "Exceptional Books of 1998" by Bookman Book Review Syndicate. A six-part series on the Texas-Mexico border, "A Rio Runs Through It," appears in *Best American Travel Writing 2002*. His PEN Texas-award-winning essay, "The Fate of the Texas Writer," is included in *Fifty Years of the Texas Observer* and his

Texas Monthly story, "Wal-marts Across Texas," is excerpted in *True Stories* by David Byrne. Davis has received numerous awards as a magazine editor and writer. He earned an M.A. in Government at Louisiana State University and studied at the University of Virginia before joining the Army in 1970, serving as a first lieutenant in South Korea. He lives in Texas.

Also by Rod Davis — Corina's Way

Efforts by Corina Youngblood—Christian minister, voudou priestess, and botanica proprietor—to stop the construction of a rival SuperBotanica, a "Wal-Mart of spiritual supplies," begin to founder until Gus Houston, a displaced former army officer, now ersatz chaplain at an exclusive girl's school, stumbles into Corina's store. When Gus hits on the idea of entering the wealthy white girls into the gospel singing competition during the Jazzfest, he triggers a series of events that has all sides evoking the spirits for good and ill. Author Rod Davis combines religion, voudou, New Age philosophy, and good old-fashioned capitalism, greed, envy, and a host of other unsavory motives in his entertaining first novel. Winner of the 2005 PEN Southwest Fiction Award

ISBN 978-1-58838-129-3
Available in hardcover and ebook formats
Visit www.newsouthbooks.com/corinasway

Praise for Corina's Way

"In the tradition of Flannery O'Connor or John Kennedy Toole: a welcome romp, told in an old-fashioned style and with traditional southern charm." — KIRKUS REVIEWS

"*Corina's Way* is a triumph in Southern storytelling . . . a bubbling pot of clever insanity. Davis' pen leaks wit and cunning on each page . . . Each chapter flows seamlessly and we discover something of ourselves in each realistically crafted individual . . . a beautiful stroke of fiction."
— CAPITAL CITY FREE PRESS

"Davis captures the essence of New Orleans . . . [he] nails the complicated racial and religious stew that makes up bayou culture, and his witty, fast style perfectly complements the clever premise." — PUBLISHERS WEEKLY

"Davis combines religion, voodoo, New Age philosophy, and good old-fashioned capitalism, greed, envy, and a host of other unsavory motives in his entertaining first novel." — BOOKLIST

"Davis sets an authentic tone for his first novel. The soul of the book rings true."— FOREWORD REVIEWS

"Make room on that crammed New Orleans shelf for *Corina's Way*, a multi-layered tale of suspense about our mysterious underbelly and its all-seeing navel." — ANDREI CODRESCU, author of *Messiah*

"Rod Davis's novel, *Corina's Way*, is an absorbing tale of Corina Youngblood, a New Orleans spiritual healer in the African/Haitian derived practice of 'Santos.' Corina's efforts in the healing work of the body and soul becomes a meditation on American marketplace culture, where even emotional well being can be turned into a commodity."
— WESLEY BROWN, author of *Tragic Magic*